Thomas Secker

Nine Sermons Preached in the parish of St. James, Westminster,

On Occasion of the War and Rebellion in 1745

Thomas Secker

Nine Sermons Preached in the parish of St. James, Westminster,
On Occasion of the War and Rebellion in 1745

ISBN/EAN: 9783744716178

Printed in Europe, USA, Canada, Australia, Japan

Cover: Foto ©Andreas Hilbeck / pixelio.de

More available books at **www.hansebooks.com**

NINE

SERMONS

PREACHED IN THE

Parifh of St. James, Westminster,

ON OCCASION OF THE

WAR and REBELLION in 1745.

By THOMAS, Lord Bifhop of OXFORD,
Then RECTOR of the faid PARISH,
Afterwards Lord Archbifhop of CANTERBURY.

To which are added,

His Grace's ANSWER to Dr. MAYHEW,

AND

His LETTER to Mr. HORATIO WALPOLE.

The FOURTH EDITION.

L O N D O N:
Printed for F. and C. RIVINGTON, in St. Paul's Church-yard;
and B. and J. WHITE, in Fleet-ftreet. 1795.

NINE

SERMONS

Preached in the

Parish of St. James, Westminster, on

Occasion of the

WAR and REBELLION in 1745.

By THOMAS, Lord Bishop of Oxford,

Then Rector of the said Parish;

Afterwards Lord Archbishop of Canterbury.

To which are added,

His Grace's ANSWER to Dr. Mayhew,

AND

His LETTER to Mr. Horace Walpole.

The FOURTH EDITION.

LONDON:

Printed for F. and C. Rivington, in St. Paul's Church-yard;
and B. and J. White, in Fleet-street, 1795.

THE
CONTENTS.

A 2   1 PET.

CONTENTS.

Phil. iv. 6, 7.

*Be careful for nothing: but in every Thing by
Prayer and Supplication, with Thanksgiving,
let your Requests be made known unto God.*

*And the Peace of God, which passeth all Under-
standing, shall keep your Hearts and Minds
through Christ Jesus.*

2 Cor. i. 9, 10.

*But we had the Sentence of Death in ourselves,
that we should not trust in ourselves, but in
God which raiseth the Dead:*

*Who delivered us from so great a Death, and
doth deliver; in whom we trust that he will
yet deliver us.*

JOHN

JOHN v. 14.

Afterward Jesus findeth him in the Temple, and said unto him, Behold, thou art made whole: sin no more, lest a worse Thing come unto thee.

PSAL. cxxii. 6.

O pray for the Peace of Jerusalem: They shall prosper, that love thee.

PSAL. xxix. 10.

——The Lord shall give his People the Blessing of Peace.

An

CONTENTS. vii

SER-

SER-

SERMON I.

(Preached on a General Faſt.)

2 CHRON. XV. 2.

The Lord is with you, while ye be with Him,
and if ye ſeek Him, He will be found of you:
but if ye forſake Him, He will forſake you.

THESE Words are the Beginning of a
ſerious Admonition, given by the Direction of Heaven to the Nation of
the *Jews*, as they returned from obtaining,
under the Conduct of *Aſa* their King, one of
the greateſt Victories recorded in Scripture.
Their Condition, after This, might have appeared to human Policy a very ſecure one: But
the Divine Wiſdom ſaw the greateſt of all
Dangers impending over them, that which
proceeds from forgetting God, and abandoning
Virtue. *And the Spirit of the Lord came upon*
Azariah the Son of Oded, and he went out to

B

meet

meet Aſa, and ſaid unto him, Hear me, Aſa, and all Judah and Benjamin: The Lord is with you while ye be with Him; and if ye ſeek Him, He will be found of you; but if ye forſake Him, He will forſake you. Now theſe great Truths, of which Heaven thought it needful to remind them, at the Concluſion of a proſperous War, it muſt be very much more needful that we ſhould attend to, who ſeem to be only at the Beginning of a doubtful one. And accordingly we are met here, by the Command of Authority, to conſider our Ways, and humble ourſelves before God for our Sins, as the neceſſary Means for deriving a Bleſſing on our Arms, and reſtoring and perpetuating Peace and Proſperity to our Country.

It is a melancholy Conſideration, that Creatures endued with Reaſon and Humanity ſhould ever come to employ Force againſt one another, and make the dreadful Addition of the Miſeries of War to the many unavoidable Sufferings of Life. But wicked as this is, when Paſſion and Reſentment, Deſire of unjuſt Gain, or Fondneſs of infamous Glory prompts to it: yet when Injuries of pernicious Conſequence are done to a Nation, and perſiſted in, and no competent Redreſs can be obtained, it becomes then, both

neceſſary

neceffary for particular Societies, and beneficial to human Society in general, that invaded Rights be vigoroufly afferted by the only Way left. When the Sword is drawn for Juftice alone, and ever ready to be fheathed as foon as that is granted, then Heaven may be appealed to, with Hopes of a favourable *Sentence coming forth from his Prefence, whofe Eyes behold the thing that is equal* [a]. But if the Affertors of a righteous Caufe be in other refpects a finful People, it is evidently juft for God, who hath the Cognizance of both thefe Things, to regard whichfoever of them infinite Wifdom fhall direct; and make even the injurious Party *the Rod of his Anger, and the Staff in the Day of his Indignation* [b], to correct, or deftroy, if their Wickednefs deferve it, fuch Nations, as though right in their Difputes with their Enemies, are wrong at the fame Time in Matters more important. And how little Terror foever our Enemies might give us at firft; yet now we muft be fenfible, that we know not in the leaft, how foon and how formidably they may increafe: but this we know certainly, that *there is no Reftraint to the Lord*, to punifh, as well as *to fave, by Many, or by Few* [c]. Times of

---

[a] Pfal. xvii. 2.   [b] Ifai. x. 5.   [c] 1 Sam. xiv. 6.

War

War therefore add a peculiar Strength to thofe
Admonitions, which Reafon and Scripture give
us at all Times, to confider what our State is
with regard to Him, *who doth according to his
Will in the Army of Heaven, and among the
Inhabitants of the Earth*[d].   Let us then all
confider now, whether we have Ground of
Hope or of Fear from that awful Declaration
of the Prophet, which you have heard read.

' *The Lord is with you, while ye be with Him.*
To be with God, is to preferve in our Minds a
reverent Senfe of his Being, Prefence, and Government; to keep clofe to his Laws, and
ftand on his Side againft the oppofite Power of
Darknefs and Sin.   Let us then think, if there
be need of Thought to anfwer; How is the
Reverence due to the Supreme Being preferved
among us? Have we not Perfons who even ridicule the Notion of a wife and good Maker
of all Things? Have we not thofe, who, if
they do admit a Creator, do not admit a Moral
Governor of the World; or at leaft reprefent
him fo very defective in his Adminiftration of
it, as finally to let bad Perfons be Gainers by
their Wickednefs, and good Perfons Lofers by
their Virtue: rejecting with mirthful Scorn,

[d] Dan. iv. 35.

what

what hath ever been the Hope and Support of
wife and good Men, the Belief of that future
State, in which the vifible Irregularities of the
prefent fhall be rectified? Have we not alfo
too many, who, profeffing perhaps to believe
in Natural Religion, yet fpeak of Chriftianity,
the great Means by which it is both fupported
and perfected, not only as a Falfhood, but an
Impoffibility: *Blafpheming that worthy Name,
by which we are called*[e], and difdaining to receive
from God himfelf any other Rules, either of
Faith or Life, than fuch as their own Reafon,
directed by their own Fancy, fhall prefcribe to
them? And let us fuppofe, if we can, that the
Number of fuch, as go thefe Lengths deliberately, is upon the Whole but fmall: yet what
fhall we fay of the inconfiderately guilty? Are
there not Multitudes of all Degrees, who feem
never once to have afked themfelves, whether
they believe in God or not? or if they do,
whether any Regard is due to him or none:
who flight Religion boldly, without imagining
they have ever examined it: who are perfuaded
of its Truth perhaps, fo far as they have any
Perfuafion about the Matter; but have no Notion, that they are to regulate their Conduct by

[e] James ii. 7.

B 3   it:

it: who possibly do not quite approve of profane Perfons, but are aftonifhed at pious ones;
and by their Indulgence to the former, and
their very great Pronenefs to defpife the latter,
plainly fhew, whether they perceive it themfelves or not, which Party they are on the Road
to join?

We have indeed many ftill, who frequent
Divine Worfhip: but how many of all Ranks,
and of that Rank particularly, which ought to
be an Example, and will be one either of
Good or Bad; how many that omit this Duty
entirely, or near it; and though it be an evident Part of the Law of Nature, and an exprefs Precept of Chriftianity, can yet talk, not
only of their own neglecting it, with much
Gaiety and Humour, but of other Perfons at-
tending upon it as Matter of Confcience, with
much Raillery.   And fuch an Afcendant hath
this contemptuous kind of Impiety got, that
there are many Perfons, who fincerely honour
their Maker in their Hearts, but dare not for
fear of Derifion fhew it in their Behaviour.
Let it be thought of a little, what the Appearance and Conftruction of thefe Things is:
and let thofe who are qualified for it, judge;
Is not this the one Nation upon Earth, in
                                        which

which Regard to God is taught in the greateſt
Purity, and treated with the greateſt Contempt?

But a worſe Symptom yet is, that whilſt
Irreligious Perſons are active in the Cauſe of
Infidelity; ſome of them with ſo ſelf-deny-
ing a Bigotry, as to teach it their Servants,
their very Wives and Children: the Generality of ſuch, as think themſelves very compe-
tently religious Perſons, ſcarce appear to have
any practical Impreſſions at all made on them
by thoſe Truths, which they acknowledge for
the Law of their Lives. They forget, it may
be feared, almoſt totally, the Exerciſe of private Piety; and behave in regard to publick
Devotion with a Negligence, which they would
think highly indecent towards their earthly
Superiors: allow themſelves in ſuch Levity of
Speech on the moſt ſerious Subjects, as would
ſcarce be juſtifiable in ſome of the moſt trifling
ones; form their Conduct avowedly on Principles, that have no Tincture in them of the
Faith, which they profeſs; and in effect declare themſelves to think of nothing but this
World, whilſt yet they are really perſuaded of
another to come. To this it muſt be added,
that very many, who not only believe, but

are influenced by their Belief in other Refpects, inftead of *confeffing their Lord and Mafter before Men*, as he hath moft folemnly
commanded them[f], are filent and indifferent,
whilft he is denied, or difregarded ever fo
much; and feem afhamed of a Caufe they
ought to glory in: by which Means they give
bad Perfons a Colour for pretending, that few
or none are Chriftians in earneft; and take
away from fuch, as are well-difpofed, the Encouragement of feeing how great a Number
yet remains. For, God be thanked, they are
ftill no fmall Number, who continue after all
bearing Teftimony to the Gofpel of Chrift.
But of how many Sins againft it, not a few
even of thefe are guilty at the fame Time, by
deviating from *the Form of found Words*[s], by
unwarrantable Divifions, and uncharitable Animofities; it is a great deal better that they
fhould confider, than that others fhould fay:
only thus much cannot but be faid, that thefe
Things add a peculiar Gloom to the View,
which we are taking.

Religion, it muft be owned, hath never been
practifed any-where, as it ought. But have

[f] Matt. x. 32. Mark viii. 38. Luke ix. 26.   [s] 2 Tim. i. 13.

not

not both the Practice and Profeſſion of it decayed moſt remarkably, in this Nation, within
the Compaſs of but a few Years? Is not the
Proſpect before us, that of its declining yet
much lower in the Generation that is coming
on? And what do we imagine this will end
in? If God is, it muſt be a Matter of ill De-
ſert, either wilfully or thoughtleſsly to treat
Him, as if he were not. If he hath given a
Revelation of his Will to Mankind, it cannot
be innocent to neglect it, as if he had given
none. And if he is the righteous Governor of
the World, he will ſupport his Government by
puniſhing where Guilt appears. If the Guilt
be National, it muſt be expected the Puniſhment will be ſo too. And though it were not,
yet amidſt the innumerable Connexions of
Things, one Part of a Society cannot ſuffer,
but the Whole muſt partake.

What Judgments in particular God will execute at any Time on impious Nations, we cannot ſay. All Nature is in his Power: and
they, who offend, have every thing to fear.
But one ſure Method of Correction, (a very merciful Method, as the lower Degrees of it give
Warning of the higher, but a dreadful one indeed,

deed, if that Warning be not taken) is by appointing the natural Confequences of every Sin
to be Part of its Reward. The Confequences
of Irreligion then what are they, and what muft
they be, on every Community? True Piety
cannot induce Men to injure their Country;
and comprehends peculiar Inducements to ferve
it, of the greateft Force. But in Times of
public Danger efpecially, Belief of Religion
gives a Spirit, and Defence of Religion a Motive for exerting it, which Confiderations of a
lower Nature will never equal. For what is
there that can equal the Exhortation, *Be of
good Courage, and let us behave ourfelves valiantly for our People and for the Cities of our God:
and let the Lord do that which is good in his
Sight*[a]. *Fear not, neither be difmayed: for the
Battle is not your's, but God's*[i]. Whereas, if
fome through Infidelity have no Hope in him,
and others through Wickednefs have only Fear
of him, fo far as thefe Ways of Thinking can
influence, *all Hands will be feeble, and every
Heart will melt*[k].

But indeed the Belief of a juft and good Being, who fees and will reward, is at all Times
the great Support under the Sufferings of Life,

[a] 1 Chron. xix. 13.　　[i] 2 Chron. xx. 15.　　[k] Ifai. xiii. 7.

　　　　　　　　　　　　the

the great Incitement to every thing worthy, the great Reftraint from every thing bafe. Human Weaknefs evidently wants thefe Things: and there is nothing elfe, that can always furnifh them. The virtuous Dictates of their own Minds will have little Influence comparatively on moft Men, when they are confidered no longer as the Voice of God fpeaking inwardly to them. And the Penalties of human Laws, without thofe of the divine Law fuperadded, will often be evaded, and not feldom defperately braved. For if once Men think there is nothing beyond Death, they will foon come to think there is nothing in it, which ought to with-hold them from preferring a fhort Life fpent as they like, to a long one fpent otherwife. Feeling themfelves free from the Terrors of Religion, they will fly out into Profligatenefs, merely to fhew they are free: And it will be Encouragement enough to them, to purfue every Appetite, Paffion, and Fancy, without Referve; that whatever Inconveniencies may happen to arife from it, one Moment can deliver them from all at once, whenever they pleafe. How then will they act in the numberlefs Cafes, to which the Power of the Magiftrate either cannot or is not likely to

reach

reach at all, or but imperfectly at beft? How, for Inftance, will the Properties, and even the Lives of Men be fecured, when Perjury is no longer dreaded? A Confideration of peculiar Weight in this Country: where, with amazing Inconfiftence, we are multiplying Oaths, as if we could depend upon them for every thing; and flighting the Care of Religion, which alone can give us Caufe to depend on them for any thing. But in general, What or Whom can we poffibly hope Mankind will regard to any conftant good Purpofe, if they will not regard God: And how can we pretend to regard him, whilft we go on, as we do? Nor let it be thought, that the Belief of a future Recompence is neceffary to the lower Part of the World alone: though if it were, they will never preferve it long, when they fee their Superiors have it not. But the higher Mens' Station, and the greater their Power is, the more is the Importance, both to others and themfelves, that they be ftrongly influenced to do Good and not Evil, by this only Motive that can never be outweighed.

It is very true, neither Irreligious Perfons are always fo bad, nor Religious ones always

fo

fo good, as their Notions lead them to be: But ftill every Way of Thinking produces, more or lefs, its natural Effects. The deeper Root Religion takes, the more Benefit will fpring from it: and the wider Irreligion fpreads, the more Mifchief it will bring forth. At prefent it muft endeavour to appear as harmlefs as it can, to recommend itfelf: and fome Degree of the good old Impreffions will remain, and have Influence for a Time, even on thofe who have done their beft to wear them out. But when Profanenefs fhall once have attained its Maturity, then it will be felt, if Men are refolved not to fee it before, which were in the right: the weak and credulous Creatures, who contended for honouring God: or the Perfons of fuperior Knowledge and Freedom of Thought, who fcorned and forfook him.

But we muft remember, our Maker is forfaken, when Virtue, the Law He hath given to Mankind, is tranfgreffed; as well as when his Worfhip is deferted, or his Being denied. Let it then be a fecond Article of Inquiry, What our Condition is in this Refpect.

The Confequence appears a very plain one, that when Religion decays, Morals muft. How-

However let us look into Fact. In fpeaking of Virtues and Vices relating to the Public, no Matters of Controverfy ought fo much as to be hinted at in this Place: a Place to be kept facredly feparate from the Contefts of Parties; and only employed, when Occafion requires, to call on every Party alike, as in the Name of God, to confider their Doings. Where Divifions and mutual Accufations run fo dreadfully high, there muft be great Faults on one Side or other; 'tis well, if not on all. And all fhould confider very ferioufly, what they are aiming at, and by what Means; what they are rifquing, and to what good End. But That above the reft fhould be confidered, which it may be feared is often thought of leaft, what muft become, whilft each Side is fupporting itfelf by the Methods too common, what muft become of the Virtue and Integrity of this People, the moft important Part of all they have to be concerned for. Every other Sort of Lofs Nations have often recovered, and rifen again from the loweft Ebb: but Lofs of Probity and Principle, this affects the Vitals of Society: and whatever accidental Advantages may feem to arife from it in any Cafe for a Time; if the Diftemper grows, and

it

it is the hardest in the World to stop, its Conclusion must be fatal.   And let it not be objected that Countries of very little Virtue and public Spirit have flourished notwithstanding. For how have they flourished?   In a State of Freedom?. No.   Outward Prosperity hath been joined with domestic Oppression: or if Intervals of Ease have been felt; they have always been precarious, and generally short.

Impartial Reflections on these Matters will shew us very clearly the Guilt and the Danger of our Sins with Respect to the Public.   But we shall see both in a yet stronger Light, if we reflect farther, How very little Zeal we express, in the Midst of all our Vehemence about disputed Points, for the Promotion of Things indisputably right.   Proposals for Reformation are treated in the Gross, as mere Chimeras; mighty little Harm apprehended from the most flagrant Immoralities, but dreadful ill Consequences to Liberty from restraining them: Laws treated with Contempt by those who should obey them, and this connived at by those who should execute them; still every one complaining immoderately of others, for what no one will himself contribute to amend.

But

But indeed public Virtue, though it were genuine, will never be confiftent and univerfal, while private Vices are indulged. And to what a deplorable Degree thefe abound amongft us, needs not be faid, how much foever it needs to be thought of. The Intemperance, the promifcuous Lewdnefs, the Want of Induftry and Frugality, the Difregard to Authority and Order, the Profligatenefs of all Kinds, that hath overfpread in a moft uncommon Manner the lower Part of the People, every Body fees. And would but fome of higher Condition reflect, how much they have funk themfelves to a Level with their Inferiors, in fome of the worft of their Qualities ; and indeed contributed to make many of them fo bad as they are, and themfelves defpifed by them at the fame Time; it might be hoped the Confideration would be ufeful. But not to fay more of thefe: The Faults of too many, who are accounted, and are in Comparifon, decent and regular Perfons; their improvident Expenfivenefs, pernicious many Ways; their Living to Amufements and Pleafures only, and overlooking the moft ferious Obligations of Life; forgetting the Infpection of their own Conduct, their Families and Affairs; neglect-

ing

ing their very Children, at leaft in the important Point of their Religion and Morals: Thefe are fad Inftances of perfonal Guilt, and make a great Addition to the national Danger.

But when to the above-mentioned Epidemical Sins, every one hath added, after examining himfelf faithfully, the feparate Tranfgreffions of his own Life, and the inward *Plague*, which he hath permitted to infect *his own Heart*[l]; unknown perhaps to Men, but *naked and open to Him, with whom we have to do*[m]: then we fhall have no Doubt left, whether the total Amount be not abundantly fufficient to juftify Heaven, in whatever Judgments it may inflict on Us and our Country. And if, for Inftance, by our Contempt of true Religion, we fhould open a Way for Popifh Superftition to overfpread us, after a fhort preparatory Reign of Atheiftical Diffolutenefs; if our Abufes on all Hands of the Bleffings of a Free Government fhould introduce upon us a Slavery of our own creating; if the finful Exceffes, that we have fuffered Wealth and Plenty to lead us into, fhould bring on us, as

[l] 1 Kings viii. 38.   [m] Heb. iv. 13.

.C   they

they naturally do, Poverty and Diftrefs; and our domeftic Enmities deliver us up to our common Adverfary: *who fhall have Pity upon thee, O Jerufalem, or who fhall bemoan thee; or who fhall go afide to afk of thy Peace* *?

The common Anfwer to all Reprefentations of this Sort, is, That the World hath always been bad; and therefore we have no peculiar Reafon to fear. But if it hath been always a Place of Wickednefs, it hath always been a Place of Mifery too, by Means of that Wickednefs. Continual Effects have been ever neceffary to keep both from increafing. And if we, whom God hath treated with fuch diftinguifhing Mercy, will not ufe thefe Efforts, but abandon ourfelves to Sin; as he doth think fit to make fome Examples of his Juftice from Time to Time, what fitter Example he can make, is hard to fay.

Perfons however will flatter themfelves, that thefe, at the worft, are Dangers of very diftant Times. And every fingle Sinner in the World flatters himfelf in juft the fame Manner. Yet the Confequences of their Sins do overtake Men, and may overtake Nations too,

* Jer. xv. 5.

with

with furprifing Suddennefs. And the Sentence, recorded in Scripture, is perfectly juft:
*They of the Houfe of Ifrael fay, The Vifion that
he feeth is for many Days to come; and he prophefieth of Times that are far off. Therefore
fhall none of my Words be prolonged any more:
but the Word which I have fpoken fhall be done,
faith the Lord God*. And they fhall know, that
I am the Lord; and have not faid in vain, that I
would do this Evil unto them*.*

Other Perfons there are, who acknowledge
the Profpect to be bad, and Evil perhaps impending: But the only wife Part in their Opinion is, to let Matters go as they will, and enjoy themfelves as long as they can: Why
fhould they be uneafy before the Time
comes? Now if it were certain, that nothing
could do good, this might be reafonable in a
worldly View of Things: but where every
one may contribute, both by amending himfelf
and awakening others, to prevent Ruin; there
to be indolent, is as contrary to Humanity, as
it is to Religion. And therefore the Word of
God hath taken fevere Notice of it, as a great
Crime. *Ye have feen the Breaches of the City
of David, that they are many:—And in that Day*

° Ezek. xii. 27, 28.　　ᵖ Ezek. vi. 10.

　　　　　　　did

*did the Lord God of Hosts call to Weeping, and to
Mourning, and to girding with Sackcloth: and
behold Joy and Gladness, eating Flesh, and drink-
ing Wine: Let us eat and drink, for To-morrow
we die. And it was revealed in mine Ears by
the Lord of Hosts: Surely this Iniquity shall not
be purged from you, till ye die, saith the Lord
God of Hosts [s].*

But even they, who are concerned for the
Public, may yet express that Concern in a very
faulty Way. Many seem to think they have
fully done their Duty, as soon as they have
been angry at those, whom they apprehend to
have any Way occasioned what is amiss: angry, perhaps at the wrong Persons, perhaps in
a wrong Manner: such as only tends to increase
Guilt, and hasten Mischief.

The first Complaint, generally speaking, is
of those in Authority. And undoubtedly the
People have a Right to complain, whenever
the common Concern is administered ill. But
then it should be considered, that we may,
through Ignorance or Prejudice, expect from
Authority, either what it cannot do, or what
is not fit to be done: we may expect more than

<hr>

[s] Isa. xxii. 9, 12, 13, 14.

is

is reasonable to expect from Men like ourselves, though it be fit: and even supposing them very much to blame, we may conduct ourselves upon it so as to be equally or yet more to blame. Want of Reverence to Laws and Superiors is one of our great Evils: and all Opposition to whatever is thought wrong, should be accompanied with the strictest Care not to augment this Evil. But our Duty requires us peculiarly to beware of raising Domestic Uneasinesses too high, when a foreign Enemy may take Advantage of them: and at all Times it requires us, to preserve most religiously the Loyalty and Honour due to the supreme Power: especially now, when our present Establishment is our only human Hope of having all that is valuable to us secured to ourselves, and transmitted to our Posterity.

Next to the Rulers of a Nation, its Instructors are usually the great Object of Censure: and we acknowledge there is Cause. We have not been so serious and religious, so zealous and diligent, so disinterested and humble, so mild and charitable, as we ought. The Public must have suffered by this: we have suffered by it ourselves: and, unless we repent, we have Ground to expect a yet fuller Execu-

tion,

tion, than we have experienced already, of what Heaven inflicted on our Predeceffors in the *Jewish* Nation: *Therefore have I alfo made you contemptible and bafe before all the People, according as ye have not kept my Ways*'. Yet we cannot but hope, that a very confiderable Part of the Accufations brought againft us, would appear, upon Enquiry, to be without Foundation. But however that be, we muft remind you, that Our Faults will be no Excufe for Your Tranfgreffions: and we earneftly beg, that they who complain we do not the Good we ought, would at leaft not hinder, but give us Opportunity, and affift us rather, to do both Others and Themfelves the Good we would.

But even they, who proceed from Complaints to Endeavours of amending Things, will fail unhappily of their End, if they truft to worldly Methods alone, and leave Religion and Virtue, the great Support and Cement of human Society, out of their Schemes. This will be merely palliating for a little while: and doing what the Scripture, in perfect Conformity with plain Reafon, hath long ago condemned, as doing nothing. *Becaufe they have feduced my People, faying, Peace, and there was no Peace:*

' Mal. ii. 9,

and

*and one built up a Wall, and others daubed it with untempered Mortar: Therefore, thus saith the Lord God, I will rend it with a stormy Wind, and bring it down to the Ground, so that the Foundations thereof shall be discovered; and it shall fall, and ye shall be consumed in the Midst thereof, and ye shall know that I am the Lord**. Indeed every Page of the prophetical Writings recommends itself greatly to thinking Persons, by the most forcible and convincing Expressions of the utter Inefficacy of every Expedient for public Good, that is not accompanied with true Virtue and true Piety.

These, therefore, it is our most important Interest to restore and promote: to represent with Earnestness, and yet with Mildness, to such as are deficient in either, how wrong in itself, and how hurtful to the World, their Conduct is: and to be zealous in doing our own Duty, whether They will attend to theirs or not: Persons of Rank and Influence, by setting an Example worthy of Imitation, and shewing different Regards to the Good and the Bad; Persons intrusted with public Power, by behaving in their several Stations uprightly; Parents and Masters, by the prudent Exercise of their

* Ezek. xiii. 10—14.

C 4

private

private Authority; and every one, at leaft, by
reforming himfelf.   This, if it do nothing farther, will be fecuring his own Happinefs: and
the more fingle Reformations there are, the
nearer will be our Approach to an Univerfal
one. We are called indeed perpetually to Repentance: but the prefent National Call, if it
be not hearkened to, will much aggravate the
Guilt, not only of the profane Defpifers of it,
but thofe alfo, whofe Compliance with it is
merely external; who dare to approach the
Searcher of Hearts, and mock him by faying
to him, without Sincerity, fuch Things as we
have joined in faying this Day.

 On the Times appointed for Confeffion of
Sins, it hath always been a Rule, as the Word of
God plainly fhews, for Perfons to abftain in a
confiderable Degree from their ufual Food; not
as thinking it a Duty of any Value in itfelf,
for that were a fuperftitious Imagination; and
nothing can be more exprefs againft every Superftition, than Scripture is: but partly to make
an Acknowledgment of more than ordinary
Solemnity, by their Actions as well as Words,
of their Unworthinefs to partake of the common Bleffings of Heaven; and chiefly to fpend
thofe Hours in Humility of Spirit, and cool
                                Reflection

Reflection for their future Good, which they have spent too frequently in dangerous Levities, or sinful Indulgences. It is not then the Abstinence, it is not the outward Humiliation, nor even the real Serioufness of a Day, which God requires of us; but that these Things be made subservient to our lasting Benefit: that preserving on our Minds the Impression of what we have said and heard here, we go Home and retire into ourselves; think over our several Duties, public and private, with respect to our Maker, our Fellow-creatures, and the Regulation of our own Hearts; and after renewing our Applications for Pardon and Grace, set right, without Delay, whatever hath been wrong: that we form Resolutions to think often of our own Conduct, to follow steadily the most effectual Methods for preserving it such as we ought, and not to suffer the Opinions and Customs of an inconsiderate World, to wear out of our Minds the Regard we owe to the Author and End of our Beings.

But besides these Obligations, there is yet another, which particularly deserves our Attention at this Time; that when we ask Mercy of God, we shew it to Man. And accordingly the Scripture joins closely together Fasting and giving

ing

ing Alms; which therefore we fhould join too, each according to his Ability: but always remembering, that no one Part of our Duty whatever will be accepted as an Equivalent for tranfgreffing any other; but we muft *break off our Sins by Righteoufnefs*, as well as *our Iniquities by fhewing Mercy to the Poor* [t], if ever we expect that our Charity fhould avail towards procuring our Pardon.

And now would we but employ the prefent Solemnity, in determining confcientioufly to practife thefe Things: befides the good Fruits, it could not fail to produce in each of us fingly; we might hope, on very juft Grounds, to experience nationally the fame happy Effects of it, which we read the *Jews* did, from making the fame Determination, upon hearing the Admonition of the Text. *They gathered themfelves together, and they entered into a Covenant to feek the Lord God of their Fathers. And they fware unto him with a loud Voice: And all Judah rejoiced at the Oath. For they had fworn with all their Heart, and fought him with their whole Defire, and he was found of them: And the Lord gave them Reft round about* [u].

[t] Dan. iv. 27.   [u] 2 Chron. xv. 10, 12, 14, 15.

SER-

SERMON II.

(Preached on a General Faſt.)

1 P E T. v. 6.

Humble yourſelves therefore under the mighty Hand of God, that he may exalt you in due Time.

HUMILITY of Heart and Behaviour is a Duty ſo deeply founded in the Nature of Man, that though we knew of no Power above us, we ought yet to think modeſtly of ourſelves, from a Conſciouſneſs of our Infirmities; and pay a mutual Deference one to another, in proportion to the different Pre-eminences, be they ever ſo ſmall, by which we are ſeverally diſtinguiſhed. But the leaſt Apprehenſion of a perfect Being ſuperintending us, muſt ſurely magnify beyond Expreſſion the Senſe, how very imperfect we are: and convince us, that the utmoſt Reverence, of which we are capable, towards ſuch a one, if ſuch a
one

one there be, will fall vaftly fhort of what we
owe.　Now the Exiftence of a powerful and
wife, a juft and good, Ruler of all, is at firft
Sight a poffible Thing.　And were we fure of
no more, the Notion is fo refpectable in itfelf,
fo beneficial to human Society, and fo peculiarly
comfortable to every honeft Mind, that paffing
it over with a fcornful Neglect, inftead of at-
tending to it ferioufly, would be a Haughtinefs
of Spirit, blameworthy and fhocking to a great
Degree.　But the Reality of this Notion is
undeniably proved, by the plaineft Obfervations
on every Part of the Univerfe, and the ftricteft
Inquiries into its general Conftitution: by the
natural Prepoffeffions of common Men, the
acuteft Reafonings of fpeculative Men, and the
moft univerfal Confent, that ever any invifible
Truth obtained, of all Men.　Yet farther, to
leave no Plea for Ignorance of it, or of its
Confequences, the Creator hath made himfelf
known to his Creatures by exprefs Revelation:
and declared, what he is, what he expects from
them, what he hath decreed concerning them.
How monftrous a Difpofition of Soul muft it
be then, that can pride itfelf in ftanding out
againft fuch Evidence of fuch a Doctrine: can
take upon it to cenfure the Works of the Almighty,

mighty, without underſtanding a ſingle Part of them thoroughly; can triumph in the Thought of an ungoverned and fatherleſs World, of Wickedneſs unpuniſhed, and Virtue unrewarded; and hold thoſe in utter Contempt, who entertain better Hopes!

Our Nation affords, I fear, more than a few Perſons, guilty even of ſuch Pride againſt God, as this. But it affords Multitudes of a Sort, if poſſible, yet more unaccountable; who believe in him, and ſlight him. Acknowledging a Sovereign Lord of the World, without ſtanding in Awe of him, is doubtleſs a moſt aſtoniſhing Inconſiſtency: and yet I conceive it will appear, on Inquiry, the main Source of thoſe great and many Sins, for which we are met here to expreſs our Concern. Now if this be our Caſe, a little Reflection will ſhew it to be a very dangerous one: and the Apoſtle hath pointed out the only Cure, that ſince, as the preceding Verſe teaches, *God reſiſteth the Proud, and giveth Grace to the Humble,* we ſhould *humble ourſelves* unfeignedly *under his mighty Hand,* which hath been, and is, in ſeveral Reſpects, heavy on us; that ſo, inſtead of depreſſing us lower ſtill, *he may exalt us* again *in due Time.*

There

There are not many comparatively, but in their cooler Hours at leaft, believe the Author of Nature to be alfo the wife and juft Lawgiver and Ruler of Mankind. Nay, lamentable as the Apoftacy of our Days hath been, the Generality ftill entertain a Perfuafion, grounded on the firmeft Proofs, that he hath notified the Conditions of eternal Felicity by Jefus Chrift. But, having this *Knowledge of God*, do they *glorify him as God* [a]? Do they pay any Homage to him, do they cultivate any Regard for him? Do they confider him as the Giver of all Good, to whom their Thanks are due for every Thing they enjoy; as the Judge of the whole Earth, who fhall reward every one according to his Works? Will they, in Obedience to that Reafon, which he hath beftowed on them, refift their vicious Appetites and Paffions: will they, on the Authority of that Revelation, which he hath fuperadded, receive any Thing, but what they can fee of themfelves to be true; or do any Thing, but what they can fee of themfelves to be requifite? Is it not indeed their ftated Practice to fet their own Inclinations and Fancies above all his Affertions and Laws: difdaining to mind what is right or wrong, even

[a] Rom. i. 21.

        when

when it relates to this Life; and much more, to be fwayed by the Tendencies, which Doctrines or Precepts may have, to fit them for the Happinefs of another?

Nay, fuch as imagine themfelves perhaps very fteady Believers, and fufficiently good Chriftians, do not many of them, though lefs profeffedly, and without diftinctly feeing it, yet almoft as effectually make their Choice juft as they like, in what Things their Chriftianity fhall confift; and what they will go on to think or practife, however plainly forbidden in any one's Judgment, but their own. Are they at all willing to feek, with ferious Humility, what the Gofpel teaches? Are they withheld from any Sin which it forbids, merely by the Fear of their Lord and Mafter? Do they perform any Duty which it enjoins, merely from Love to their Redeemer? Try them but in one Point. The facred Writings have repeatedly directed a regular Attendance on public Worfhip and Inftruction. Yet they neglect it perpetually, on Pretences, for which they would neglect fcarce any one Thing befides: when they condefcend to come, they would ufually be underftood to do it as Matter of Prudence, or Propriety, and Compliance with Cuftom; but by no Means

of

of Obedience to God. And in general, they
fubftitute the Fafhions and Ufages of what they
call the World, that is, of the Perfons with
whom they are pleafed, and whom they defire
to pleafe, in the Place of the Divine Commands. This wretched Rule they follow againft
their Confciences firft: to this by Degrees
they bend their Confciences afterwards: and
when once they have accomplifhed that, they
will not reflect, they will not hearken, they
will not bear the Mention of an Argument or
a Hint to the contrary; but exclaim againft it
as abfurd, before it can well be brought out;
let Reafon or Scripture fay what they will: till
at laft, not even yet renouncing their Faith,
they have hardly a fingle good Impreffion from
it left: no Gratitude to God, no Hope in him,
no Dread of him; no Thought of themfelves
in earneft, as his Creatures; nor any Recollection, how profligate a Treatment this is of our
Maker, of our Saviour, of the holy Spirit of
Grace. We do not know, I believe, nor fufpect very often, how inconfiderable God is become in our Eyes, and how near Advances we
have made to what is in Effect mere Atheifm.
But we have cheated ourfelves with Difguifes,
and fhifted between Religion and Irreligion, till

we

we have no Perception whereabout we are. And it is high Time for us to fix once for all, which we will ftand to. For if the Almighty deferves any Regard, he deferves a moft dutiful and univerfal one. Will we therefore pay him that, or will we avow paying him none?

But were many of us, whofe Appearance is more decent, to be examined, what there is in us beyond Appearance; were many, who have fome inward Reftraints and pious Feelings, queftioned how far they extend; and if there be not mixed with them, a much lefs indeed, but ftill a very criminal Neglect and Contempt of the fupreme Being; what do we think the Refult would be? Were fuch to be afked, how often they pray to him in private, or whether they remember perhaps, when they did fo laft; with what Attention they pray at fuch Times, or whether hurrying over a Set of unmeaning Words contents them; what Care they take in his Houfe, that their Hearts join in the Things they fay, or improve by thofe they hear; how often they meditate, as in the Prefence of God, on their Duty, and their Condition with Re- -gard to another Life; whether in Truth they almoft ever think of a future State, as their principal Concern, or have not inwardly chofen

their

their Portion here; whether they indulge no
secret Immorality, are chargeable with no In-
justice or Unmercifulness; what Expreſſion, or
what Tincture, there is in their common Con-
verſation and Behaviour of a Chriſtian Spirit;
what Zeal they have, what Expences they are
at, what Methods they encourage, what Pains
they take, for promoting the preſent and eternal Welfare of their Fellow Creatures: how
muſt they anſwer? Nobody hath a Right, it
may be, to put ſuch Queſtions to you: but
ſurely they are very important ones for you to
put to yourſelves. And for God's Sake do it:
and preſs your Souls home to make an honeſt
Reply. For if Religion be any Thing, theſe
are moſt material Things. Do you then find,
that you have hitherto been, in Relation to
them, ſuch Perſons as you ought? And if not,
do you experience a proportionable Concern for
your Failures? Are you even now reſolved to
become ſuch? And will you remember and
keep to what you reſolve: or run away from
your Convictions to the firſt Employment or
Amuſement you can hope to loſe them in, or
however ſuffer them to wear out for Want of
being renewed; ſo after a while, neglect your
Maker and his Laws as much as ever; and

I   poſſibly

póffibly defpife yourfelves for having once, in a Sort of Fright, thought to do otherwife? If you relapfe fo far, your Cafe will be a very dangerous, God grant it be not a defperate one.

Yet amongft all thefe blameable Sorts of Perfons, there are many perhaps not ill-difpofed, were they left to follow their own Judgments quietly, towards becoming fincerely and throughout religious. But the World would wonder at them, their Acquaintance would ridicule them: and that they cannot bear. But which is your God then? The World, or the Maker of it? And which is it fitter you fhould humble yourfelves under? The rightful Authority of the greateft and beft of Beings; or the ufurped Tyranny of a few vain Mortals, whofe Friendfhip means you no Good, and whofe Enmity can do you no Harm? But fo it is; we are cowardly one to another, and brave only againft *Him, who hath Power to caft into Hell*[b].

Even the loweft Part of Mankind, they alfo now have, learnt from their Superiors to lift themfelves up in Defiance of the Moft High: to plead openly and boldly for Gratifications, exprefsly prohibited by his Commandments;

[b] Luke xii. 5.

to prefer their Diverfions or their Idlenefs before his Worfhip; fome of them to *fit in*, and
others to furround *the Seat of the Scorner*[c].
For poor Wretches, that know nothing elfe,
imagine they know enough however to be above
Inftruction in their Duty, to contemn God's
Word, and fcoff at his Minifters.

Such is the Condition, and I appeal to the
Obfervation of you all, alas! to the Confciences
of too many of you, if it be not daily more and
more, if it be not, I had almoft faid, univerfally, the Condition of the People of this Land,
efpecially this City. *Help, Lord: for the godly
Man ceafeth, for the faithful fail from among
the Children of Men*[d].

But how great and general foever our Tranfgreffions have been; it will be alledged, that
they cannot have arifen from a Principle fo very
fhocking as Pride, directed againft the Author
of our Beings, but from inconfiderate Indulgence of lefs heinous, though ftill blame-worthy
Difpofitions. But were there, and O that there
were, much more Room for this Plea than there
is, yet bare Inconfideratenefs and Forgetfulnefs
of God is, in no fmall Degree, Contempt of
him. However, fome Offenders have not ad-

[c] Pfal. i. 1.   [d] Pfal. xii. 1.

ventured

ventured on fo direct Impiety as others.   And we ought to judge with all poffible Tendernefs of every one's Cafe, befides our own; but it concerns us beyond Expreffion not to flatter ourfelves in that.   And we may difcern with Certainty the true State of it by this one Mark. If Want of Thought hath occafioned our ill Behaviour, we fhall be thankful for Admonition, and readily change our Courfe: if Pride, we fhall be difpleafed with it, and tempted to go on.   But whether we have difobeyed God wilfully or inadvertently, we have great Caufe to humble ourfelves before him with deep Contrition: and bewail our own perfonal Guilt in the firft Place; then the Sins of thofe, who make up the fame Community with us: for he cannot correct Them, but we muft fuffer at the fame Time.

Now fuppofing we did not at all feel ourfelves particularly under his mighty Hand at prefent, yet furely we ought to recollect with great Awe, that in Reality we are under it always.   His Government of the World is without ceafing carried on, however filently, yet fteadily and powerfully, to that one End, which a Being of perfect Holinefs muft propofe to himfelf ultimately, the Manifeftation of his Glory, in the

Punishment of the Wicked, and Reward of the
Good.   Were both to be entirely deferred till
after Death, as the chief Part of both will, yet
how near is that to us all; and how very near
to many of us, who perhaps are the fartheſt of
any from ſuſpecting it! Though were it as diſ-
tant as it can, yet the Connection of it with
eternal Enjoyments or Sufferings being as certain as tnat God is holy and true, the practical
Inference would be juſt the ſame, as if it were
overtaking us this very Moment. But indeed,
unleſs we will abſolutely ſhut our Eyes, we
muſt ſee Judgments from above, both naturally
flowing from our Sins, and additionally inflicted
on them, in the mean while.

All Wickedneſs by the righteous and wiſe
Appointment of Providence, in the ordinary
Courſe of Things produces Miſery: and the
great Reſtraint from all Wickedneſs is the Fear
of God.   While Men continue to reverence
Him, there will always be ſome Hold upon
them, to keep them back from committing
Evil, or bring them back to repent of it.   But
when once that Band is broken, which it is of
late in this Nation, beyond any other in the
Chriſtian, or perhaps the Heathen World,
ſlighter and weaker Ties will ſoon give Way

one

one after another, till by Degrees every Thing is set loose. And how very fast accordingly our Morals and our Prudence have been forsaking us, ever since we have begun to forsake Religion, and to find out that our Maker is unworthy of our Notice, a little Reflection will shew us too plainly, if indeed any be needful. Do we not see Probity and Integrity, Friendliness and natural Affection, visibly decayed? Persons of all Ranks living above their Ranks; and first distressing themselves and their Families by vain and vicious Expences, then descending to every Baseness, that will enable them to proceed in this wrong Way, and every Folly that will drive away Remorse for an Hour, though by furnishing Cause for its Return with more Bitterness than ever: crouding their whole Time with absurd and dangerous Diversions, and infected with a Rage for Pleasure and Shew, be the Consequences what they will, that hath taken Possession of High and Low, Young and Old, to a Degree unknown before; and in many fears not, in some affects, to display itself, on the Days set apart for the Worship of God, nay for solemn Penitence and Humiliation? Do we not see almost every Body

D 4   treating

treating the groffeft and moft pernicious Immoralities, of what they gently ftile the gay
Kind, as no Faults at all in one Sex, and daily
approaching nearer towards affording them open
Countenance in the other: making on any
Occafion indeed, very little Diftinction, though
it be of unfpeakable Importance to make a great
one, between good People and bad; or, to fay
the Truth, rather inverting than laying Claim
to the Pfalmift's Character: *In whofe Eyes a
vile Perfon is contemned; but he honoureth them
that fear the Lord*. Do we not fee them,
educating their Children, and managing their
Servants as if it were on purpofe to have them
wicked: plainly perceiving them to be miferable in Confequence of it; perpetually involving
themfelves in grievous Uneafineffes and Difficulties from it, and making frequently heavy
Complaints of it; yet never once reflecting to
Purpofe, whence it comes, or what would
mend it: but ftupidly acquiefcing in what they
have the neareft Concern to prevent; and take
it for granted, that fuch of Neceffity is to be
the Condition of their Families, from one Generation to another?

* Pfal. xv. 4.

And

And if thefe fruits have fprung in private
Life from our Difdain of Piety, what muft it
have produced in public ? Juft what we were
to expect from a Number of fuch Creatures put
together ; and from the fixed Decree of Providence, that *they, who plough Iniquity, and fow
Wickednefs, fhall reap the fame'.* Rulers and
Magiftrates having permitted the Authority
that ordained them, to fink, have, by a Confequence, which they might eafily have forefeen, loft their own; Refpect to every Kind of
Superiors is worn out; and next to the Laws
of Heaven, thofe of our Country are regarded
leaft. The Nature of Things, and the Word
of God, have made Uprightnefs and Induftry
the Supports of Society, and Religion the Support of Them. But we have imagined we could
do better than this: we have been laying other
Foundations, and bringing thefe into utter Dif-
efteem, as it were by Confent on all Sides; till
they, who defire moft to act upon Principle,
find, it may be feared, fcarce any Remainder
of Principle among us, left to act upon. We
have *trufted in the Staff of a broken Reed,
whereon if a Man lean, it will go into his Hand,*

' Job iv. 8.

and

and pierce it [a]. *We have forsaken God, the Fountain of living Waters, and hewed us out broken Cisterns, that can hold no Water* [b]. We have indeed been worse than negligent, we have been jealous of Religion; fearful, that Bigotry, Enthusiasm, Superstition, and all Manner of Evils would flow from it: and so, without taking the least Care to guard against them, or prevent the Increase of that Communion, in which they are most intimately mixed with it, Piety in general hath been made the Subject of Invective and Derision, till we are at present immersed in Profaneness and Profligateness: and, as Extremes beget one another, directly in the Road to be over-run after a while by Popery, the Schools of which are multiplying continually in our Streets. We have thought the Morals of our People totally undeserving of Regard, unless it were to corrupt them, that we might enjoy *the public Benefits of private Vices:* and the Consequence hath been, to say of others no more than hath been said, that our Poor, the Strength and Riches of a Nation when regulated well, are every where destroying themselves and their Posterity by their Intemperance and promiscuous Lewdness; and be-

[a] Isa. xxxvi. 6.   [b] Jer. ii. 13.

coming,

coming, in the mean Time, an infupportable Burthen by their Idlenefs and Extravagance. We have thought that neither God nor Man were to reftrain what we are pleafed to call Liberty; and thus we have plunged into a Licentioufnefs, that hath brought upon us many of the Inconveniencies, and almoft all the Difcontent, of Slavery.

Nor hath the Almighty omitted to fuperadd, though with a gentle Hand, Corrections intirely his own, to the Sufferings, which we have chofen to inflict on ourfelves by Means of the ftated Connections, which he hath wifely and juftly eftablifhed. We had long been poffeffed of the Bleffing of Peace, without making any one good Ufe of it: and he hath permitted a War to come upon us, of which we forefee neither the Duration nor the Event. We had long enjoyed healthy and plentiful Seafons, without acknowledging Him for the Giver of them : and we have fince been vifited with Sicknefs in all our Borders; and fuch Dearth, as few, if any of us, ever knew before. *Our Heavens have been made as Brafs, and our Earth as Iron*[l]; and we would not underftand it to be a Chaftifement: *the former and the latter Rain*[k] have

------

[l] Deut. xxviii. 23.   [k] Deut. ii. 14. Jer. v. 24.

been

been restored to us, and we have not owned it to be a Mercy. Now, if lighter and shorter Judgments will not awaken us, heavier and longer muft. For fo the Prophet foretells: *Lord, when thy Hand is lifted up, they will not fee: but they ſhall fee* [l]. And how much greater Evils God may yet caufe us to fee, lies hid in the Treafures of his own Foreknowledge. We are at prefent in a Condition, that may, in various Refpects, very naturally and very foon become extremely dreadful. And what elfe we can do to better our Profpect, is neither eafy for any Perfon to difcover, nor indeed the Concern of every Perfon to inquire: but there is one Thing, which alone of itfelf will do incredible Good; and every Thing befides, very little without it; which we all have in our Power, and all feel to be our Duty. *Come, and let us return unto the Lord our God: for He hath torn, and He will heal us: He hath ſmitten, and He will bind us up* [m].

Both Particulars and Nations, which fall into a bad Way, are ftrangely unwilling, for the moft Part, to underftand the Truth of their own Cafe. Such was the Difpofition of God's ancient People, admirably defcribed by the Pro-

[l] Ifa. xxvi. 11.   [m] Hof. vi. 1.

phet

phet *Hosea: His Strength is devoured, and he knoweth it not: yea, grey Hairs are upon him, and he knoweth it not. And the Pride of Israel testifieth to his Face: and they do not return to the Lord, nor seek him, for all this*[a]. Nay, when the Disease is much too notorious to be denied, Persons will be ascribing it to other Causes, and inventing other Cures, than the right one; putting Confidence in Schemes unconnected with Reformation, and perhaps mending bad with worse. But to these the Almighty himself hath expresly denounced: *Woe to the rebellious Children, saith the Lord, that take Counsel, but not of me; that cover with a Covering, but not of my Spirit; that they may add Sin to Sin: that will not hear the Law of the Lord; which say, Cause the Holy One of Israel to cease from before us. Wherefore, thus saith the Holy One of Israel: Because ye despise this Word, therefore this Iniquity shall be to you as a Breach ready to fall, swelling out in a high Wall, whose Breaking cometh suddenly at an Instant*[b]. Healing Sores in a palliative, unsound Manner, only occasions their bursting out again with more threatening Symptoms. If therefore we would truly mend our Case, we must

[a] Hos. vii. 9. 10.   [b] Is. xxx. 1—13.

go to the Bottom of it. We have been wicked, and we muſt repent. We have deſpiſed God, and we muſt *humble ourſelves under his mighty Hand.*

But then what ſhall we reckon is doing ſo? Is it merely appointing or obſerving a Form of Humiliation for Form's Sake? Inſtead of appeaſing God, we ſhall not ſo much as deceive Men by this: but only veil Irreligion with tranſparent Hypocriſy. Is it then being affected and warmed a little, at the Time, by what we ſay or hear in this Place; and becoming, almoſt immediately after, juſt the ſame Perſons that we were before? On the contrary, theſe tranſient Fits of Piety are mentioned in Scripture, as a very diſcouraging Sign: *O Ephraim, what ſhall I do unto thee? O Judah, what ſhall I do unto thee? For your Goodneſs is as a Morning Cloud, and as the early Dew it goeth away*ᵖ. While Perſons reflect not at all, one knows not how it may operate, if ever they come to reflect. But when, through the Grace of God, they have actually been made ſenſible of their Guilt and their Danger, and yet relapſe into it; when their Convictions have been renewed, their good Purpoſes repeated, and yet all ſuf-

ᵖ Hoſ. vi. 4.

fered,

fered, Time after Time, to fall back into nothing: what can be expected, but that Heaven
will at laft abandon thofe, who in fo fhameful
a Manner abandon themfelves. Our prefent Bufinefs therefore is, each of us to imprint on our
Minds now fuch deep Sentiments, as may influence us ever after, that devoutly conforming
our Lives and our Souls to the Will of God, is
the very End of our Being: to recollect and
confefs before him, how grievoufly and how
long both we in particular, and this Nation in
general, have neglected the Obedience we owe
him: to acknowledge, that we are altogether
in his Hands, as private Perfons and as a People: to confider whatever hath befallen us, as
lefs than our Iniquities have merited; to pre-
pare ourfelves, with meek Refignation for whatever more he may pleafe to inflict on us: yet
earneftly petition him, that whatever becomes
of our temporal Concerns, *our Spirits may be
faved in the Day of the Lord Jefus*[a]; and that
if it be confiftent with his Holinefs and Wifdom, he would fpare us even in this World,
*not for our Righteoufnefs, but his own great
Mercies*[b], in Chrift our Redeemer, for the Honour of his Name, and the Prefervation of his

[a] 1 Cor. v. 5.   [b] Dan. ix. 18.

true

true Religion eftablifhed amongft us; to form folemn Refolutions againft every Sin, againft every Occafion of Sin, for the future: begging at the fame Time that Grace of our Sanctifier, which alone can make them effectual: and do all thefe Things not only in Profeffion, as Matter of outward Decency, but from the Bottom of our Souls; not only with a fudden Fervor, excited here in the Congregation, but deliberately at Home, before *our Father which feeth in fecret* [*].

How eafy, or how hard, it may be for any of us to bring our Hearts really into fuch a Frame as this, He only knows, who knows all Things. Perhaps it is a Sort of Language, and a Way of Thinking, to which fome of us have never been ufed, and which others have long difufed. If it be, we have fo much the more Need to take it up without Delay.   For our Maker and our Judge is intitled to the moft lowly Submiffions from his guilty Creatures: and there is neither any Meannefs in making, nor any Greatnefs in refufing, them.   In all Cafes, the juft and the right is the worthy and the honourable Behaviour.   But in this, above all, it is the neceffary one too.   Obftinacy cannot fupport

[*] Matt. vi. 6.

us :

us: Diffimulation will not conceal us: it is God we are concerned with, and our only Refource is to throw ourfelves on his Mercy. The very beft of us have Caufe to lament our Failings, to reiterate our Vows, to implore his Forgivenefs and Affiftance, yet more ardently than we have done. -In proportion to our Tranfgreffions and Deficiencies; our Self-Abafement, our Penitence, our Supplications, our Efforts of Amendment, ought to Increafe. And that our Performance of thefe Obligations will be followed, bad as our State is, with the happieft Confequences, Reafon affords comfortable Hope, the whole Tenor of Scripture exprefsly declares, and the Text with peculiar Strength implies: *Humble yourfelves under the mighty Hand of God, that he may exalt you in due Time.*

But I muft not now enter on the Illuftration and Proof of this important Connexion. May our prefent Humiliation give an experimental Proof of it, by effectually inclining us to *be reconciled to God*[1]; and inducing Him to direct our public Counfels into the Way of national Profperity, and our private Conduct into that of eternal BlefTednefs.

[1] 2 Cor. v. 20.

E

[illegible] Difficulty [illegible] not conceal, as it is God [illegible] concerned with, and our only Business [illegible] us have Cause to think [illegible] our Feelings, to [illegible] in our Vows, to implore his Forgiveness [illegible] demonstrate Philosophy have [illegible] done. In proportion to [illegible] Transgressions, and [illegible] Deficiencies, our Self-Abasement, our Peni- [illegible] tence, our Supplications, for Others of Mankind [illegible] because [illegible] [illegible] these Obligations, my [illegible] [illegible] with the happiest con- [illegible] that affords considerable Help, the [illegible] the Glory of God, which [illegible] will fly to [illegible] now. I endeavoured by my before [illegible] from the Reason, both the general Duty [illegible] [illegible]

SERMON III.

(Preached on a General Faſt.)

1 PET. v. 6.

Humble yourſelves therefore under the mighty Hand of God, that he may exalt you in due Time.

AT our laſt Meeting on the ſame moſt neceſſary Occaſion, which calls us together now, I endeavoured to lay before you, from theſe Words, both the general Duty of Man's *walking humbly with his God*[a], and the particular Reaſons, which we of this Nation have, for exerciſing a very deep Humility towards him, as we have been particularly guilty, beſides various other Sins, of that unſpeakable ſhocking one, Pride againſt him. Too many amongſt us have dared to treat the Faith, if not of his Being, yet of the only Thing which makes it valuable, a juſt and good Pro-

[a] Mic. vi. 8.

E 2

vidence,

vidence, with utter Contempt: abſurd as it is, that the wiſe and powerful Maker of the World ſhould not be the Ruler of it, and that the Ruler of the World ſhould not *reward every one according to his Works* [b]. Much greater Numbers, if they do not deny his Moral Government, yet almoſt intirely diſregard it: attend on his public Worſhip but ſeldom, and then viſibly as Matter of mere external Decency; never condeſcend to pay him any Homage in private; nor through their whole Behaviour conſider him, in the leaſt, as, what they profeſs to acknowledge He is, the Lawgiver, the Inſpector and Judge, of their Lives and Hearts: but ſecurely follow Paſſion, Appetite, Cuſtom, Fancy, as the Guide of their Conduct; and openly ridicule thoſe that do otherwiſe, call themſelves Chriſtians perhaps; but are totally void of Reverence for every Doctrine of Chriſtianity, that is above their Comprehenſion, for every Precept that contradicts their Inclination; and ſtrangely negligent even of natural Piety and ſocial Virtue. Larger Multitudes yet imagine, that they are mighty Religious Perſons, if they preſerve but a tolerable Regularity in the outward Acts of Devotion,

[b] Matt. xvi. 27.

Juſtice

Juſtice and Temperance: though not proceeding from any inward Principle of Love and Duty to God, not accompanied by any Senſe of their needing his Pardon through the bleſſed Jeſus, or his Help through the Influences of the Holy Spirit; not carried on to an uniform Habit either of Obedience or Reſignation, or animated by the Hopes of a better World. Indeed they moſt commonly live, and often die, as unconcerned about his future Diſpoſal of them, as if it were not a Matter of Moment at all, inſtead of being the only real one, that belongs to our Condition.

But, if poſſible, we have ſlighted him ſtill more, conſidered as a People, than ſeparately. We have enjoyed the greateſt national Bleſſings, without the leaſt national Thankfulneſs for them. In particular he hath bleſſed us with the cleareſt Knowledge of the ſeveral Obligations incumbent on us: and we have ſhewn the moſt abſolute Scorn of all Methods for promoting or ſecuring the Practice of them, even in thoſe Points, on which our public Welfare moſt confeſſedly depends. Nor have we hitherto received the Warnings, or even the Corrections of the Almighty, which have begun to overtake us, with more Reſpect, than his Mer-

 cies.

cies. You have juft heard the Cafe of the barren Fig-tree read in the Gofpel for the Day: *Behold, thefe three Years I come, feeking Fruit, and find none: cut it down, why cumbereth it the Ground*[e]*?* Brethren, what is our Cafe? The prefent is the fifth Year that we have profeffed to obferve a folemn Faft, on Account of our Sins and our Dangers, without making the leaft Reformation in any fingle Article. Nay, we have continually increafed in Neglect of Religion, in Gaiety and Madnefs for Pleafure: till we are come to purfue our Diverfions openly on the moft facred Day of the Week; and fome (for, in every Inftance, while the Offence is renewed, the Complaint muft) cannot perfuade themfelves to abftain from them, or from inviting large Companies of others to join in them, even on thefe Anniverfaries of peculiar Humiliation.

Such Outrages on Piety and common Decency as thefe, muft, when repeated after Notice taken of them, and Warning given againft them, which hath been faithfully done by the Minifters of God's Word, be deemed premeditated Infults, not Inadvertence and Forgetfulnefs. Yet Forgetfulnefs of the Moft High can

[e] Luke xiii. 7.

never

never be a flight Offence: and is greatly ag-
gravated by the ftrong Admonitions to remember him, which not only his holy Word and
our Confciences, would we hearken to them,
give us perpetually, but his Providence alfo
hath given us of late. The natural Confequences, and fuperadded Punifhments of our
Difregard to him, have appeared very plainly
for fome Time, and are daily becoming more
vifible and fenfible, in the Sins, and Follies,
and Diftreffes of private Life, in the general
Want of public Order and public Spirit, in Burthens and Uneafineffes; in Threatnings and
actual Attempts from Abroad to deprive us of
the Liberty we have abufed, and the Religion
we have fcorned; and fink us down into the
Slavery, and Superftition, and Wretchednefs,
that we have deferved to feel. Hitherto, indeed, the Storm hath not fallen upon us: but
it ftill hangs over us more heavily, than moft
of us have ever known: our Efforts to difpel it
have fucceeded very imperfectly: The Difficulty of renewing thofe Efforts muft be augmenting each Year: our Enemies are multiplied
in a dreadful Manner: and what Affiftance we
may expect from our Friends, God only knows.
One Thing, indeed, may afford fome Confola-

E 4

tion

tion to us. We have manifested, on Occasion of our Danger, an universal Zeal for that Establishment, which is the only human Means of preserving us from it. Had we failed in our Loyalty, we had completed our Wickedness: and should any Temptation hereafter intice or provoke us to fail in it, we and our Posterity are intirely undone. But there can be no sure Dependence on their Dutifulness to their King, who are undutiful to their God: or on their Attachment to the common Interest of the Society, who prefer every present Gratification to their own everlasting Welfare. Or if there could; a profane and wicked People will never have equal Spirit in Defence of the Community, for they have not equal Motives to it, with a pious and virtuous one. Or supposing their Courage ever so great: their Wealth, their Strength, their Union, their Assiduity, their Observance of Rules, their mutual Confidence, will be less: and those Vices, which have brought us already so far on our Way towards Ruin, must at Length, if we persist in them, bring us to it, merely by producing their natural Effects.

But could we have Hopes of escaping these, the Honour of the Divine Government is concerned

cerned not to let a national Contempt of it go unpunished, even in this World: and all Reliance on human Wisdom and Power, without Regard to God, will prove in the End fatal Self-Deceit. *When the Lord shall stretch out his Hand, both he that helpeth shall stumble, and he that is holpen shall fall down: they shall all fail together*[d]: *The Anger of the Lord shall not return, till he have performed the Thoughts of his Heart: in the latter Days ye shall consider it perfectly*[e].

But surely then we had much better consider it *in this our Day*[f]: and, as another Text awfully exhorts, *give Glory to the Lord our God, before he cause Darkness; and while we look for Light, he turn it into the Shadow of Death*[g]. Too many, of all Ranks, will probably slight whatever of this Kind is said, even from Scripture itself. But still our Commission is: *Son of Man, I send thee to the Children of Israel; to a rebellious Nation, that hath rebelled against me, they and their Fathers unto this very Day: and thou shalt say unto them, Thus saith the Lord; and thou shalt speak my Words unto them, whether they will hear, or whether they will*

---

[d] Isa. xxxi. 3. [e] Jer. xxiii. 20. [f] Luke xix. 42.
[g] Jer. xiii. 16.

forbear[h]. Men in Power and high Stations more especially, and they who aspire to them no less, have always been disposed to look with great Disdain on the artless and unwelcome Directions, which Religion suggests for Deliverance from Danger. They have more refined Contrivances, on which they rest; and scorn the plain Methods of Reconciliation to God, and trust in him, through our blessed Redeemer, as fitted only for the Populace to hearken to. But the Scripture hath provided an alarming Denunciation against Them in particular. *Hear the Word of the Lord, ye scornful Men, that rule this People which is in Jerusalem. Because ye have said, We have made a Covenant with Death, and with Hell are we at Agreement; when the overflowing Scourge shall pass through, it shall not come unto us; for we have made Lies our Refuge, and under Falsehood have we hid ourselves: Therefore thus saith the Lord God, Behold, I lay in Zion for a Foundation a Stone, a tried Stone, a precious Corner Stone, a sure Foundation: he that believeth, shall not make haste*[i]. *Judgment also will I lay to the Line, and Righteousness to the Plummet;*

[h] Ezek. ii. 3, 4, 7. x. 11.   [i] Or, be ashamed. See Rom. ix. 33.

and

*and the Hail shall sweep away the Refuge of Lies,
and the Waters shall overflow the hiding Place.
And your Covenant with Death shall be disan-
nulled, and your Agreement with Hell shall not
stand.   Now therefore be ye not Mockers, left
your Bands be made strong* [k].* Another Sort of
Perfons, extremely apt to defpife the Thought
of Reformation, indeed all ferious Thought
whatever, are they who abandon themfelves to
Indolence and Voluptuoufnefs, and the Study of
luxurious Elegance and Delicacy. But for thefe
likewife there is in the Treafury of the Prophets a Menace in Store, which contains, alas,
much too exact a Defcription of our own Times.
*Wo unto them that are at Eafe in Zion, that put
far away the Evil Day, that lie upon Beds of
Ivory, and stretch themfelves upon their Couches,
that eat the Lambs out of the Flock, and the
Calves out of the Midst of the Stall,* (the Luxury
of the Table had then made but a fmall Progrefs) *that chant to the Sound of the Viol, and
invent to themfelves Inftruments of Mufick, that
drink Wine in Bowls, and perfume themfelves
with the chief Perfumes* [l]*, but are not grieved*

---

[k] Ifa. xxviii. 14.—18, 22.   [l] In our Tranflation it is, anoint
themfelves with the chief Ointments. But this, though literal,
gives a different Idea now from what it did then.

for

*for the Affliction of Joseph. Therefore now shall
they go captive with the first that go captive, and
their Banquet shall be removed* [m]. Others again
are by no Means indifferent about the Storm,
which they see gathering; but have no Belief,
that Amendment, or any Thing, can disperse
it: and therefore will take no Pains in what
they conceive will produce no Good. But at
least to themselves Amendment will produce
the greatest Good: and Resolutions not to
amend, will bring, both upon Them and others,
more certain and speedy, and total Destruction;
which else, after all, may perhaps be avoided.
For hear the Declaration of God in this Case.
*Now therefore speak to the Men of Judah, and
to the Inhabitants of Jerusalem, saying: Thus
saith the Lord, Behold, I frame Evil against
you; return ye now every one from his evil Way,
and make your Ways and your Doings good. And
they said, There is no Hope: but we will walk
after our own Devices, and we will every one do
the Imagination of his evil Heart. Therefore
thus saith the Lord, Ask ye now among the Heathen, who hath heard such Things. I will scatter
them, as with an East Wind, before the Enemy:*

---

[m] Amos vi. 1, 3—7.

I will

I will shew them the Back, and not the Face, in the Day of their Calamity.

So that, whether it be Confidence, or Despair, that hinders Reformation, the Threatnings, you see, are the same. And the full Execution of these Threatnings, together with the Cause of it, is thus recorded in the Book of Chronicles. *The Lord God of their Fathers sent to them by his Messengers, because he had Compassion on his People, and on his Dwelling-Place. But they mocked the Messengers of God, and despised his Words, and misused his Prophets, until the Wrath of God arose against his People, till there was no Remedy. Therefore he brought upon them the King of the Chaldees, who slew their young Men with the Sword in the House of their Sanctuary, and had no Compassion upon young or old: he gave them all into his hand*.

How near we have approached to them in our Guilt, is too visible: how easily we may come to resemble them in our Punishment, is not less so. The Hand of God is plainly lifted up over us: the only Question is, Will we *humble ourselves under it*, or will we not? Will we yet acknowledge, that He is the Sovereign of the World, and obeying him the only Way to

* Jer. xviii. 11, 12, 13, 17.   * 2 Chr. xxxvi. 15, 16, 17.

I   profper?

profper? Will we yet *feek him, while he may be found*[p]; confefs our Sins, change our Conduct, and petition for his Mercy? There have been Circumftances, in which Repentance itfelf would not ftop the Courfe of temporal Punifh- ments, though it will always prevent eternal ones: in which God hath faid to his Prophets, *Pray not for this People for their Good. When they faft, I will not hear their Cry; and when they offer an Oblation, I will not accept them: but I will confume them by the Sword, and by the Famine, and by the Peftilence*[q]. Even to this Extremity we may reduce ourfelves: but that we are already in it, no Way appears. The general Rule of his Providence is, *At what In- ftant I fhall fpeak concerning a Nation, and con- cerning a Kingdom, to pluck up, and to pull down, and to deftroy it: if that Nation, againft whom I have pronounced, turn from their Evil, I will repent of the Evil that I thought to do unto them*[r]. And it ought to be our Perfua- fion, that we are within the Rule. Our Caufe is unqueftionably good: and though we have been, moft of us, lamentably wicked, yet through his Grace many have preferved their Integrity; and either for their Sake, or his

[p] Ifa. lv. 6.   [q] Jer. xiv. 11, 12.   [r] Jer. xviii. 7, 8.

Mercies Sake, we ſtill enjoy great Bleſſings. He hath been far from forſaking Us, to the Degree that We have forſaken him: elſe our State were wretched indeed: and would we but now *humble ourſelves* throughly *under his mighty Hand,* there is no Room to doubt, but *he would exalt us in due Time.*

Whenever he calls upon us to uſe the Inſtrument, he ſurely deſigns us to attain the End, for which it was formed. Now penitent Reformation is the natural, as well as the appointed Inſtrument for exalting both particular Perſons and Communities. Religion works indeed by Terror at firſt, and lowers the high Spirits of the Guilty: but only to raiſe them again on ſolid Grounds, inſtead of the treacherous Props which kept them up before. Without it, there is no Dignity in the Condition of Man: and how ſhould there be any expected in his Deportment? If Perſons either believe not in one, who ſees and rewards, or cannot hope that he will reward Good to them: if all that they promiſe themſelves be here, and they apprehend, that neither Annihilation or Miſery awaits them hereafter; they will of Courſe be many of them dangerous and miſchievous, the

Generality

Generality of them bafe and vile, attend folely to the Indulgence of their Fancies and their Senfes, *eat and drink, for To-morrow they die*[*]. Or if any Sparks of Worth do remain, unextinguifhed by fuch a mean Way of Thinking, they will have only an occafional and partial Influence. Or could it, in fome few, be a conftant and uniform one, yet they will be very few: and the Body of a People, if they are without Confcience towards God, will be without Honour and Probity towards Men, without Prudence and Magnanimity in the Conduct of themfelves, profligate and defpicable in all Refpects. But on the contrary, true Religion, for I fpeak not of fuperftitious Perfuafions and Obfervances, true Religion places Men above fordid Interefts, low Pleafures, and worldly Anxieties: teaches them to dread nothing, but offending their Maker; to fet their Hearts on nothing, but pleafing Him; and to have no Conception of pleafing him by any other Means, than rational Piety and genuine Virtue: it excites them by the nobleft of Motives to whatever is ufeful and eftimable; and reftrains them by the ftrongeft Terrors from whatever is bad and hurtful: obliges them to right Beha-

[*] 1 Cor. xv. 32.

viour

viour in the higheſt Proſperity, and ſupports them in it under the heavieſt Adverſities: inſpires Men with the moſt earneſt Concern for doing their Duty; and frees them from all Concern about the Conſequences of it in this World, by preſenting to their View the endleſs Recompences of a better.   Such, in ſome Degree, is the Influence even of natural Religion: but unſpeakably more powerful will that be found, *whereby are given unto us exceeding great and precious Promiſes, that by theſe we might be Partakers of the Divine Nature* [t].

Then farther, the Sentiments, which thus dignify every one's Behaviour ſingly, muſt have the ſame Influence upon all, conſidered as forming a Community.   Publick Welfare will never be conſulted as it ought, while Men act merely on ſeparate ſelfiſh Bottoms: nor ever fail to be conſulted, when a well-founded Faith in God animates their Zeal for general good.   Slights and Provocations, Difficulties and Riſques, private Advantages, and party or perſonal Attachments, may very eaſily ſway and bias all, that act from temporal Motives: but are nothing to ſuch as act from This; the only one that cannot poſſibly be at any Time overbalanced.   So

[t] 2 Pet. i. 4.

F

long

long as the State of Affairs is calm indeed, Government may go on very fmoothly, without
much Principle in thofe who are employed by
it, or live under it: perhaps the more fmoothly
for a while, in fome Cafes, the lefs Principle
there is.   But when Storms rife, as after fuch
Calms they will rife, then is the Time to fee,
in what the real Strength of Society confifts:
who will ftruggle, who will hazard, who will
be faithful to the laft.   They, that fear God,
certainly will: and we can have no Certainty
(how fhould we?) of any other.   Amongft
the truly religious, becaufe they are fuch, there
will be fecure and mutual Truft, faithful Oe-
conomy, and unwearied Application: their
Counfels will be fteady, their Undertakings juft,
their Execution bold, their Confidence in Heaven ftrong, and their Adherence to a righteous
Caufe unmoveable! Seldom, if ever, will a
State, which proceeds in this Manner, fail of
Succefs.   And were they to fail ever fo greatly,
nay, to be overwhelmed ever fo intirely, they
would fall with more Reputation and more
Happinefs, than others flourifh. But there is
always Reafon for better Hopes.   A Nation,
reverencing the Sovereign of the Univerfe, will
be reverenced by all around them, as *a wife*

and

*and understanding People, which hath the Lord
nigh unto them*[u]. Their Friends will know,
they can depend on them: their Enemies will
know, they have the utmost Efforts to fear
from them: both will know, and they themselves too, that even in their last Extremity,
Providence may be expected to fight for them.
*Great are the Troubles of the Righteous: but
the Lord delivereth him out of them all. The
Lord delivereth the Souls of his Servants: and
they, that put their Trust in him, shall not be
destitute*[w].

But then it must be observed, that such as
have long been Sinners, and are at last become
penitent, (the former is certainly our Case,
would to God the latter were!) if Relief doth
not appear immediately, ought to wait for it with
much Patience, and be well satisfied if they are
exalted in due Time: in God's Time, not their
own. Wickedness ruins Nations by Degrees:
Reformation may restore them by Degrees. An
imperfect Reformation will be likely to bring
forth but imperfect Fruits. And the completest
Reformation of a Few may prove insufficient to
save the Whole. Still these are Reasons, only

[u] Deut. iv. 6, 7.   [w] Psal. xxiv. 20, 22.

why

why All fhould repent: not why None fhould,
unlefs All will, which it is impoffible to forefee.
For be the Generality ever fo incorrigible, and
their Deftruction ever fo abfolutely decreed on
that Account: there is Encouragement enough,
notwithftanding, for thofe who do humble
themfelves, and return to a better Mind. *Seek
ye the Lord, all ye meek of the Earth, which
have wrought his Judgment. It may be ye fhall
be hid in the Day of the Lord's Anger*[x]. At
leaft, whatever fuch may fuffer in common with
others, far from being a Mark of his Anger
towards Them, will contribute largely to improve their Virtues, and increafe their future
Reward. So that in every Event they may *caft
all their Care on God, for he careth for them*[y].
Undoubtedly they will feel the Uneafinefs,
which human Nature muft from whatever is
painful to it: and in particular, a tender Concern for, Multitudes, who have none for themfelves. But ftill they will fubmit with Compofednefs and reverent Approbation to the fevereft Sentences of Heaven; and reflect with
Joy, that their chief Intereft is fafe, though
inferior Comforts be loft.

[x] Zeph. ii. 3.   [y] 1 Pet. v. 7.

Let

Let us therefore *acquaint ourselves with God,
and be at Peace* [z]: *For he will keep those in perfect Peace, whose Mind is stayed on Him* [a].
Whoever they are, that, sensible of their Offences and their Weakness, apply for the Pardon obtained by Jesus Christ, and the Grace
communicated by the Holy Spirit: who, in
their private Capacity, honour God, study to be
harmless and useful amongst Men, and govern
themselves by the Rules of Virtue; who also,
in their public Capacity, earnestly *pray for* and
impartially seek the *Peace of Jerusalem* [b], the
Welfare of their Country, civil and religious;
not led by Interest, Resentment or Vanity, but
having at Heart real common Good; and who
in their whole Conduct encourage and restrain
themselves as the Case requires, by the Faith
of a Future Recompence: whatever may befall
the Society, of which they are Part, it shall be
well with them. Whatever else they may undergo, others will have nothing to reproach
them with, they will have nothing to reproach
their own Souls with; and *in the Darkness
Light shall arise unto them* [c]. All such Persons
therefore, after doing conscientiously what is

---

[z] Job xxii. 21.   [a] Isa. xxvi. 3.   [b] Psal. cxxii. 6.
[c] Psal. cxii. 4.

F 3

incum-

incumbent on them, not only may, but ought
to be without Solicitude: and fhould let the
Foundation of their Peace be known; that all
around them may perceive, how vaftly preferable the Confolations of Religion are to every
other Method of making themfelves eafy. The
pious Man doth not labour to quiet his Thoughts
by obftinately fhutting his Eyes, or plunging
into Exceffes, or taking off his Attention by
Amufements: but can with Tranquillity look
towards the evil Day, and fee it coming: wait
for it, and bear his Share of it, lefs or greater;
being affured, that *all Things work together for
his Good*[a]. A very different State from theirs,
who know they have deferved the Judgments
of God, who know they have contributed to
bring them down on their own and others
Heads; who have nothing to cheer them, when
the Clouds gather on every Side of them; nothing to direct them, when the blackeft Tem-
peft pours upon them, but the momentary
Glimmerings of human Hope, ftruck out by
their own Imaginations; and if they fhould efcape, if they fhould outwardly profper again for
the prefent, will only be tempted by it to *trea-
fure up to themfelves* hotter *Wrath againft the*

[a] Rom. viii. 28.

Day

Day of Wrath[e], and final Judgment. But hear, I intreat you, how the Word of God expreſſes the Caſe of each: and may its enlivening Exhortation to the former, and its terrifying Admonition to the latter, ſink deep into your Breaſts. *Who is among you, fearing the Lord, that walketh in Darkneſs, and hath no Light? Let him truſt in the Name of the Lord, and ſtay upon his God. Behold, all ye that kindle a Fire, and compaſs yourſelves about with Sparks; walk in the Light of your Fire, and in the Sparks which ye have kindled: this ſhall ye have of mine Hand, ye ſhall lie down in Sorrow*[f].

[e] Rom. ii. 5.   [f] Iſa. l. 10, 11.

SER-

SERMON IV.

2 SAM. X. 12.

*Be of good Courage and let us play the Men for
our People, and for the Cities of our God:
And the Lord do that which seemeth him
good.*

MANY of you, I hope, remember, that
I discoursed to you upon these Words,
a year and seven Months ago [*]: when
God, for our Sins, threatened us first, with
what, for the Continuance of them, he hath
at length permitted to fall on Part of this Land.
The Renewal, and nearer Approach, of the
same Danger, requires a more earnest incul-
cating of the same Exhortations. For perhaps
we may now lay to Heart the Things we did

[*] *February* 26, 1743-4.

not

not then.   It is very true, the Pulpit ought
never to be prophaned, and I truſt never hath
or ſhall by me, to ſerve the Purpoſes of Party-
Intereſt; or intermeddle with any Points of a
Political Nature, about which the Friends of
their Country, that think at all, can poſſibly
be of different Opinions.   But the preſent is a
common Cauſe, affecting every one of us, without Diſtinction, in what is moſt important to
us: and God forbid, that the Miniſters of the
Goſpel ſhould be either unwilling or afraid to
ſpeak, when his Providence calls on them ſo
loudly, to lift up their Voice.   Should the
Storm, which is now beating on many of our
Fellow-Subjects, be diſperſed by infinite Goodneſs ever ſo ſoon and ſo intirely, without reach-
ing Us; it may yet be of unſpeakable Uſe, to
have made the proper Reflections and Reſolu-
tions, whilſt it was approaching towards us.
And ſhould the Almighty ſuffer us to feel it,
as we have well deſerved; nothing, but thinking and behaving rightly under his Judgments,
can give us Hope of his Mercy to moderate and
ſhorten them.

Now whatever is requiſite for theſe Ends, is
clearly comprehended in the Words of the Text;
which

which bring naturally to our Thoughts the three following Particulars.

I. The Interests we have at Stake. *Our People, and the Cities of our God.*

II. The Spirit, which we ought to shew in defending them. *Be of good Courage, and let us play the Men.*

III. The humble Dependance on Heaven, which we ought to exercise at the same Time. *And the Lord do that which seemeth him good.*

I. The Interests we have at Stake. *Our People, and the Cities of our God:* in other Words, our Civil Rights, and our Religion.

The Defence of their Persons and Possessions against lawless Power, and the secure Enjoyment of the Means of Happiness here and hereafter, were the great Motives, that induced Men to submit originally to Government. And every particular Government is good or bad, as it answers or fails of answering these Purposes. Now in our own, as it stands at present, our Liberties are greater than those of any other Nation upon Earth: we enjoy them so fully, that we abuse them beyond Example: and, I believe, no one Person amongst us, of Knowledge

ledge and Confideration, doth or can fufpect
our King of having the leaft Defign to infringe
any Branch of them. The private Property of
the very Meaneft is as fafe from the Violence
and Oppreffion of the Greateft, as good Laws
and an impartial Execution of them can be
hoped to make it. And for the public Burthens
we labour under, we have laid them on ourfelves, by Reprefentatives of our own Choice,
for Ufes, which we and our Fathers, very juftly
in the main, thought neceffary: In particular
for the moft important Ufe, of fecuring the
Nation, from Time to Time, againft the Mifchief that now once more hangs over us: which
if we at laft get rid of, all we have fpent is well
laid out; and if we fubmit to, all is thrown
away.

Still, there may doubtlefs have been Faults
committed, in Relation both to thefe and other
Matters. But then, Part of the Faults commonly charged may be imaginary; for we are
all as fallible, as thofe whom we blame; and
few of us in fo good a Situation for judging.
Part may be of fmall Confequence; and therefore no Ground for any great Refentment. Part
may have arifen from our own Mifconduct, as
much, if not more, than from that of our Superiors.

periors. Part again may have proceeded from excufable Miftakes or Infirmities of theirs; for which, as we need Allowance in ourfelves, we fhould make Allowance in others: efpecially in Princes, for the fame Reafon as in Parents; and to a fit Degree, in thofe alfo that are employed by them. But whencefoever apprehended Grievances may have come, we have legal, conftitutional, peaceable Means for redreffing them; with uncontrolled Liberty to ufe thofe Means, if we will. And fuppofe they have not operated fo fpeedily, or fo effectually, as we may wifh: yet, if Force may be ufed inftead of them, upon every Failure or Delay, efpecially when caufed merely by Difference of Opinions amongft ourfelves, no Society can ever fubfift. And if we are too corrupt a People to expect any Good from mutual Perfuafion; much lefs can we expect it from mutual Violence.

Then laftly, as for our Religion; the leaft valued, I fear, yet infinitely the moft valuable of all our Bleffings; and which guards and fences the reft, in a Manner that nothing elfe can: our Religion, I fay, is undeniably the moft rational and worthy of God, the moft humane and beneficial to Men, the furtheft from being either tyrannical or burdenfome, the freeft from
Super-

Superftition, Enthufiafm, and Gloominefs of any in the World. It is eftablifhed with fuch Care, that the Support of it is infeparable from that of the Civil Government: yet happily with fuch Moderation, as to bear hard on none who diffent from it. The Practice of it indeed, we muft own, hath not been inforced on its Profeffors, fo generally or fo carefully as it ought, either by the Authority or the Example of thofe, whofe Duty it is. Would to GOD it had! GOD grant it may! But ftill, they who have not duly excited Men to Piety, have not reftrained them from it: and every one's Difregard to it is principally chargeable on himfelf alone.

This I apprehend to be a true and a modeft Account of our prefent Condition: for I have put the Advantages of it at the loweft, in order to fay nothing that can be difputed. And what are we to change it for, if the Attempt, now making, fhould fucceed? Indeed what have we to expect before it can fucceed, (for every one muft be convinced, that it will not be tamely fubmitted to,) but a wide and horrid View, in Proportion as it makes a Progrefs, of Bloodfhed in the Field and out of it, and of Ravage at the Pleafure of a rude and uncivilized People, to

the

the imminent Hazard of every Thing, and every
Perfon, dear to us? Judgments, which this
Ifland hath been long without experiencing:
but how long, and how heavily it may groan
under them now, unlefs a fpeedy Check be
given to this Rebellion, God only knows. For
a conquering Enemy, had he the Will, which
is dreadful to truft to, hath often not the Power
of reftraining the Defolations of Fire and
Sword, when once they are begun.

But fuppofe this Beginning of Sorrows over:
what muft follow?

With Regard to our Civil Concerns: How
large Numbers are there, who have no other
Security for a confiderable Part, it may be the
Moft, or the Whole of their Property, than
the Continuance of the Government now in
being; in whofe Hands it actually is? And
fhould that Government fail: as it cannot be
hoped, that what hath been lent for its Support, and proved one of its main Supports, will
be regarded very favourably by thofe who come
to overturn it; how terrible may the Diftreffes
of fuch Perfons be, and how much farther than
themfelves muft they extend? To all their Do-
meftics, all their Dependants, all that have
Dealings or Concerns with them. What Multitudes

titudes are there again, whose Fortunes are intirely, or principally, built on Royal Grants,
judicial Determinations, or Acts of the Legislature, made within the last six and fifty Years?
which, in Case of a Change, will all become
questionable, as done by incompetent Authority, and lie at the Mercy of we know not
whom. The Person, who now threatens us,
comes attended with a large and an indigent
Train of Followers, collected from each of the
Three Nations, who will think, and do their
utmost to make him think, that the long Sufferings of many of them, and the present dangerous
Services of many more, can never be rewarded
with sufficient Bounty. And when Revenge,
and Poverty, and Avarice, are set on Work together, what Forfeitures may be claimed, what
Misdemeanors and Treasons charged, in a Nation, which will be looked on as the Whole of
it involved in Treason, for so many Years past;
or how unfairly the plainest Laws in our Favour may be interpreted to admit of such Attempts, or even wrested to serve them; which
of us all can so much as guess, or who can be
assured of his own Safety?

But besides these Hazards to the Properties
and the Lives of particular Persons, in what

State

State will be Commerce and Poſſeſſions of the Nation be? Think, what innumerable Debts the Pretender to His Majeſty's Crown muſt needs have contracted in ſo long a Space, during which he hath had nothing of his own to ſubſiſt on: think, what immenſe Sums foreign Princes may charge on Account of moſt expenſive Wars, which they may plead were begun or carried on for his Service: and how dreadfully this Nation may be exhauſted, to ſatisfy but a ſmall Part of theſe Demands: for which it will make no Amends, to annihilate the preſent Incumbrances on our public Revenues, by a ruinous Breach of the public Faith. Think alſo, once more, what fatal Conceſſions the Powers who ſupport the preſent Invaſion, and who will be wanted for a continual Support, even were it to ſucceed; what fatal Conceſſions they will aſſuredly require in Return, of Places on which our Trade depends, of Indulgences in Trade to themſelves, of Reſtrictions upon Us; which will reduce us to a Condition impotent, precarious, and deſpicable.

I ſay not this, or any Thing, to raiſe in you a Spirit of unchriſtian Bitterneſs, either againſt the ignorant Wretches that have been deluded into this Rebellion, or even againſt their Lead-

G

ers.

ers. Let them be judged of with all the Charity, let them be treated with all the Mercy,
which their Cafe will poffibly allow: only let
us fee the Mifchief, that their Succefs would
bring on us, and exert ourfelves accordingly to
prevent it.

But were we ever fo fafe in other Refpects:
what Security can we have with Refpect to our
happy, envied, legal Conftitution; when that
Power of fufpending and difpenfing with Laws,
and levying Money without Law, which lays
every Provifion, that can be made in Favour of
the Subject, wholly at the Sovereign's Feet;
and yet was not only claimed, but exercifed immediately before the Revolution, fhould come
of Courfe to be eftablifhed as a juft Prerogative,
by what will be called a Reftoration? The
Rights, that we have enjoyed as indifputably
our own, from that Time to this, may then be
accounted feditious and treafonable Pretences;
and every Expreffion of Fondnefs for any Remain of Liberty, be deemed a Step towards
Rebellion: as indeed it will be thought but
natural, to fufpect and ftifle the leaft breathing
of that Spirit which once delivered us, in order
to prevent another Change. Efforts notwithftanding will, in all Likelihood, be made to-

wards

wards one: how bloody and how fatal, who can tell? The Apprehenfion of thefe Efforts will be a much ftronger Plea, than in the late King *James's* Time, for keeping up a charge-able and dangerous ftanding Force, perhaps a foreign one. The Dread of that Force will in-timidate fome; and the Principle of turning to their own Advantage what they cannot help, will intice others, to go every Length of Com-pliance that they are required. And a Prince, coming in on the Bottom of Right Hereditary and Indefeafible, will think he hath the cleareft Title to Abfolute Power. His Partizans, even whilft he is out of Poffeffion, have openly avow-ed that he hath: and what can be expected then, if he fhould get into it! The mere Ex-ercife of fuch a Power very probably will not fatisfy: but Declarations and Oaths be invented, for the Acknowledgment and Support of it; which, it will be impoffible for us, either to make with Innocence, or to refufe with Safety.

Then for the State of our Religion: No one Inftance can be given, that Popery ever fpared Proteftantifm for any Continuance, after it was able fafely to opprefs it. But leaft of all will Favour be fhewn here, longer than Neceffity obliges. For, to whatever Tendernefs many

G 2

of

of that Communion may be inclined; as, no
Doubt, there are Numbers amongst them of
mild and worthy Persons: yet the uncharitable
Part will assuredly prevail, as they always have
done every-where; and falsely imputing to our
Religion that pretended Disloyalty, which proceeded only from their illegal Attempts to overturn the whole Constitution, will not fail to
argue, that the same Cause must produce again
the same Effect, and therefore must not be permitted to subsist. Think then, all that love
the Church of *England*, all that believe the
Doctrines of the Reformation to be the Truth
of Christ, what a Condition it will be, either
to profess and practise the Falsehoods and Im-
pieties, of which you are so thoroughly convinced, or to be driven from this, and every
other Place of God's public Worship into Corners: nay, in a while, to be dragged out thence
also, and sacrificed to that *Mother of Abominations*, which hath so long been *drunken with
the Blood of the Saints* [b].

And let even them who are indifferent, or
Doubters, or Unbelievers in Religion, reflect
on this at least: that, as they are always in-
veighing against Superstition, so the Church of

[b] Rev. xvii. 5, 6.

Rome

Rome is over-run with it to the higheſt Degree
poſſible: and, as they are always exclaiming
againſt the Wealth and the Power of Eccleſi-
aſtics; ſo the Wealth and the Power, the Pride
and the Tyranny of Popery, are unſpeakably
the greateſt, that ever the World knew. And
if they will notwithſtanding go at preſent upon
their favourite Maxim, that All Religions are
the ſame, it will be a juſt Judgment of God to
make them feel the Difference.

But to theſe Things it may be anſwered, that
the moſt ſolemn Obligations have unqueſtion-
ably been entered into, by him who claims the
Crown, for our intire Security, both in Church
and State. Nor indeed could any thing ſeem
in Speculation more likely: becauſe nothing is
more apparently requiſite in all common Policy.
And yet, ſurprizing as it is, no one clear and
explicit Declaration of this Kind was made by
the Pretender at the Time of the laſt Rebellion:
nor can I hear of any made by him at preſent.
And I beg you to conſider, if he will not promiſe plainly now, what will he do afterwards?
For as to any good Words, given by another in
his Name, what can be eaſier for him, than to
diſavow them, as going beyond the Commiſſion
which he granted? But ſuppoſe the ſtrongeſt

G 3

Aſſurances

Affurances given by himfelf: were they not
given by the bloody Queen *Mary* to her Proteftant Subjects, who had fully merited them
by their Zeal for raifing her to the Throne?
And did fhe not perfecute them immediately,
and burn them in little more than a Twelvemonth? Were they not given by the late King
James? And had he not ftrong Motives of Gratitude, as well as Confcience, to keep them?
And yet did he keep them for the fmalleft Part
of four Years? How can we then flatter ourfelves, that any one, who claims under him,
will be at all more favourable to that Religion,
and thofe Liberties, which have been all this
Time the capital Enemies to his Pretenfions?
The moft formal Declarations, that he can
make, have been over and over, and long fince
the Revolution, declared by the Authority of
the See of *Rome* :" utterly null and void from
" the Beginning, whenever they are prejudicial,
" in any Manner, and the leaft Degree" (I ufe
the very Words of Pope *Clement* XI. in the
very Cafe of Stipulations made in Favour of
Proteftants) " to the Catholic Faith, the Sal-
" vation of Souls, or to any Rights of the
" Church whatfoever; even though fuch En-
" gagements have been often ratified, and con-
" firmed

" firmed by Oath[*]." Let therefore the Pretender to the Crown make Promiſes ever ſo full and expreſſive, let his natural Diſpoſitions to keep them be ever ſo favourable; yet, as he profeſſes Subjection of Conſcience to the Pope's Determinations, under whoſe Eye he hath long reſided, in whoſe Dominions his Son, who hath now invaded us, was born and educated, and by whoſe Bounty they have both been all along ſupported; he cannot refuſe to break any Ties, which ſhall be declared ſinful by his infallible Guide; who may purpoſely have connived at his engaging in them, in order to his breaking them at a proper Time. But if he were to refuſe it; can we imagine, that all his Succeſſors too will be ſo obſtinately undutiful, as to ſpare a Religion which they mortally hate, when they believe extirpating it will intitle them to heaven, and atone for all the Sins of a wicked Life?

It muſt be acknowledged, Popery hath appeared milder of late, than in former Ages. Yet even our Days have known the Executions of *Thorn*, and the Baniſhments of *Saltzburgh*: and *France*, this very Year, hath been perſe-

[*] Clem. XI. Pont. Max. Epiſt. & Brevia. fol. Romæ, 1724. tom. ii. p. 179.

                              cuting

cuting and murdering our Proteftant Brethren for the Profeffion of their Faith. Nor hath the Church of *Rome* ever given up any one of the Claims, which it may have forborn to exercife: and, fhould it once regain fo much of its an⌐ cient Power, as would neceffarily follow from prevailing here, it would foon refume its ancient Fiercenefs in Proportion.

Shall we perfuade ourfelves then, that Fear will reftrain a Popifh Prince from attempting to overturn our Religion and Laws? But what if his greateft Fear fhould be that of Damnation for not attempting it? which was the known Cafe of King *James,* and may be that of others after him. Or what if it fhould be held the fafeft Way, in a political View, to make thorough Work at once, by the Affiftance of Foreigners, now preparing to invade us?

Still it may be faid, that whoever becomes our King, will at leaft, for his own Intereft, be careful of the Trade and Power of the Nation. But how can he, if he would; when he muft undoubtedly have promifed the contrary to foreign Powers already? And if he is capable of deceiving Them, how fhall We truft him? But fuppofing he hath promifed them nothing: yet, if he prevails by their Help, what can he

be

be elſe, than a Deputy and a Viceroy, ſubject
to the Commands of our moſt formidable Adverſaries?

This Conſideration ought in Reaſon to alarm
even thoſe who wiſh well to his Cauſe, even
thoſe who profeſs his Religion; and make them
utter Enemies to his coming in ſuch a Manner,
however deſirous they may be of his coming
otherwiſe. For can we, or can they, make
Terms with the Power of *France*, when we
have once given it a footing in the Heart of our
Country; or hope, that any Terms, which are
made, will ever be obſerved? Will that moſt
ambitious and perfidious Crown loſe ſuch an
Opportunity of weakening us by our own
Strength, making us dependent on itſelf for
ever, and Tools to enſlave the reſt of *Europe?*
Will it not treat both us, and the King it ſets
over us, as the Tyrant of *Babylon* did the Prince,
whom he gave to the *Jews? He hath made a
Covenant with him, and taken an Oath of him;
he hath taken alſo the Mighty of the Land; that
the Kingdom might be baſe, that it might not lift
up itſelf; but that by the keeping of his Covenant
it might ſtand* [a].

[a] Ezek. xvii. 13, 14.

Such

Such then being the View of our Dangers, let us proceed to confider.

II. The Spirit, with which we ought to defend ourfelves againft them. *Let us be of good Courage, and play the Men.* Thefe Words may feem to exprefs the Duty of the Soldiery alone. And, without Queftion, they exprefs that peculiarly: and, joined with the following ones, clearly fhew, that a ftrong Senfe of Religion, and a virtuous Concern for the common Welfare, are the two Principles, that will give military Perfons Bravery and Succefs; as they did to thofe, whofe Hiftory the Text relates. But, ftill the more literal Tranflation is, *Be ftrong, and let us ftrengthen one another*[e]. In this Senfe they concern us All: this therefore I fhall follow.

And if ever Caufe required exerting and joining all the Strength, and all the Courage we have, This is that Caufe. For the Attack is made by our Enemies, foreign and domeftic at once, on every Thing dear to us, Civil and Sacred: and Confcience towards God, as well as private Intereft and public Good, demands our utmoft Zeal in fuch a Conteft.

[e] See Gen. xxv. 22. xli. 2.   2 Kings xiv. 8, 11.

The

The Plea, which some would use to check this Ardour, as if the Government we live under ought not to be supported, because the late King *James* and his Son were set aside by the People, is absolutely groundless. For indeed King *James* set himself aside; abandoned the Government wilfully, rather than administer it according to Law: and by so doing, left the Nation at Liberty, or rather under Necessity to provide for itself in the Manner it did; especially as he carried away the Person, whom he called his Son, along with him. And had he not been carried away; all the World knows, it was generally and strongly suspected, that he was not the Queen's Child; and the three Estates of the Kingdom, the only fit Judges of a doubtful Succession, fixed it without taking Notice of him. But had none of these Things been so; that unhappy King, seduced by *Romish* Bigots, had invaded, with a high Hand, the Religious and Civil Rights of his People: instead of giving the least Hope of Amendment, he was going on with Rapidity to the utter Destruction of both. And Subjects were not made for Princes, to be treated as their absolute Property, and descend from one to another like Cattle, let them be used as they will: But

Princes

Princes were made for their Subjects; to govern
them legally, and seek their Good. What is
the Duty of the one, is the Right of the other:
and where there is a Right, there ought to be
a Remedy. Common Remedies are ever to be
used in common Cases: and if they are insufficient, single Persons ought to bear every Thing,
and Nations, every Thing that can be borne
without Destruction; rather than break the
public Peace, and established Order of Government. But in extreme, imminent, universal Dangers, Methods of the last Resort, if
necessary and likely to succeed, are fully war-
ranted; by the Nature of the Thing, by our
original Constitution, by ancient Practice upon
it, and royal Recognitions of it.
 The Scripture indeed commands what Reason
itself doth, Subjection to the supreme Powers.—
But how many other Commands are there,
which confessedly admit of proper Exceptions?
And were this to admit of none, yet the Scripture doth not determine, in whose Hands the
supreme Power is lodged. And where it is
divided, as it is with Us, between the King
and his great Council, by whose joint Authority every Statute is expressed to be made: he,
who refuses to stand to that Division, as the

late

late King *James* did openly, both by Word and Deed, renounces the Authority that belonged to him under it; and other Authority he hath none. Or fuppofe even this doubtful; the Scripture requires Subjection: But to whom? To *the Powers that be*, the actual, vifible Governments of every Country. Thefe it declares *are ordained of God*; and that *they who refift, fhall receive Damnation*[f]. Not the leaft Hint given, of enquiring into the Juftice of an Eftablifhment in its firft Rife, long ago: a Thing which few Subjects can do, and perhaps few Governments can bear. Not the flighteft Intimation, of adhering for ever to the Family of an abdicated Prince, and going on, Age after Age, to afcribe the fovereign Authority over a Nation, to a Perfon that hath no Means of exercifing any one Act of Authority. The Neceffities of Mankind render it abfurd: the Practice and the Notions of Mankind have always been contrary to it. Heathens, *Jews*, Chriftians, Papifts, Proteftants, all the World have agreed in the Point with univerfal Confent; excepting a fmall Handful of Men in this one Age and Nation: Perfons greatly to be pitied, and highly to be efteemed, while they fubmit

[f] Rom. xiii. 1, 2.

peaceably

peaceably to Inconveniences for Confcience
Sake; but furely guilty of as indefenfible a Sin-
gularity, as ever was.

There may indeed often be a Doubt, and
fometimes it may laft a good while, which are
the Powers that be: whether a Government is
yet to be confidered as eftablifhed, or not. But
in our own Cafe, if a Duration of fo many
Years, and the peaceable Succeffion of fo many
Princes, and the repeated Acknowledgments of
the whole People of thefe-Kingdoms, and of all
the Sovereigns and Nations of the Earth, do
not make it a clear Point, in whofe Hands the
fupreme Authority of this Country long hath
been, and actually now is: nothing of fuch a
Nature can ever be clear at all. Very few of
Us have either known, or lived under any other
Government: we have all of us claimed, and
enjoyed the Protection of this: we have acted
in Purfuance of its Authority; we have prayed
continually for its Prefervation; we have many
of us bound our Souls by folemn Oaths, and
fome of us by repeated ones, to maintain it:
in fo doing, we maintain at the fame Time,
every Thing that is valuable to us and our
Pofterity: and there cannot be a firmer Tie
upon us, than thefe Things together: nor more

4

abandoned

abandoned Wickednefs, than to break through it.

Strengthened thus then within ourfelves, let us proceed to *ftrengthen one another.* God knows, inftead of this, we have taken great Pains to weaken one another, by feparate Intereſts and Views, Animofities and Refentments, unkind Sufpicions, and unjuft Imputations. What Party or Sort of Men hath been moft to blame in this Refpect, were it ever fo eafy to fay, would be very unfit: when the plain Concern is, not to accufe and recriminate, but all to unite in what affects all fo nearly. They therefore, who have hitherto thought the Danger of fuch an Attempt fmall, let them now fhew they were far from wifhing it greater. They who have been diffatisfied with particular Meafures of Government, let them now give Proof, that they were not difaffected to the Government itfelf: and if poffibly in any Thing they may have oppofed too far, take this fitteft Opportunity of making Amends. This will demonftrate the Uprightnefs of their Intentions; give Weight to their Sentiments on other Matters, and pull down the falfe Hopes, that our Enemies have founded on our domeftic Difputes. But then, at the fame Time, if the

Zeal

Zeal of any for the prefent Eftablifhment, hath tempted them to judge too hardly concerning the Affection of others towards it, they ought now candidly to acknowledge their Error: embrace thofe as true Friends, who approve themfelves to be fuch in the Day of Trial; and remember for the future, that Strength is attained, not by Divifion, but by Union. Indeed we fhould all remember, inftead of aggravating what our Oppofers have done amifs, to reflect ferioufly what we and our Friends have been faulty in: and perhaps we fhould moft of us find, it hath been a great deal too much.

But it is not mutual good Temper alone, that our Cafe requires; but mutual Affiftance and Encouragement, to be given with Spirit by each of us, according to his Ability, and the Nature of his Station, to all around him: by ranking ourfelves openly on the Side we are of; joining our Counfels, contributing our Money, hazarding our Perfons, if need require it; by inftructing, undeceiving, exciting, fortifying, as many others as we can. That Part would be indifferent, Part timorous, and All refift weakly, was the great Thing, that the Adverfaries of the Government promifed themfelves,

and

and its Friends were apprehenfive of. God be thanked, both of them in fome Degree have feen their Miftake. Let us go on to complete the Conviction, by a daily Increafe of refolute Activity. *Strengthen ye the weak Hands, and confirm the feeble Knees: fay to them that are of a fearful Heart, Be ftrong, fear not*[t].

One Thing more, to be mentioned under this Head, is, that if the prefent Endeavour to ruin us fhould increafe, though it were confiderably, the public Expence neceffary to defend us, we are furely neither to wonder, nor to murmur at it; but bear with Chearfulnefs what may be inconvenient, in order to prevent what muft be ruinous; and confider well, that were this Defign to take Place, we fhould probably pay much more to Foreigners, as a Reward for enflaving us, than now to our own Governors, as the Means of keeping us free.

But human Means alone, human Prudence and Strength, be it ever fo great, is no fufficient Ground of Confidence. For *the Moft High ruleth in the Kingdom of Men, and giveth it to whomfoever he will*[u]. We muft never forget therefore,

[t] Ifa. xxxv. 3, 4.   [u] Dan. iv. 17.

H   III. An

III. An humble Dependance on Heaven for
the Event of all. *And the Lord do that which
seemeth him good.*

What it will seem good to him to do with
Us, when we confider our National Wickednefs and Ingratitude to him, it muft be acknowledged we have great Caufe to fear. He hath
blefled thefe Nations beyond moft, if not any
other Part of the World: and we have turned
all his Blefſings into Occaſions of Sin. He hath
given us Wealth: and we have applied it to
the wicked Purpofes of Diffolutenefs and Luxury.   He hath given us Liberty: and we have
abufed it to the bitterest Hatred, and the groffeft
Licentioufnefs.   He hath given us true Religion: and we have flighted and fcorned it;
caft off the Worfhip of God, received the
Mercies of his Providence without Thankfulnefs, and the Threatnings of it without Humility: nay, ridiculed the Obligations even of
Probity and moral Virtue, till we have fcarce
Principle enough left to be concerned for any
Thing, but prefent Pleafure and prefent Intereft. Our Abhorrence of Popery is gone: our
Zeal againft Slavery is degenerated into Faction:
our Zeal for the Government, into private Self-
* ifhnefs.

iſhneſs.   We daily accuſe one another of theſe Things: we never think of reforming ourſelves. And what can be, in a rational View, the probable Conſequence, in a religious one, the juſt Puniſhment of ſuch Behaviour, but that which the Divine Wiſdom has ſo clearly foretold? *For that they hated Knowledge, and did not chuſe the Fear of the Lord; they would none of my Counſel, and deſpiſed my Reproof: therefore ſhall they eat of the Fruit of their own Way, and be filled with their own Devices*[1].

It is by ſlow and ſilent, but it is by effectual Methods, that God ſhews himſelf the Governor of the World.   Princes, that neglect to ſupport His Authority, ſhall find their own decay with it.   Subordinate Rulers, that truſt to other than virtuous Arts of Government, ſhall find they have leaned on a broken Reed.   And Nations, that indulge Profaneneſs and Profligateneſs, ſhall experience them to bring on Confuſion and Ruin.   Eſcaping it in one Shape for once is nothing: in that, or ſome other, it muſt fall upon them, if they continue ſuch as they are.   And were ever ſo great Ruin to fall

----

[1] Prov. i. 29, 30, 31.

upon Us now, what would it be more, than *Samuel's* Prediction verified? *If ye shall still do wickedly, ye shall be consumed, both ye and your King*[k]. And what could we say, but acknowledge before God, with the penitent *Jews* in *Nehemiah, Thou art just in all that is brought upon us: for thou hast done right, but we have done wickedly: neither have our Kings, our Princes, our Priests, nor our Fathers* (would to God there were not the most Cause of all to add, nor we ourselves) *kept thy Law*[l].

Considering our Case in this Light then, we have small reason to *be of good Courage.* And yet, considering the divine Mercies, we are far from having any Reason to despond, if we have any Heart to repent. The Cause we are engaged in, is that of Right and Truth, and God's own Honour. Defending it valiantly, is performing one Part of our Duty to him: and deserting it, would be filling up at once the Measure of our Iniquities to the utmost. Wicked as we have been, and are, yet if we will but, *at least in this our Day, know the Things that belong to our Peace*[m], there is still abundant

---

[k] 1 Sam. 12. 25.   [l] Neh. ix. 33. 34.   [m] Luke xix. 42.

Room

Room to truſt in his gracious Protection, that we have ſo often experienced: and, provided we can but now bring our Hearts in earneſt to fear God, we have no Need to fear Man. What hath hitherto happened, is indeed more than enough to awaken us from that Supineneſs, which it is aſtoniſhing we ſhould have indulged ſo long; but not at all to make us doubtful concerning the Event, were there only any Proſpect, that we ſhould render ourſelves fit Objects of our Maker's Favour. For the Sake of a few good, there may be Mercy in Store for the reſt. The more of us become ſo, the greater is the Hope. And would but this National Alarm produce, what undoubtedly Heaven hath deſigned it for, a National Reformation; we might boldly ſay to our Enemies, in the Words of holy Writ: *Aſſociate yourſelves, O ye People, and ye ſhall be broken in Pieces: take Counſel together, and it ſhall come to nought: ſpeak the Word, and it ſhall not ſtand: for God is with us. Sanctify therefore the Lord of Hoſts, and let him be your Fear, and let him be your Dread, and he ſhall be for a Sanctuary*. For God will ſave* Sion,

* Iſa. viii. 9, 10, 13, 14.

H 3

and

and will build the Cities of Judah. *The Pofte-*
rity alfo of his Saints fhall inherit it; and they
that love his Name fhall dwell therein[*]. *Their*
Children fhall continue, and their Seed fhall be
eftablifhed before him[r].

[*] Pfalm lxix. 35, 36.   [r] Pfalm cii. 8.

SER-

SERMON V.

(Preached in 1745.)

PHIL. iv. 6, 7.

*Be careful for nothing: but in every Thing by
Prayer and Supplication, with Thankſgiving,
let your Requeſts be made known unto God.
And the Peace of God, which paſſeth all Underſtanding, ſhall keep your Hearts and Minds,
through Chriſt Jeſus.*

DANGERS are ſo conſtant, and Sufferings ſo frequent, in human Life, that
behaving properly under the Apprehen-
ſions and Experience of them, conſtitutes a very
conſiderable Part of our Buſineſs here. But
when Providence permits a peculiar Degree of
either to be our Lot, it calls us peculiarly to
think, what Methods will beſt preſerve us from
them, or carry us through them. Now theſe
are of two Sorts: Worldly Prudence, and Re-

ligious

ligious Wifdom. The Precepts of the former
it is not the Bufinefs of this Place to deliver;
but to limit and perfect them by the Dictates
of the latter: that we may neither endeavour
to fecure ourfelves by acting wrong, nor doubt
of Support in acting right. We are apt to look
on Religion, very injurioufly, as only prefcrib-
ing difagreeable Duties; whereas it fuggefts the
kindeft Advice, and fuperadds the moft comfortable Promifes: which cannot be done more
completely, in the great Point of moderating
Fear and Uneafinefs, than it is in the Text:
where we have

I. A friendly Caution: *Be careful for nothing.*

II. A moft neceffary Direction: *But in every
Thing by Prayer and Supplication, with Thankf-
giving, let your Requefts be made known unto
God.*

III. And Affurance of the happy Effect,
which this Conduct will produce: *And the
Peace of God, which paffeth all Underftanding,
fhall keep your Hearts and Minds, through Chrift
Jefus.*

I. A friend-

1. A friendly Caution: *Be careful for nothing:* Words, which neither common Reason allow us to take in their utmoſt Extent, nor Scripture itſelf. For it every-where demands from us the moſt earneſt Care about the Things of another World: and enjoins, quite as often as it needed, a moderate Care about the Affairs. of This. *Being careful* therefore muſt mean, in the Paſſage which I have read to you, as an Expreſſion mighty little varied from it, being full of Care, doth for the moſt Part, in our daily Speech; not a diſcreet and rational, but a diſquieting and tormenting Solicitude: and that principally, not concerning our Behaviour, which is the only Thing in our Power; but the Event, which is often entirely out of it. This the Original *Greek* Phraſe elſewhere uſually ſignifies, though not always. In the Sixth of St. *Matthew* it is many Times rendered, *Take no Thought.* But there alſo we muſt remember, that only what is immoderate was intended to be forbidden : which, it had been happy, if our Tranſlation had more determinately expreſſed.

Thoughtfulneſs concerning our Deportment, our Welfare, that of others, and the Public, ſo far as it will really be of Uſe, is a Duty of

indiſ-

indifpenfable Obligation.   And firft acting at
Random, then turning our Eyes from the evil
Day, when we fee it coming, inftead of confidering how we may avert it, or make the beft
Provifion againft it, will prove the fureft Way
to bring it on with its blackeft Horrors.   But
the contrary Extreme, Anxiety, is both a miferable Feeling in itfelf, and the Parent of many
farther Mifchiefs, without any Mixture of
Good.   It reprefents every Object of Terror as
vaftly greater than it is in Truth: and frequently gives far more Pain beforehand, than
the Prefence of all that we fear, is capable of
giving.   Nay, it makes us tremble at mere
Spectres: and fills us with the moft alarming
Sufpicions, fometimes of what cannot happen,
often of what is highly improbable.   And yet,
were it ever fo likely, exceffive Dread will do
nothing towards preferving us from it.   Calm
Reflection will inftruct and excite us to do every
Thing for ourfelves, which we are able to do:
and the utmoft Agonies of Difquiet can never
carry us beyond our Abilities.   Indeed very
commonly vehement Emotions either hinder us
from feeing what is fit, or difqualify us from
performing it: nay, hurry us into what is very
unfit;

unfit, and prejudicial to the Point, which we
have in View.

But were they to leave us otherwife intirely
Mafters of ourfelves, that Eagernefs of looking
farther than we can fee, which they always beget, hath a powerful Tendency to miflead us
very unhappily. Dangers, which we think we
difcern at a Diftance, may have no Reality: or
if they have, may never draw near. Dangers
that are near, may never reach us: and Evils,
that have reached us, may vanifh on a fudden.
Thefe are no Reafons againft prudent Forecaft:
but they are ftrong Reafons againft extracting
Wretchednefs out of Speculations on Futurity,
inftead of following quietly and chearfully the
proper Bufinefs of the prefent Day; fince *we
know not what another may bring forth*[a], and
confequently require us to contrive or execute,
to grieve or rejoice at. *To-morrow*, our bleffed
Saviour hath told us, *fhall take Thought for the
Things of itfelf*[b]: Time, as it runs on, will
direct us much better than we can guefs now,
what Precautions we are to take, and what
Judgments we are to form, about remote Affairs: and fince all, that appears at this Inftant
likely to fall out, or wife to do, may poffibly

[a] Prov. xxvii. 1.   [b] Matt. vi. 34.

in

in the next appear quite otherwife; we ought ftudioufly to moderate both our Actions and our Paffions, by recollecting the Mutability of the World; which would fave us a vaft deal of fruitlefs Labour, and needlefs Mifery. We every one of us think the Sorrows of Life abundantly enough: why then fhould we multiply them by long Anticipations; and load ourfelves at once with Misfortunes prefent and to come, unmindful of our gracious Lord's important Maxim: *Sufficient unto the Day is the Evil thereof* [e]? Had our Maker framed the human Mind in fuch Manner, that we muft have been *always forecafting grievous Things* [d], and fuffering every Hour, in Thought, all that through a Courfe of Years we are to fuffer in Reality, and much more; we fhould certainly have looked on it as very hard Ufage. Why then will we bring ourfelves into a State, in which if God had placed us, we fhould have complained of him, as cruel? He hath mercifully hid future Events from us, left the Forefight of them fhould make us unhappy. And we pry into them by Conjecture, and dwell upon them by Imagination, that we may be unhappy whether he will or not.

[e] Matt. vi. 34.   [d] Wifd. xvii. 11.

This

This, you fee, is more than Folly: it is evidently Sin. He intended us to live here in Comfort and Peace: and we are not at Liberty to fruftrate his Defign, by making ourfelves uneafy and wretched. Both Nature and Scripture plainly forbid it. Nor have we the leaft Ground to hope, that the Fault will be deemed a Punifhment fevere enough for itfelf. Many others are accompanied with grievous Mifery, to which notwithftanding more hereafter is defervedly threatened. And the Guilt of inordinate Solicitude is greater, than we generally apprehend. It implies, not only Difobedience to God, but Diftruft in him. It unfits us for the Offices of Piety and of common Life. By dejecting the Spirits, and fouring the Temper, it renders us different, in many Refpects, from what we fhould be, to all around us. It leads Perfons into ftrong Temptations, of raifing and cheering themfelves under their Troubles by falfe and pernicious Supports, or of feeking Deliverance from them by difhoneft Arts and Compliances. It infects others, who fee it, with the fame Apprehenfions: which may produce the fame or worfe Effects on their Quiet, nay their Innocence. And in Proportion, as difcouraging Alarms become epidemical, the

Calamity

Calamity dreaded becomes likely to happen. Still, fo much of this wrong Turn, as is really conftitutional and unavoidable Weaknefs, will certainly not be imputed as criminal. And therefore we ought not to double our Uneafi‐nefs, by adding to involuntary Anxieties a rigid Condemnation of ourfelves for them: but ftrive againft them to the utmoft of our Power; and then be fatisfied with the Confcioufnefs, that we have done fo: only not deceiving our Hearts with a Notion, that we have refifted Fears, which in Truth we have indulged.

But fome will fay, " How can we refift " them ? Muft we not of Neceffity be terrified " at what we perceive is terrible: be concerned " about what we are fenfible is of great Con‐ " cern to us? Where is the virtue of pretend‐ " ing to blind ourfelves, or even of doing it " actually, if we could?" None at all certainly. But the Rule prefcribed you is, not to fhut, but open your Eyes, and contemplate the whole of your Cafe deliberately and impartially. For perhaps it is not fo bad, perhaps not near fo bad, as you conceive, though you were to look on it only in a worldly View. And yet were outward Appearances, and our own Strength, all that we had to look at, there would be no

Wonder,

Wonder, if fometimes our Hearts fainted within us at the Profpect: for the ftouteft and the proudeft Hearts have fainted, before Us, on like Occafions.   But the never-failing Foundation of Comfort is this.   A Being infinitely powerful, wife, and benevolent, fuperintends the Univerfe continually: thefe Attributes afford us large Ground of Hope; and, that our own Unworthinefs may raife no Doubt, his exprefs Declarations give us full Affurance, that if we fly to him with humble Faith, *he will not fuffer us to be tempted above that we are able, but will, with the Temptation, alfo make a Way to efcape*[e].   The moft ufual Anxiety of Men is about the daily Neceffaries of Life. With Refpect to thefe therefore he condefcends to argue with us particularly; and the Argument will hold as well concerning lefs common Exigencies: that fince he fuftains the Vegetable Part of the Creation, which can do nothing for itfelf, and the Animal, which cannot do near fo much as we: certainly he will take of Us, on doing what we ought, a Care proportionable to the Superiority of our Nature.   For in this lies the Force of our Saviour's Reafoning. And, when he faith, *Behold the Fowls of the*

[e] 1 Cor. x. 13.

Air;

Air; they sow not; neither do they reap; yet your heavenly Father feedeth them: Are ye not much better than they[1]? He doth not mean, that they take no Pains, and therefore we are to take none.   They take a great deal, in seeking Food, and contriving Security against Dangers, for themselves and for their Young, according to the Extent of their Faculties.   And we are to take as much, in Proportion to the Extent of ours.   But then, as Providence furnishes to Them, so far as consists with its wise Purposes, whatever they need, and cannot acquire by their own Power: the same Providence will certainly watch over Us with more peculiar Tenderness, even in the present State; besides that what we suffer now shall increase our Happiness hereafter.   And therefore, since They are easy in Their Condition, well may We in Ours.   For it would be strange indeed, if that Order of earthly Beings, which enjoys the greatest Favour beyond all Comparison, should be the only one discontented. Reflect then: where human Care ends, the Divine Care begins.   The Duty of To-day is our Business; the Event of To-morrow is our heavenly Father's: and surely you do not wish to remove

[1] Matt. vi. 26.

it

it out of his Hands into your own; or furmife,
that you can poffibly be unfafe, while under
the Protection of Him, with whom *the very
Hairs of your Head are all numbered*[s].   Here
then we have a fecure Refuge againft Inquietude.
But let us remember: If, having it, we ufe it
not: if, profeffing Faith in God, we allow
ourfelves to be as much difconcerted and per-
plexed on every Alarm, as they that *have no
Hope, and are without God in the World*[h]; we
either think unworthily of him, or behave quite
unfuitably to what we think; and our Guilt is
greater, as our Temptation to it is lefs.   When
therefore, on being troubled and caft down, we
are inclined to lay the Blame on accidental or
natural Lownefs of Spirits, or whatever Excufe
occurs, let us *take Heed, left there be in us an
evil Heart of Unbelief*[i], or Difobedience.   If
there be, amending That is the Way to *uphold
him that was falling, and ftrengthen the feeble
Knees*[k].

But in vain fhall we attempt any Thing beneficial to us, if we truft to ourfelves for Succefs.
And therefore, to make his Caution effectual,
the Apoftle fubjoins,

[s] Matt. x. 30.   [h] Eph. ii. 12.   [i] Heb. iii. 12.
[k] Job iv. 4.

I   II. A moft

II. A moſt neceſſary Direction. *In every Thing by Prayer and Supplication, with Thankſgiving, let your Requeſts be made known unto God.*

The uſual Method is, to be *careful about many Things*[1], and pray about Nothing: but the right one is, to be careful about Nothing, but pray about every Thing, which is of Importance enough to be laid before the Lord of All. The Movements of our Hearts indeed, though unuttered, are clearly diſcerned by him: and he foreſaw from Eternity whatever we ſhould wiſh on every Occaſion. But the Scripture ſpeaks in the Language of Men: and calls that *making known our Requeſts to God,* which is only expreſſing before him what he is perfectly acquainted with already, in order to imprint more efficaciouſly, on ourſelves and others, the Sentiments concerning him, which belong to our Condition.

Applying to the Almighty in our Difficulties immediately reminds us, on whom we and all Things depend: and brings it ſtrongly to our Thoughts, that the moſt threatning Dangers cannot advance one Step farther, than infinite Wiſdom ſees it proper they ſhould, and infinite

[1] Luke x. 42.

Goodneſs

Goodnefs permits.   Placing ourfelves in his Prefence awes and compofes our worldly Fears; not by a fervile Dread of him, forcibly over-coming them, and fubftituting itfelf, a ftill worfe Terror, in their Stead; but by a filial Reverence, mixed with humble Reliance on his Favour, which calms and revives us in fuch Manner, that we perceive our Solicitudes to va-nifh even whilft we are confeffing them; and quickly fmile at what we fhuddered at before. Then, befides, venting our Defires to Him, fhews us in the fulleft Light, which are finful, and to be repreffed, if we hope for Acceptance with him: and begging his Help, muft power-fully admonifh us, that we are not to think of helping ourfelves by Methods difpleafing to him; but adhere ftrictly to our Duty, and be affured it will lead us out of whatever Perplexities it leads us into. *Commit thy Way unto the Lord, and put thy truft in him, and he fhall bring it to pafs*[m].   Further yet, praying to *our* Father which is in Heaven, leads us to confider him as our common Father: who is concerned, not only for us, but for all our Friends; and ex-pects us to be zealous for the general Good, as well as our own; and on no Account to with-

[m] Pf. xxxvii. 5.

                                    draw

draw from the Service of the Body, of which he hath made us Members. Piety therefore, excites the trueſt and firmeſt public Spirit; but ſmooths and tempers, at the ſame Time, that Roughneſs and Vehemence, which too frequently renders it ineffectual and hurtful, by promoting, as it doth beyond all Things, an humble Opinion of ourſelves, and Meekneſs towards others.

With ſuch Diſpoſitions, we ſhall be duly qualified for the Mercy we intreat: and they who are, will never fail to receive it. For *this is the Confidence which we have in him*, ſaith the beloved Diſciple, *that if we aſk any Thing according to his Will, he heareth us. And if we know that he heareth us, whatſoever we aſk, we know that we have the Petitions which we deſired of him* [n]. We are ſure of the very Favours we beg, if they are conducive to his Glory, and the Happineſs of his Creatures: which doubtleſs the Deliverance of this Nation from its Enemies muſt be, ſince we profeſs and ſupport his holy Truth, would we but penitently conform our Conduct to it. And his long Forbearance under our Provocations gives us Room to expect every Inſtance of Mercy, in Caſe of

[n] 1 John v. 14, 15.

our

our Amendment. What indeed the humble Applications of a few may do for others, He only knows. But for themſelves they will certainly obtain infinitely greater Benefits, than ſharing in the higheſt Degree of earthly Proſperity. Now the ſole Reaſon of our praying for any Thing is, that we ſuppoſe it will be good for us. And therefore we pray for nothing of this World abſolutely, but on that Condition. So that if God, who knows beſt, withholds it becauſe it will be otherwiſe, he grants our Requeſt in the general, though he refuſes it in the particular: and if we are wiſe, far from being overwhelmed by the ſevereſt Diſpenſations, we ſhall not only be contented, but glad, in ſuch Meaſure as human Infirmity and Sympathy permit, that *His Will ſhould be done, not Ours*.

For this Cauſe the Apoſtle, when he might have ſaid, what moſt People would have thought very ſufficient, that we ſhould *make our Requeſts known unto God* with Reſignation, choſe to ſay more, that we ſhould do it *with Thankſgiving*. And indeed we ought to be heartily thankful, not only for the many and great Bleſſings, temporal and ſpiritual, national and

* Luke xxii. 42.

I 3 perſonal,

perfonal, which God continues to us in the Midft of his Corrections, (O that we would all think ferioufly, how many and great they are) but even for his Corrections themfelves: and much more for the Alarms and Warnings, the Liftings up of his Rod, which are defigned to prevent the Neceffity of heavier Judgments. What he doth with this View, though it produce terrifying Apprehenfions, is the moft real Kindnefs; the only Kindnefs, that we permit him at prefent to fhew. Many, we may hope, will be influenced by fuch awful Notices, to amend their Ways. But at leaft we need not fail of being influenced ourfelves to what is right. And then, whatever the Event be to thofe around us, to Us it fhall be happy: if in no other Refpect, yet in That, which, beyond all Comparifon, is of the greateft Confequence: *Our light Afflictions which are but for a Moment, fhall work out for us a far more exceeding and eternal Weight of Glory* [v].

Knowing thefe Things, well might the Apoftle add in the Text

III. An Affurance of the bleffed Effect, which raifing our Thoughts from Earth to

[v] 2 Cor. iv. 17.

Heaven

Heaven will produce. *And the Peace of God, which paffeth all Underftanding, fhall keep your Hearts and Minds, through Chrift Jefus.*

Bad Perfons, as they have never any well-grounded, have feldom any long-continued Peace of Mind, even in Profperity: and much lefs can they hope for it in Troubles and Dangers. If they have not been juft and merciful, they are confcious of ill-deferving Behaviour to their Fellow-creatures. If they have not been uniformly virtuous and religious, they know they have acted undutifully and ungratefully to their Creator. If they have not by due Application for Pardon reconciled themfelves to Him, the Guilt of their Sins remains upon them: and the whole Creation is a Weapon in his Hands againft them. They may be ftupidly unmoved by thefe Confiderations: they may affect to hide their Convictions, or ftrive to run away from them into whatever prefents it-felf. But ufually the livelieft and ftrongeft natural Spirits will fink under them, in a Time of fevere Trial. Or fuppofing they do not; the more obftinately fuch Perfons hold out, and the more gaily they go on, the heavier in all Like-lihood will be their prefent Ruin, but the dread-

I 4

fuller

fuller certainly their final Sentence. For fooner or later, and with full Recompence for ever fo long Delay, the folemn and repeated Denunciation muft be verified, *Whatfoever a Man foweth, that fhall he alfo reap*[q].

But the obedient and devout Soul, which looks beyond worldly Appearances, and refts itfelf on the divine Providence, is intitled, whatever outward Commotions happen, to the trueft, the fteadieft, the moft delightful inward Compofednefs: to that *Peace of God*, that Senfe of being in Friendfhip with Him, that Feeling of Comfort and Joy flowing from him, *which paffeth all Underftanding*; exceeds the Conceptions of thofe who have not experienced it, and fhall exceed hereafter the prefent Conceptions of thofe who have. Yet the fincerely Good may not conftantly enjoy a very high Degree of This. The Imperfection of their Goodnefs, the Lownefs of their Spirits, Errors of Judgment, fudden Alarms, Afflictions uncommonly grievous, may leffen, may interrupt it: or God may, for fecret Reafons of infinite Wifdom, *hide his Face from them*[r] for a Time. But, ordinarily fpeaking, their Tranquillity and Confolation will be found proportionable to their

[q] Gal. vi. 7.   [r] Pfa. xiii. 1.

Improve-

Improvements in real Religion. And, though undoubtedly Seasons of Difficulty and Hazard will give some Uneasiness to the best Minds; yet no more, than is moderate, and very tolerable: no more, than leaves them, on the whole, in a peaceful State; and able to *cast*, if not *all*, as they should, yet the most of *their Care on Him, who careth for them* .

Let us therefore try ourselves by this Rule, whether we have indeed practical Faith and Confidence in the Almighty. And if not, let us instantly labour to obtain it, by a total Forsaking of *our Iniquities, which have separated between Us and Him* , and humble Addresses *for Grace to help in Time of Need* The common Resource is to the Help of Man alone: *there be many that say, who will shew us any Good?* but the Language of a well-instructed Heart is, *Lord, lift thou up the Light of thy Countenance upon us* . *Some put their Trust in Chariots, and some in Horses: but let us remember the Name of the Lord our God*: provide for our Security with the utmost Prudence, and defend our Cause with the boldest Zeal: but still rely on Him alone, *who giveth Victory unto*

 1 Pet. v. 7.   Isa. lix. 2.   Heb. iv. 16.
 Psa. iv. 6, 7.   Psa. xx. 7.

Kings.

Kings [y]. Every other Aid may fail: but God cannot. *He is able to save by many or by few* [z]: *to break the Arm of the Wicked* [a], *and disappoint the Devices of the Crafty* [b]. *He stilleth the Raging of the Sea, the Noise of its Waves, and the Madness of the People* [c]. Under his Conduct, the *Things,* that seem the most *against us* [d], may prove the very Means of our Deliverance: and the fiercest Storms drive the Ship with more Speed into a safe Harbour. Therefore *say to them, that are of a fearful Heart, Be strong, fear not: behold your God will come with a Re-compence; he will come and save you* [e]. All, who are penetrated with these Truths, though timorous naturally, and while the Danger is dif-tant, shall when it draws near, *out of Weak-ness be made strong, and wax valiant in Fight* [f]: not with a tumultuous and transitory animal Courage, but a calm and stedfast Resolution, *keeping,* as the Apostle expresses it, *their Hearts and Minds,* quieting their Passions, fixing their Judgments, and by Consequence determining their Behaviour. The Reasonings of such Per-sons will be those of the Psalmist: *God is our Hope and Strength, a very present Help in Trou-*

[y] Psa. cxliv. 10.   [z] 1 Sam. xiv. 6.   [a] Psa. x. 15.
[b] Job v. 12.   [c] Psa. lxv. 7.   [d] Gen. xlii. 36.
[e] Isa. xxxv. 4.   [f] Heb. xi. 34.

ble.

ble. ' *Therefore will we not fear, though the Earth be moved, and though the Hills be carried into the Midst of the Sea: though the Waters rage and swell, and though the Mountains shake at the Tempest of the same. The Rivers of the Flood thereof shall make glad the City of God, the holy Place of the Tabernacle of the Most High.' God is in the Midst of her, therefore shall she not be removed: God shall help her, and that right early. The Nations make much ado, and the Kingdoms are moved: but God sheweth his Voice, and the Earth shall melt away. The Lord of Hosts is with us, the God of Jacob is our Refuge*[g].* These are the Grounds, and there cannot be stronger, on which a good Person, unless he is wanting to himself, *will not be afraid of any evil Tidings: for his Heart standeth fast, and believeth in the Lord*[h]. Nay, were it not the Pleasure of God to deliver his People from their Enemies, even in that Case, they would be enabled to *suffer according to his Will, and commit the keeping of their Souls to him in well-doing, as unto a faithful Creator*[i].

But then we must ever observe, by whose Means alone this unconquerable Firmness, this inconceivable Serenity, is to be acquired. *The*

---

[g] Psa. xlvi. 1—7.   [h] Psa. cxii. 7.   [i] 1 Pet. iv. 19.

Peace

Peace of God shall keep your Hearts and Minds, through Christ Jesus. For as, without Faith in Religion, Persons very often have no Refuge at all in the Storms and Troubles that overtake them; so, without Faith in the Christian Religion, they are liable still to most uneasy and disheartening Fluctuations; from Doubts, how far Providence extends; Doubts of their own Title to Forgiveness and Favour; Doubts of the Existence and Duration of a future Reward: to all which the Gospel hath put the happiest End; informing Mankind with Certainty of every Thing that could induce them to act right with chearful Perseverance; and confirming the highest Expectations, which they can possibly entertain, by that equally convincing and affecting Argument: *He that spared not his own Son, but delivered him up for us all, how shall he not with him also freely give us all Things*[k]? Thus then *we have Hope, as an Anchor of the Soul, sure and stedfast, and which entereth into that within the Veil*; lays hold on the promised State of invisible Glory, *whither the Forerunner is entered for us*, to take Possession already in our Name, *even Jesus*[l]: whose gracious Words to his Disciples we ought to have constantly pre-

[k] Rom. viii. 32.   [l] Heb. vi. 19, 20.

sent

fent to our Thoughts, when Clouds arife and
darken our Profpect, hang over our Heads, and
feem ready to burft upon us. *Thefe Things have
I fpoken unto you, that in me ye might have Peace.
In the World ye fhall have Tribulation: but be
of good Cheer: I have overcome the World*.
Peace I leave with you: my Peace I give unto
you: let not your Heart be troubled, neither let
it be afraid*.*

        m John xvi. 33.   n John xiv. 27.

SER-

... to ... Thoughts, when Clouds arise and
dark ... Prospects, hang over our Heads, and
... ly to burst upon us. *That Things have
spoken unto you, that in me ye might have Peace.
In this World ye shall have Tribulation; but be
of good Chear; I have overcome the World.*
*Peace I leave with ... my ... I give unto
you: let not your Heart be troubled, neither let
it be afraid?*

SERMON VI.

(Preached in 1746, on the Victory at CULLODEN.)

2 COR. i. 9, 10.

But we had the Sentence of Death in ourselves,
that we should not trust in ourselves; but in
God which raiseth the Dead:

Who delivered us from so great a Death, and
doth deliver; in whom we trust, that he will
yet deliver us.

OUR gracious Sovereign having appointed,
of his own mere Motion and Personal
Piety, a solemn Acknowledgment to
Heaven, for our late Victory over the Rebels,
to be inserted in the Prayers of this Day, permit me, as far as I am able, to be a *Helper of*
your Joy * on that happy Occasion. And may
God effectually dispose us all to *rejoice before*

* Verse 24.

Him

Him [b] in fo wife and religious a Manner, as may lay a fure Foundation for his *rejoicing over Us to do us Good* [c]; for his going on to *comfort us again, after the Time that he hath afflicted Us, the Years wherein we have fuffered Adver-fity* [d].

I hope it may promote this bleffed End, if we confider our Condition in the fame Views in which the Text places before us that of the Apoftle St. *Paul*, comprehending an Account,

I. Of his Danger: *A great Death, of which he had the Sentence within himfelf.*

II. Of his Defender from it: *God, who had delivered, and did ftill deliver him.*

III. Of the Reafons, for which he was firft permitted to fall into this Danger, then brought out of it: *that he might not truft in Himfelf, but might truft in God, which raifeth the Dead:* as accordingly he declares he doth, for Deli-verances yet future.

I. His Danger: *A great Death, of which he had the Sentence within himfelf.* Death, being the Extremity of temporal Sufferings, in the *Hebrew* Idiom, which expreffes every Thing

[b] Deut. xii. 12.   [c] Jer. xxxii. 41.   [d] Pfa. xc. 15.

ftrongly,

ftrongly, fignifies any very dreadful Evil or Hazard. Thus *Pharoah*, on the Plague of Locufts, begs of *Mofes*; *Entreat the Lord your God, that he may take away from me this Death only* [e]. But more efpecially Hazard of Life goes under that Name. Whence *David* fpeaks of himfelf, as *counted with them that go down into the Pit; free among the Dead, like the Slain that lie in the Grave* [f]. Now St. *Paul*, to ufe his own Phrafe towards the latter End of this Epiftle, had been *in Deaths often* [g]. And therefore the Term, *fo great a Death*, muft denote, that on the Occafion, to which he refers, his Peril was eminent, peculiarly terrible, and, humanly fpeaking, unavoidable. His own Words are, *we were preffed out of Meafure, above Strength, infomuch that we defpaired even of Life* [h]. Farther Particulars cannot now be difcovered, excepting one, which he adds, of fmall Confequence to Us, that this Trouble came to him in *Afia*. But by his Manner of notifying it, and the Warmth of his Defcription, it muft have been recent, fince he wrote the former Epiftle.

[e] Exod. x. 17.   [f] Pfal. lxxxviii. 4, 5.
[g] Chap. xi. 23.   [h] Ver. 8.

K

How

How lately we have been in like Diftrefs, you all know. How *great a Death* we muft have fuffered, had our Enemies prevailed; how total a Deftruction of every Thing valuable to us on Earth, that can be deftroyed by Man; I endeavoured to fhew you at the very Beginning of their Attempt: and the whole Body of the Nation, God be thanked, have expreffed the ftrongeft Deteftation of it. May neither the Horror of the impending Ruin, nor the frightful Probability there was of its overwhelming us, ever be forgot. Recollect, I intreat you, what your fucceffive Apprehenfions have been for many Months paft: on the early and intire, and eafy Defeat of our Forces by the Rebels; on the defencelefs Condition in which the Ifland then was; on their paffing afterwards, unhurt, by two Armies pofted to intercept them, and approaching towards this Capital; on the Profpect of powerful Affiftance to them from Abroad; on the credible, though happily falfe, Intelligence of our being actually invaded; on the fafe Retreat of our domeftic Enemies into the North, to join, as it was affirmed and believed, with foreign Succours there; on our fecond Difappointment in Battle, a fatal one it might have proved; on the con-

tinual

tinual Dangers, to which that heroic Prince was expofed, whofe Prefence and Conduct, and Courage and Activity, were fo effentially neceffary for animating our difpirited Troops; on the Reaffembling and Succeffes of our Foes, after a feeming Defpondency and Difperfion; on the Largenefs of their Numbers, the Advantages of their Situation; and laftly, on the ftrong Report of what was but too poffible, a complete Victory obtained by them, when indeed one had been obtained over them, of which we were ignorant. Had we not often, during this Period, *the Sentence of Death within ourfelves?* Were we not *troubled on every Side; without were Fightings, within were Fears*[1]; *Mens Hearts failing them for Fear, and for looking after thofe Things which were coming on the Earth*[k]? And had we been afked, at fome Junctures efpecially, as the Prophet was, in Language akin to that of the Text, *Can thefe dry Bones live?* Can this exhaufted Nation rife up again, and fhake off the Preffures, from every Quarter, under which it labours? What other Reply, at beft, could we have made, than His? *O Lord God, thou knoweft*[l]. For furely the wifeft of Men did not know: nor could the

[1] 2 Cor. vii. 5.   [k] Luke xxi. 26.   [l] Ezek. xxxvii. 3.

braveſt anſwer for the Event, after it had been ſo frequently contrary to what we thought the moſt rational Expectations. Of this only there was Certainty, that we had the loudeſt Call to adopt the Pſalmiſt's Prayer: *O God, thou haſt caſt us off, and ſcattered us; thou haſt alſo been diſpleaſed: O turn thee unto us again. Thou haſt moved the Land, and divided it: heal the Breaches thereof, for it ſhaketh* ᵐ. And praiſed be his Name, that we can now add the Words which follow thoſe: *Thou haſt given a Token for ſuch as fear thee, that they may triumph becauſe of thy Truth* ⁿ.

And we have accordingly triumphed in this comfortable Earneſt of Proſperity, returning to us after ſo long an Abſence, with a Joy as cordial and univerſal, as perhaps this Nation ever expreſſed. May both our Friends and our Enemies know it, and draw the natural Concluſions from it, to the Encouragement of the former, the Diſmay of the latter. But then, if we *triumph* only for the Safety of our Perſons and Properties, and not *becauſe of God's Truth, and pure Religion;* if we rejoice, and overlook the Author of our Joy, *the Giver of all Victory;* we ſhall fall inexcuſably ſhort of our Duty, and

---

ᵐ Pſal. lx. 1, 2.   ⁿ Verſe 4.

the

the Example fet us by the Apoftle: who fubjoins immediately to his Account of the Danger, which he had efcaped,

II. A thankful Mention of his Defender from
it: *God, who had delivered, and did ftill deliver him.*

It is evidently both as eafy for the Supreme
Being, and as worthy of him, to govern the
Univerfe, as to create it.   Indeed the only Purpofe, for which Divine Wifdom could create
it, muft be to conduct every Part of it to a right
End: and the fmalleft Parts are no more be-
neath his Attention, than the greateft; for He
is infinitely above all.   What Reafon thus
teaches, holy Scripture confirms with important
Additions: informing us, that a future Day is
appointed for the full and final Difplay of his
Juftice and Goodnefs towards the Children of
Men; but that in the mean Time his Providence is active, fo far as the Conftitution of
Things eftablifhed by him permits, and not
the leaft Occurrence comes to pafs, without the
fuperintending Care of *our Father, which is in
Heaven*[*].   We are often indeed ignorant, by
what Means he acts: for he is able to influence,

* Matt. x. 29.

K 3   upper-unperceived, not only the Course of inanimate Nature, but the Minds of rational Agents, and to produce the greatest Events from the flightest Occasions. We are often equally ignorant of his Views in acting: for *we know but in Part* [p]; whereas *all Things are naked and open to the Eyes of Him with whom we have to do* [q]. The Imperfection of our Discernment therefore must be no Hindrance to our Faith: but our plain Duty is to reverence implicitly those Proceedings of His, the Manner and Grounds of which are hid from us: as well as to pay him more particular Acknowledgments on Account of such as we understand.

For in many Cases the Hand of God is clearly visible: but no-where more than in the Correction, and yet Preservation of *States professing his holy and eternal Truth* [r]: as indeed there cannot be on Earth fitter Objects of his righteous Providence. Thus in all Ages he hath watched over his Church. Thus more especially he hath treated this Church and Land, ever since the Reformation: *visiting our Offences with the Rod, and our Sin with Scourges; nevertheless his loving Kindness hath he not utterly*

----

[p] 1 Cor. xiii. 9, 12.   [q] Heb. iv. 13.
[r] Office for *November* 5.

taken

*taken from us, nor suffered his Truth to fail[1].
Many a Time have they fought against me from
my Youth up, may Israel now say; yea, many a
Time have they afflicted me from my Youth up,
but they have not prevailed against me. The
Ploughers have ploughed upon my Back, and made
long Furrows: but the righteous Lord hath hewn
the Snares of the Ungodly in Pieces[2].* And surely
in the Troubles, which we have undergone of
late, a pious and thoughtful Mind may trace
evident Footsteps of Divine Interposition. Why
else, on the one Hand, did our Enemies increase, prevail, and escape, so surprisingly, for
so long together? Why, on the other, did they
so unaccountably miss the fairest and most pal-
pable Opportunities of Undoing us effectually;
neither pursuing at Home the Advantages they
had gained, nor procuring the Succours, which
their Friends Abroad in all Prudence ought to
have sent them? And why, lastly, have they
allowed us to obtain so decisive a Victory, in a
few Moments, at the Expence of so little Blood
lost on our Side, (would God their own, poor
deluded Wretches, could have been spared)
when both from the Encouragement of their
preceding Successes, and the Necessity of exert-

[1] Pf. lxxxix. 32, 33.　　　[2] Pf. cxxix. 1—4.

K 4

ing

ing themſelves to the utmoſt in this Criſis of their Fate, a very obſtinate Engagement was to have been expected? Whence have theſe Things happened thus, but that *God ruleth in the King-dom of Men*[u]? *The Lord maketh the Devices of the People to be of none Effect, and caſteth out the Counſels of Princes. But the Counſel of the Lord ſhall endure for ever, and the Thoughts of his Heart from Generation to Generation. Bleſſed are the People, whoſe God is the Lord Jehovah; and bleſſed are the Folk, that he hath choſen to be his inheritance*[w].

Let us learn therefore, and acknowledge, for it is a very bad Sign if we are unwilling, that both our Dangers and our Deliverances are from above. This will in no Degree leſſen the Guilt of our Enemies: for they were prompted by their own Wickedneſs unjuſtly to attempt, what Heaven for Our Wickedneſs might juſtly have permitted. Nor can it ever be a Plea for yield-ing tamely to their Enterprizes, that God makes Uſe of them to ſerve his Purpoſes. We know not the Extent of thoſe Purpoſes; which he will certainly execute, as far as they extend: and are therefore to do our evident Duty. If he ſuffers our Adverſaries to attack our moſt

[u] Dan. v. 21.   [w] Pſ. xxxiii. 10, 11, 12.

valuable

valuable Rights, he both impowers and commands Us to defend them: and they, who
confider themfelves as his Inftruments for this
End, will act with unfpeakably more Faithful-
nefs and Zeal, than fuch as are induced by
worldly Motives alone; which frequently other
worldly Motives, and fometimes very trifling
ones, may outweigh: whereas there is no
Counterbalance to a Principle of Confcience.
Nor doth it in the leaft detract from the Merit
of our Soldiers and Commanders, that *the Salvation of the Righteous cometh of the Lord, who
alfo is their Strength in the Time of Trouble* [x].
Every Pre-eminence is more eftimable for being
his Gift; every great Action, for being done
by his Guidance: and the higheft of thofe,
who have wrought this Deliverance for us, are
furely the moft deeply fenfible, that the nobleft
of their Diftinctions is, being employed by their
Maker, and Fellow-Workers with him, for
the Support of genuine Religion, virtuous Liberty, and public Happinefs. This Way of
Thinking will infpire the moft compofed Moderation, along with the moft undaunted Bravery: and whoever makes it the Bafis of his
Conduct, will be intitled to all Demonftrations

[x] Pf. xxxvii. 40.

of

of Refpect from Men ; and yet abundantly contented with *the Honour, that cometh from God
only* [y].

Every Thing that befalls us therefore, adverfe
or profperous, let us look on it as proceeding
from the juft and good Pleafure of our heavenly
Father: humble ourfelves before him in all our
Afflictions ; and, which is our prefent Concern,
be thankful to him in all our Rejoicings. *If
the Lord himfelf had not been on our Side, let
Ifrael now fay, if the Lord himfelf had not been
on our Side, when Men rofe up againft us : they
had fwallowed us up quick, when they were fo
wrathfully difpleafed at us : yea, the Waters had
drowned us,——the deep Waters of the Proud
had gone over our Soul. But praifed be the
Lord, who hath not given us over for a Prey
unto their Teeth* [z]. This is the Language, that
exprefles the Truth of our Cafe : and it is of infinite Importance, that we own it unanimoufly.
For the Sovereign Difpofer of the Univerfe will
neither be denied nor forgot, without vindi-
cating the Glory of his Name : and he hath
long ago pronounced the Sentence : *They regard
not in their Mind the Works of the Lord, nor
the Operation of his Hands ; therefore fhall he*

----

[y] John v. 44.   [z] Pf. cxxiv. 1—5.

break

I

break them down and not build them up [a]. But the Duty and the Neceffity of fuch Regard will more diftinctly appear, by confidering,

III. The Reafons, for which the Apoftle was firft brought into Danger, then brought out of it: that he might learn by the former *not to truft in himfelf*; and by the latter, *to truft in God, which raifeth the Dead.*

Now if there was Need of improving St. *Paul* in this Leffon, much more is there of teaching it others. And never perhaps was any Nation, at leaft which made Profeffion of Faith in Chrift, fo deplorably inattentive to it, as ours. Our Wealth, our Fleets, our Valour, have been for many Years paft, till very lately, our continual Boaft. And in vain had the Scripture forewarned us: *Curfed is He, that trufteth in Man, and maketh Flefh his Arm, and whofe Heart departeth from the Lord* [b]. How then fhould God convince us of fo pernicious an Error; and fhew us, that we were not fufficient of ourfelves? By the very Method, which he hath taken. *He hid his Face, and we were troubled* [c]: Storms rofe around us; and the moft

---

[a] Pfal. xxviii. 6. [b] Jer. xvii. 5. [c] Pfal. clv. 29.

dangerous,

dangerous, where we thought there was nothing to produce any: our Navy proved no Protection; our Valour funk into panic Terrors;
our *Riches* were on the Point of *making themfelves Wings and flying away*[d]; a general Bank-
ruptcy threatened us; and what the *Kings of
the Earth, and all the Inhabitants of the World
would not have believed, the Adverfary and the
Enemy were* near *entering into the Gates of Jerufalem*[e]. Who could poffibly have apprehended that the landing of fix or feven Men
fhould have put this great Nation into fuch
Confufion? Who could ever have conceived,
that the Difturbers of our Peace fhould have
multiplied and conquered as they did; fhould
have advanced and retreated, and ranged at Will
through our Land, with fo perfect Security,
for fo long a Time? And what is all this, but
a Call from God to know ourfelves, and abafe
our Pride before him: a practical Declaration,
that no Flefh fhall glory in his Prefence[f].

But neceffary as this Inftruction is, yet fingly
it is not enough. When irreligious Perfons
have found by Experience, that they cannot
rely on their own Strength, they have no other
left to rely on: and fo are tempted to defpair
in their Minds, to fail in their Duty, to feek

[d] Prov. xxiii. 5.   [e] Lam. iv, 12.   [f] 1 Cor. i. 29.

Refuge

Refuge in cowardly and treacherous Artifices for their own Prefervation. But very different are the Sentiments of the pious Man's Heart. Let ever fo unexpected Calamities happen, let ever fo alarming Dangers approach, with ever fo little Appearance of furmounting them: ftill he knows, that nothing can be fo dangerous, as to defert the Poft, in which God hath placed him; and that *He, who is faithful unto Death, fhall receive a Crown of Life*[a]. At the fame Inftant therefore, that he faith, *There be many that fight againft me, O thou Moft Higheft*, he is enabled to fay alfo, *neverthelefs, though I am fometime afraid, yet put I my Truft in Thee*[b]. And this is the Spirit, which God intends to excite, by fending, after extreme Perils, remarkable and fudden Deliverances. From thefe it is natural to learn Faith in Him, *that raifes the Dead*, that reftores from the moft helplefs Condition; and fince *he hath delivered*, to form reviving Hopes, that *he will yet deliver*; which we may and ought to do now. He hath given us a Victory fpeedier, cheaper, completer, than we could even have flattered ourfelves with. He hath given it by the Means of a young Prince, whofe confeffed Abilities, vigilant At-

[a] Rev. ii. 10.   [b] Pfal. lvi. 2, 3.

tention,

tention, unwearied Diligence, and intrepid Firmnefs, on all Occafions, as well as his wonderful Succefs on the prefent, afford us the jufteft Ground of Perfuafion, that he is chofen by Providence for the Service and Support of his Father, his Family, his Country. And the fame God, who hath *begun to fhew his mighty Hand* [1], can, with the fame Eafe, accomplifh his good Work, and bring it to Perfection.

But then, alas! what avails it that he can, unlefs we have Caufe to truft that he will? And whence fhall we have this? Thankfulnefs for paft Mercies undoubtedly is the Way to fecure future. And juft now we feem in earneft thankful. But if our Gratitude prove to be fuperficial and fhort-lived, like that of the *Jews, They fang Praife unto him: but within a while they forgat his Works, they would not abide his Counfel*; what can we expect elfe, than Judgments like theirs? *Then he lift up his Hand againft them, to overthrow them* [k]. Our State, though vaftly altered for the better, is ftill a very undefirable, indeed a very melancholy one. Our Burthens are unavoidably augmenting, and our Strength wafting. Foreign Force may foon

---

[1] Deut. iii. 24.　　　[k] Pfal. cvi. 12, 13, 26.

renew

renew our inteſtine Commotions: or even,
without their Intervention, ſubject us all directly to it itſelf. The Failures of our Friends
give us, Year after Year, new Reaſon to ſay
with the Pſalmiſt : *O. be Thou our Help in Trouble : for vain is the Help of Man*[l]. *Put not
your Truſt in Princes, nor in any Child of Man :
for there is no Help in them.* *Bleſſed is He, that
hath the God of Jacob for his Help, and whoſe
Hope is in the Lord his God*[m]. But we cannot
hope for the Continuance of his Protection,
unleſs we anſwer the Intention of it : which
the Nature of the Thing, as well as Holy Writ,
aſſures us is, *that being delivered out of the Hands
of our Enemies, we may ſerve him without Fear*[n].
It is not then, that we may ſin againſt him
without Fear : that we may return ſecurely to
the Follies and Vices, the Impiety and Profaneneſs, from which we abſtained, while his
Hand lay heavy upon us. Then we profeſſed
to obſerve Days of Faſting and Prayer. And
what was the Language of them ? " Spare us,
" good Lord, that we may ſafely go on to be
" as bad as we have been, and worſe ?" Surely
not. Some indeed expreſſed, even in the Midſt
of Danger, an open Scorn of them: others

[l] Pſal. lx. 11. [m] Pſal. cxlvi 3, 4. [n] Luke i. 74.

were evidently kept from it by mere outward
Decency.   Many however were awakened,
fpoke and thought ferioufly, refolved well, prayed heartily.   But are they not moft of them already, or fhall we not .find them foon, re-
lapfed again into their old Neglect ? For fuch
hath always been the Courfe of human Nature,
unlefs carefully reftrained by confcientious Vigilance. *When he flew them, they fought him,
and turned them early, and inquired after God:
and they remembered, that God was their
Strength, and the high God their Redeemer.
Neverthelefs, they did but flatter him with their
Mouth, and diffembled with him in their Tongue.
For their Heart was not whole with him: neither continued they fledfaft in his Covenant*. After
this Feint of Reformation, they grew, as Men
always do, wickeder than before.   And I beg
you attend to the final Confequence. When
God faw this, he was wroth, and took fore Dif-
pleafure at Ifrael: He delivered their Power
into Captivity; and their Beauty into the Enemy's
Hand*.*

If therefore it be afked, what we fhall. do to
fhew our Thankfulnefs acceptably, the Anfwer
is plain : *Walk in all the Commandments and*

---

    * Pfal. lxxviii. 34—37.   ᵖ Ver. 60, 62.

Ordinances

Ordinances of the Lord blameless [q]; but practise those with more especial Zeal, which either our Circumstances particularly require, or our Hearts tell us we have particularly transgressed.

Common Prudence is one Part of our Duty; which we have unaccountably slighted. We have increased Amusements and Gaities to a Degree unexampled, just when Providence hath called us most loudly to thoughtful Considera-tion. We have increased Expensiveness to an equal Degree, when perhaps our own Fortunes, but certainly those of Multitudes, whom our Example tempts and often almost forces to Imitation, are incapable of bearing it. And both these Indiscretions have produced personal Miseries and national Inconveniencies without Number. We have disregarded, and affected to disregard, the Care of our Families, and the proper Business of our several Employments, though sometimes perhaps important ones, not only to indulge our Appetites, but to gratify our Caprices: Behaviour, in every Rank and Station, fruitful of Mischief; but in the higher, of most dreadful and extensive Mischief. In

----

[q] Luke i. 6.

L   Matters

Matters of national Concern, we have followed
our private Interests, Resentments, Friendships,
instead of Truth, and Right, and general Good.
We have framed and supported useless and
hurtful Distinctions and Divisions; and been
unjustly vehement in mutual Reproaches; till
our Enemies were encouraged to fancy, that
one half of us was ready to join them. We
have vilified our Governors, till we had almost
disowned the Blessings of Government: and it
was very near being too late, that our Affection
to an Establishment, on which our whole Happiness depends, revived, after an Indifference,
that foreboded immediate Ruin. Let us never
forget more what we have been so seasonably
convinced of now: but always esteem as highly
our Laws and Liberties, and the august House
that secures them, as we did in that Hour,
when the Hazard of losing them was most imminent. But let us amend in every other Point
also: and while there is yet *Space to repent*[r],
become a sober-minded, frugal, industrious,
honest, and united People. For we cannot else
continue a free one: neither the Justice of God,

[r] Rev. ii. 21.

hor the Connections of human affairs will permit it.

, Thefe then are fundamental Rules of private
Prudence. With thofe of public Wifdom we
have no Concern here, beyond two particulars.
The firft is our Obligation to pray, that God
would incline thofe, who are in Authority over
us, to confider ferioufly what have been the
Caufes of our Troubles, and direct them to
proper Remedies: would enable them to preferve, both in Punifhments and Precautions,
the true Medium between too great Severity
and too great Indulgence: would inftruct them,
how to reconcile all that wifh well to the Community; and how to prevent others from renewing any more our Sufferings, or their own.
The Second is, our confequent Obligation to
diftruft our own Judgment, rather than theirs,
in Matters of fuch Difficulty; and to ufe our
faithful Endeavours, that what they determine
may become effectual.

But how rightly foever we are difpofed in
thefe Refpects, if we continue to entertain the
fame Contempt of Religion, which we have
manifefted for a long Time paft, it is in vain
to *truft, that God will* continue to *deliver us.*

 How

How much, or how little Forbearance he may exercife, cannot be faid: but fooner or later, *except we repent, we muft perifh*[*]. For, let us think of it or not, He is the Ruler of the World: and he will approve himfelf to be fuch, by inflicting on thofe, who flight him, the Vengeance they deferve. Indeed, could he leave them to themfelves; as *the Fear of the Lord is the Beginning of Wifdom*[†], fo cafting it off is the Inlet of Folly. Religious Motives are the only ones, that can, in all Cafes, either prompt to what is right, or reftrain from what is wrong, with fufficient Force: and when this Tie is broken, no other will hold. Reafon plainly fhews it: Scripture hath repeatedly foretold it: the Experience of all Ages confirms it: and there is no Room left for us to carry the Trial further, without utter Deftruction. We have been finking for a great while, in Proportion as we grew vicious and prophane, till at laft we were plunged in the very Depth of Diftrefs. Once more however, after feeming quite rejected, we have received a kind Encouragement. But if we let Judgments and Mercies

[*] Luke xiii. 3.   [†] Pfal. cxi. 10. Prov. ix. 10.

both

both be loſt upon us ; what can there remain, but final Ruin ?

Think then with yourſelves, why ſhould we not now return to God ? Gratitude is a generous Principle of Action: and he hath furniſhed us with an Opportunity for it.   Hope is a nobler one than Fear alone.   And who can tell, what Hope there may be yet for this Nation, would we but apply to our offended Father with virtuous Penitence ?   He can raiſe us Friends where we leaſt expected it, and change the Hearts of our bittereſt Adverſaries.   For *he refraineth the Spirit of Princes, and is wonderful among the Kings of the Earth*[u]. *When the Ways of a Man pleaſe the Lord, he maketh even his Enemies to be at Peace with him*[w].   But if their Enmity continues, he can check, he can break their Power, at its very Height: and *ſtrengthen the Hands*[x], direct the Counſels, proſper the Undertakings of his People ; ſo that *no Man ſhall be able to ſtand before them*[y].   *For His is the Greatneſs, and the Glory, and the Victory, and the Majeſty*[z]: *For the Kingdom is the Lord's and*

[u] Pſal. lxxvi. 12.   [w] Prov. xvi. 7.   [x] Neh. vi. 9.
[y] Joſh. i. 5.   [z] 1 Chron. xxix. 11.

He

*He is the Governor amongſt the Nations [a]. Let
it be thy Pleaſure, O Lord, to deliver us: make
Haſte, O God, to help us. Let all thoſe that
ſeek thee, be joyful and glad in thee; and ſuch
as love thy Salvation ſay alway, The Lord be
praiſed [b].*

[a] Pſal. xxii. 28.   [b] Pſal. xl. 16, 19.

SER-

SERMON VII.

(Preached *October* 9, 1746, on the Day appointed for a General Thankf-giving for the Suppreffion of the Rebellion.)

JOHN v. 14.

Afterward Jefus *findeth him in the Temple, and faid unto him, Behold, though art made whole: Sin no more, left a worfe Thing come unto thee.*

AFTER feven yearly Fafts, we have now through God's Mercy, before we have deferved it, one Day of general Thankfgiving: and furely our Concern is to employ it fo, that we may hope for more. Now there can be no wifer or kinder Direction for this Purpofe, than that of our Lord in the Text. He had juft healed the Perfon to whom

he

he fpeaks, and therefore certainly did not mean
to ufe him harfhly in thefe Words: but indeed
to fhew him ftill greater Goodnefs, than he had
done already; as much greater, as Spiritual and
Eternal Welfare is than Temporal. His Cure
had been the heavieft of Misfortunes to him,
had he behaved improperly upon it. But *Jefus
found him in the Temple*, whither probably he
went with a devout Heart, to give God Praife.
This promifed well concerning him: yet by no
Means rendered a ftrong Warning to him fu-
perfluous. Permit me therefore, finding You,
and God be thanked that I find fo many of you,
in the Temple on a like Occafion, to treat you
in a like Manner. And think it not ftrange, I
befeech you, if at prefent you hear not folely
the Voice of Joy, though never was a jufter
Occafion for it, but are exhorted, even now,
to *ferve the Lord in Fear, and rejoice unto him
with Reverence*: I hope many Teachers of
his Word will dwell this Day on the fame Subject: for the Advice, here given by our gracious Mafter, comprehends every Thing that our
Condition requires.

* Pfal. ii. 11.

J. A

I. A thankful Senſe of the Bleſſing, which we have received. *Behold, thou art made whole.*

II. A firm Reſolution of virtuous Obedience in Return for it. *Sin no more.*

III. A prudent Conſideration of the Danger of behaving otherwiſe. *Leſt a worſe Thing come unto thee.*

I. A thankful Senſe of the Bleſſing, which we have received. *Behold, thou art made whole.*

At this Time laſt Year, and for many Months after, we had a very afflicting Senſe of the Judgments, that threatened us: the whole Nation had it, and with the utmoſt Cauſe. Our Religion, our Liberties, our Lives, our public Independence, our private Properties, were all at Stake. Our Forces were few, unſuccefsful, and diſheartened: the Rebels were numerous, fluſhed with Victory, and increaſing. Then beſides what appeared, we knew not how much more Evil we had to apprehend, from Abroad or at Home, from the Fury of our Enemies, from the Coldneſs of our Friends. The Danger too was no leſs imminent than great: and muſt ſoon cruſh us, if not ſoon averted. We ſaw, and felt, and trembled at it; we exerted ourſelves againſt it, with a Spirit, never known

amongſt

amongſt us before: and God forbid we ſhould
have forgotten, God forbid we ſhould ever forget, the Impreſſions that we had ſo lately, firſt,
of the Terrors impending over us, then of the
Felicity of their ſudden Diſperſion.

It is true, we are not yet perfectly *whole.*
Far from it, Heaven knows. But what would
we have given once for ſo happy an Approach
towards it, as we now poſſefs? Our domeſtic
Foes are fallen in Battle, or cut off by Juſtice,
or driven into other Lands, or abſconding in
Corners of their own, impoveriſhed and diſ-
armed, and taught by Experience neither to
rely on themſelves, nor their faithlefs Allies.
Our Soldiery have recovered their antient Courage and Character. The Nation in general
hath united in active Loyalty: we are known
and truſted one by another; known and dreaded
by our Adverſaries, who had ſtrangely miſtaken
our inteſtine Diviſions, bad as they were, for
ſomething much worſe. Our Diſtemper is at
leaſt expelled from our Vitals, and driven to
the extreme Parts. We have Notice, we have
Time, to provide againſt a Return of it: and
poſſibly at preſent *France* may be feeling from
us, in her own Dominions, a ſmall Share of
the Sufferings, which She projected for Ours,

6

while

while We are enjoying in Peace all that we feared to lose. Whatever we may want therefore to make our Happiness complete, we ought to be most deeply sensible, that our Portion of it is remarkably large: so large, that there is not surely a Nation upon Earth, with which any one of us, in the Midst of all that we have to complain of and lament, would be willing on the whole to change Conditions.

But then, as often as we consider to how comfortable a Degree we are *whole*, we should always recollect, by what Means we were *made whole*. Our Saviour was not afraid the poor Man, whom he cured, should forget that he had regained the Use of his Limbs, but how he had regained it. And if He, who had been miraculously healed, yet had need of being reminded to whom he owed his Health: much more should we, who have been saved by the ordinary Methods of Providence, be careful to fix it in our Hearts, whence the inestimable Benefit was derived. And here let us allow their full Proportion of Praise, even to the human Means: to the Justice and Mildness of his Majesty's Government, and the Prospect of continued Security and Tranquillity under his Descendants; Blessings, which the Risque of

losing

losing exited the most vigorous Efforts for preserving; to the Valour, the Prudence, the Vi-
gilence, the Activity of his illustrious Son; to
the Bravery and Indignation, thus inspired into
his Officers and Troops; to the unexampled
Unanimity, Zeal, and Liberality of his faithful
Subjects, the Nobility, the Gentry, the Clergy,
the Commonalty of the Realm. Let us ever
acknowledge our Obligations to the Merits of
all these. But still let us remember, that Men
are only Instruments in the Hand of the Almighty. We have owned this all along by our
Prayers: let us own it sincerely in our Thankfgivings also; and not receive, without suitable
Gratitude, what we begged with such uncommon Earnestness. It is just as true at this Hour,
as it was then, that *except the Lord keep the
City, the Watchman waketh but in vain* [p]. From
his Displeasure came our Danger: from his
compassionate Goodness, our Deliverance.
Therefore despise not either *the Chastenings* or
the Mercies *of the Almighty. For he maketh fore
and bindeth up: he woundeth, and his Hands
make whole* [q]. It cannot be less criminal towards God than Men, it is unspeakably more,
to ask Assistance, and when we have had it, not

[p] Psal. cxxvii. 2. [q] Job v. 17, 18.

acknow-

acknowledge it.   He doth not indeed want our Acknowledgments; but he hath still an equal Right to them; and that he requires them not for his own Sake, but for ours, is surely no Reason, why we should with-hold them.

But you will say, " We do acknowledge " God's Mercy in delivering us, and will never " deny it." But if after a While you never think of it more, you might almost as well deny it. Or if you think of it, and are not moved by it, that is worse than forgetting it.   Or suppose you have ever so warm a Feeling of his Favours, yet if you refuse to make a proper Return for them, this is worst of all.   And what Return doth he demand ? Some hard and unnatural, or expensive and ruinous Service ? No: the most reasonable Thing in itself, and the most beneficial to us and our Fellow-Creatures, that possibly can be: what the Text expresses,

II. A firm Resolution of virtuous Obedience. *Behold, thou art made whole: sin no more.*   God hath been gracious to you: be dutiful to him. Sin is at all Times equally absurd and ill-deserving.   It is setting up our own perverse Will against the Authority of our Maker and Sovereign Lord; our own Passions and Caprices,

against

againſt the Wiſdom of our heavenly Father! thinking, that we can proſper in Oppoſition to the Almighty; or if not, preferring Rebellion and Miſery to Fidelity and Happineſs. But to ſin on, directly in the Face of diſtinguiſhing Mercies, juſt vouchſafed, this is the moſt ſhocking Aggravation of the worſt Thing in the World: a Crime ſo heinous, that perhaps you may reſent being thought bad enough to need a Caution againſt it. But the impotent Man, whom our Saviour healed, was not, that we know, a Sinner beyond others. And therefore, could we of theſe Nations truly ſay, that we are not ſuch neither; ſtill the Caution, given Him, would be a ſeaſonable one to Us. We have at leaſt ſinned enough to deſerve what we have ſuffered, which is more than a little. And had we deſerved nothing farher; yet, as *Elihu* remarks in the Caſe of *Job*, *Surely it is meet to be ſaid unto God, I have borne Chaſtiſe-ment, I will not offend any more* [d].

But, to ſee, how far ſuch Advice is neceſſary for us, it will be requiſite, not to keep in Generals, but deſcend to Particulars. And they muſt be ſuch, as relate to each of us in our private Capacities: for I am not ſpeaking now to

---

[d] Job xxxiv. 31.

Bodie

Bodies of Men, or to single Persons in high Stations. May God bestow plentifully on all such, Grace to consider, what the Warning, *sin no more*, directs Them to, while we consider, what it directs Us to. And I apprehend the present Occasion calls upon us to avoid, for Time to come, four Kinds of Sin especially: to disregard Religion no more; to misbehave towards our Rulers no more; to encourage Party-Disputes and Contentions no more; to indulge extravagant Pleasures and Amusements no more.

1. To disregard Religion no more. Perhaps this is the Nation upon Earth, where it is regarded the least, (our Neglect of God's Worship in our Churches, our Families, our Closets; the impious Talk, the infidel Books, that abound every-where, afford lamentable Evidences of it) though we have confessedly the greatest Blessings to incline us to be religious, and the most rational Instruction how to be so. Notwithstanding this, who is there amongst us, of any Age, who doth not perceive, how much commoner and opener both Indifference and Profaneness are grown within his own Time, within a small Part of it? Who was there amongst us lately, of any Thought, that did not

strongly

ftrongly fear we were become fo intirely unconcerned about the Matter, that even Popery
would have had no Terrors for us? God ·be
thanked, it hath proved otherwife.   And permit
me to add, let Them be thanked alfo, by whofe
long defpifed and reproached Labours, a Spirit
of Piety had ftill in fome Meafure been kept
alive : and by whofe earneft and feafonable Exhortations an unexpected Degree of Proteftant
Zeal was principally raifed.   Do us the Juftice
then to bear it in Mind, that you wanted our
Help, and you had it.   The Enemies of the
Government avowedly hate us for what we have
done : if its Friends will not love us for it, our
Cafe is hard indeed.   But, however you think
of Us, learn at leaft to think of the Religion
we profefs, as the trueft Support, indeed as an
effential Part, of our happy Eftablifhment.
Not that preferving it for political Purpofes
alone will be at all fufficient : they, who aim
at no more, will come fhort even of that.   God
will difappoint them; Men will fee through
them : and Infection will fpread from Hypocrify, as well as Profligatenefs, though not quite
fo faft, yet till at length the whole Frame is
corrupted and deftroyed.

You

You may plead, that however prophane the Nation may be, we are anfwerable each for him-felf only. But indeed, fo far as our Behaviour can properly influence, we are anfwerable be-yond ourfelves. Do we then endeavour to dif-countenance Irreligion, and encourage Seriouf-nefs in thofe who belong to us, in thofe with whom we converfe? Do we, as our Saviour hath enjoined us, *confefs Him before Men*[e]? Or do we not on many Occafions outwardly appear *afhamed of Him,* while inwardly our Hearts condemn us for it?

But were we to anfwer for ourfelves alone, what Anfwer could we give? We are as good as others, perhaps. And what, if others be very bad? Will that excufe Us from being what the Word of God, and our own Confciences, tell us we ought to be? If not, are we indeed fuch? Is Concern for our future Happinefs, is Reverence and Love of God, the great Princi-ple within our Breafts? Do we really love him, the better for thefe very Mercies, for which we are now met to praife him? We hope fo, perhaps. But what proof have we given of it. By ferving him better fince? And if none, while the Motive was frefh upon our Minds, what is to be expected afterwards, unlefs the

[e] Matt. x. 32.   Luke xii. 8.

M   prefent

prefent Call awaken us, as Heaven grant it
may?

2. The next Point of Inſtruction is, to miſ-
behave towards our Rulers no more. The
Connexion is inſeparable, *Fear God: Honour the
King*[f]. *For by him Kings reign, and Princes
rule*; *Nobles and all the Judges of the Earth*[g].
For which Reaſon we are to reſpect, not only
the Perſon of our Sovereign, but, to uſe the
Apoſtle's Words, *All that are in Authority*[h].
For without a Number of ſuch, Government
cannot be adminiſtered. And Profeſſions of
Duty to Him, with unjuſt Bitterneſs againſt
thoſe whom he intruſts, and cauſeleſs Oppoſition to the Meaſures they adviſe, betray either
groſs Inſincerity, or pitiable Weakneſs, or an
Impetuoſity of Temper, that ſhould be better
governed. This however doth not reſtrain
thoſe, to whoſe Rank or Office it belongs, from
uſing the faithful, though poſſibly ſometimes
unpleaſing, Freedom of giving ſuch Counſel,
or propoſing ſuch Laws, as public-ſpirited Prudence appears to direct. Nor doth it reſtrain
any one from expreſſing, in a proper Manner,
his Opinion of whatever public Meaſures may
conſiderably affect Him, or the Whole, pro-

[f] 1 Pet. ii. 17.　　[g] Prov. viii. 15, 16.　　[h] 1 Tim. ii. 1.

vided

vided he hath Ground to think himself a Judge of them. But it ought to reſtrain all Perſons from being vehement, and judging harſhly, where perhaps they are unqualified to judge at all: from indulging ſuch Behaviour, ſuch Language, or even ſuch Notions, as are injurious to Governors, or hurtful to the Ends of Government; as may excite or cheriſh Diſloyalty, or unreaſonable Diſſatisfaction, or barely promote Unconcernedneſs about thoſe, whom Providence hath ſet over us.

How far we have been guilty of theſe Things, it is much fitter that each one ſhould think ſeriouſly for himſelf, (for it is a very ſerious Matter) than that any one ſhould take upon him to tell others, eſpecially from this Place. I ſhall only ſay therefore, that every Sort of Perſons may have been guilty: ſome by wrong Compliances, and Abuſe of Power and Favour; ſome by ill-founded Complaints and Reſentments; all by diſguiſing ſelfiſh Views under plauſible Pretences. But whoever the Criminals are, the Crime is very great. Not only thoſe in Authority ſuffer by it, when they ought not, which alone is grievous Injuſtice, but the Community in general ſuffers deeply with them. The wrong Things of this Kind,

                    which

which are said and done, give the Ill-designing
dreadful Advantages against their Superiors;
and hurry the Inconsiderate, even they who mean
well, into Wildnesses almost incredible. Nay,
the Wise and Good are insensibly cooled and
alienated by them. And then is the Juncture
for attempting to overturn a Constitution. We
have felt this: and therefore we shall be inex-
cusable, unless we remember it; remember to
abstain from all Appearance [i] of Undutifulness;
to *keep our Mouths with a Bridle, while the
Wicked* or the Weak *are before us* [k]; on no Occasion to expect more from our Rulers, than
we justly may from human Creatures, like ourselves; to bear it patiently, if our most equitable Expectations are not always answered;
and *accept* and acknowledge *every worthy Deed
they do,* and surely they have done many, *with
all Thankfulness* [l]. Acting thus, very probably,
might have prevented the late Rebellion, and
may prevent another.

    3. A further Caution, closely connected with
the preceding, is, to encourage Party Contentions no more. For they always break in, and
usually to a high Degree, be it ever so unde-
signed at first, on the Respect owing to our Go-

    [i] 1 Theff. v. 22.   [k] Pfal. xxxix. 1.   [l] Acts xxiv. 2, 3.

vernors.

vernors. Or could that be avoided, one Side will be tempted to patronife, for the Sake of Popularity, what they know, or eafily might know, is wrong; to oppofe what is ufeful, or even neceffary; to conftrue the worthieft and wifeft Conduct unfairly; to prefer the Support of their Caufe before the Service of the Public; to imagine or pretend, that the Prevalence of it will produce every defirable Effect; when both Reafon and Experience demonftrate, that little, if any, Good is like to follow from it, and poffibly much Harm. The other Side, in Return, are tempted to reject what they ought to forward; to infift on what they ought to give up; to opprefs their Adverfaries by fuperior Power; to accufe them of being what they are not, till perhaps they provoke them into being what they would not be. And on both Sides thefe Difputes engage Mens principal Attention, to the Neglect of their common Welfare; drive them into doing bad Actions, and countenancing bad Perfons; make foreign Friends afraid to rely upon us; and both foreign and domeftic Enemies bold to enterprife againft us. Their late Enterprife was chiefly founded on our Divifions: which neither They, nor indeed We, could have imagined would have fuffered us to

M 3

unite

unite again&ſt; them ſo ſoon, and ſo heartily, as
we did. God be praiſed, who inclined our
Hearts to it: but let us *ſin no more*. Each Party
ſees, that the other have ſinned: each might
ſee, that they have ſinned themſelves: both
muſt ſee, that the Event was nearly pernicious:
let us take Warning for the future.

But it will be of ſmall Advantage not to oppoſe one another, if we all agree in behaving
amiſs: and therefore,

4. The laſt Caution is, to indulge extravagant
Pleaſures and Amuſements no more. It is but
too viſible, how much, living intirely to Trifles
and Follies hath increaſed in the upper Part of
the World: and Madneſs for Diverſions and
Entertainments, even in the middle and lower;
together with moſt profligate Intemperance and
Debauchery in the loweſt of all. Now vicious
Indulgencies are deſtructive to our temporal,
as well as our Spiritual Intereſts; to the Health
and Strength, that ſhould labour for and defend
the Public; to the Honeſty and Regularity,
that ſhould ſecure private Peace and Comfort.
Merely imprudent Gratifications, by devouring
Time and Money, as they do beyond Imagination, deſtroy Induſtry, and propagate Poverty;
which, we muſt be ſenſible, is making yearly

frightful

frightful Advances upon us.   And when Wick-
edness is inftigated by Neceffity, the worft of
Confequences may juftly be apprehended.
Thofe of mean Rank are then fully ripe for any
Mifchief: and what Mifchief might we not
have dreaded from them ten Months ago, had
Providence permitted the Rebels to reach our
Capital? Perfons of better Condition, when
diftreffed, will too often facrifice every other
Confideration to the urgent one of fupplying
their Wants, real or fancied; prefer their own
prefent Profit, fometimes a trifling Profit, before
the common Safety; heighten groundlefs Dif-
contents, to take Advantage of them; nay, join
in Rebellion itfelf againft their Confciences; of
which we have lately had a moft remarkable
Example, and ingenuous Confeffion [m].   May it
prove an ufeful Preventive!

A further great Evil is, that immoderate
Lovers of Pleafure will of courfe favour the
vileft Wretches, who contribute to their Enter-
tainment; and too frequently depreciate the
worthieft Character, if it be a grave one: whence
proceed Inconveniencies without Number. But

---

[m] See *Fofter's* Account of the Behaviour of the late Earl of
Kilmarnock, after his Sentence, p. 6, 7, 10, 11, 41.

M 4

were

were this defpicable Inclination hurtful no otherwife; it would be extremely fo, by taking off
the Mind from Application to Things of Moment.   Even in Perfons the leaft confiderable,
Indolence, and Inattention to their proper Bufinefs, may have extenfive bad Effects: and
when it grows general among fuch, it fenfibly
impoverifhes and weakens, and tends to ruin a
Nation.   But they, who are intrufted with
Matters of Importance, may, not only by a
Series of Neglect, but by the ill-timed Indulgence of an idle Humour for a Day or an Hour,
caufe irretrievable Mifchief to a Society, that
hath purchafed and depends on their beft Vigilance and Induftry: which therefore are due to
it, not only in Point of Honour, but of indif-
penfible moral Obligation in the Sight of God.

Thefe, I apprehend, are the chief Particulars, in which we fhould learn, from being
made whole, to fin no more.   And every one
fhould apply them to examine and direct himfelf, not to inveigh againft others: and remember, that the utmoft Punctuality and Zeal in
fome Parts of his Duty, will not be accepted,
as an Atonement for tranfgreffing or overlooking any of the reft.

III. The

III. The laſt general Head, comprehended in the Advice of the Text, is, A prudent Conſideration of what may follow, if we diſregard it : *Sin no more, leſt a worſe Thing come unto thee.* Perhaps we may think, that nothing worſe can come. And ſo perhaps thought the poor Man, to whom this was ſaid firſt : for his Illneſs had been a very deplorable one. Yet our Saviour gave Him the Warning : and let Us take it alſo. Whoever goes on to offend, after receiving ſignal Mercies, is plainly a greater Sinner : and let him not doubt, but God can ſend him a heavier Puniſhment even in this World, and make *his laſt State worſe than the firſt* [a]. Indeed, ſhould only what we have already felt return upon us : the Tenderneſs of a wounded Part will augment both the Fear and the Pain. And how little Probability of it ſoever we diſcern, as one dreadful Danger hath grown up out of nothing, ſo may a dreadfuller of the ſame Nature. Our Sins, if we amend not, will enfeeble and divide us yet more : our inteſtine Foes may take new Courage ; our foreign ones may ſupport them better : God may refuſe intirely *to go forth with our Hoſts* [b] ; and any Thing may have any Effect, that he pleaſes.

[a] Matt. xii. 45.   [b] Pſal. cviii. 11.

Hitherto

Hitherto we have only been washed by the Waves: the next Time we may sink under them: that surely would be worse. And they, who have now suffered so much from us, would with Reason become vastly more formidable to us, were they to succeed hereafter, than if they had succeeded lately.

But where is the Impossibility, that without the Help of Enemies at Home, the powerful and inveterate one, which we have Abroad, may enslave us ere long immediately to itself: and That without granting even the short Reprieve to our Religion, Liberties, and Properties, which perhaps from the former we might hope? Our only Defence against both is in God's good Providence: and our only Ground of Trust in That is, If we *sin no more*. For fresh Provocations, it must be expected, will bring on severer Judgments. Let us often recollect then, that He, who hath delivered us out of the Hand of our Enemies, can full as easily deliver us into it: and if he doth not, still hath us continually in his own. Every Thing terrible, Fire, Famine, Pestilence, waits on his Orders. At this Instant we are suffering heavily by the last, though hitherto confined to our Cattle. But how much longer and more general

a Raa Ravage it may make amongſt Them, or to what other Species of Creatures it may extend at length, and whether not to our own, which of us can ſay?

But indeed, without any other Scourge at all, Sin alone, by the natural Conſequences, which Heaven hath originally annexed to it, is able to ruin us very completely. Contempt of God and our Duty may overturn on a ſudden, but muſt undermine gradually, in Proportion as it prevails, every Bleſſing that we enjoy: fill every Family with Diſorders and Diſtreſſes, aboliſh mutual Faith and Confidence, open a wide Door to Fraud and Force, defeat the Execution of Juſtice, make our envied Conſtitution ineffectual to its great Ends, and turn all the Good of it into Evil: *till we are able to bear,* as was the ancient Complaint in like Circumſtances, *neither our Diſeaſes, nor their Remedies* [r]. The more Immorality ſpreads, the deeper Root it ſtrikes: the Difficulties of checking it increaſe; the Numbers and Vigour of thoſe who endeavour to check it, leſſen. Some Diſtempers, by the Fermentation, which they excite, work their own Cure. But Wickedneſs is a Gangrene, which deſtroys the Part it ſeizes:

[r] Liv. Hiſt. Præf.

and,

and, if it approaches towards being univerfal, muft end in Death. External Force, like an acute Difeafe, though for a Time it bears down all before it, may ftill, by the Vigour of Nature, be thrown off unexpeƈtedly: but an internal Principle of Diffolution, that hath corrupted the whole Mafs of Humours, admits no Relief.

Or fuppofe a finful Nation, either by ftopping fhort of the Extremity of Sin, or by an uncommon Delay of Divine Juftice, neither of which can reafonably be expeƈted, were to efcape temporal Ruin ever fo long: yet there will be a *worfe,* an infinitely *worfe Thing, come* without fail, and that very foon, to every Sinner in it; the final Vengeance of God in the next Life: which will be, as it ought, peculiarly fevere on thofe, who *defpife the Riches of his Forbearance and Long-fuffering; and will not know, that his Goodnefs leads them to Repentance* [q].

I am very fenfible, that this may appear a comfortlefs, an intimidating Manner of fpeaking to you: and exceedingly unfuitable to fo joyful a Solemnity, as the prefent. By why then will not all who hear me, why will not

[q] Rom. ii. 4.

this

this whole Land refolve on that Amendment,
without which no true Comfort can be adminiftered to them? Relieve us then from the
Neceffity, for we muft deal faithfully with you,
of faying on Thankfgivings juft the fame terrifying Things, that we do on Fafts. It would
afford us the higheft Delight to omit them, on
both : to fet before you only pleafing Views,
and defcribe your Condition in the Language of
the Pfalmift : *Happy are the People, who are in
fuch a Cafe: yea, bleffed are the People, who have
the Lord for their God*. It is intirely your
own Fault, that Motives of Fear are ever mentioned to you. Our gracious Maker hath fur-
nifhed us plentifully with a much better Ground
of Obedience, by the numerous Mercies, which
we have long enjoyed, and ftill continue to enjoy. Think but a little of the natural Advantages of this Ifland; of the Civil, the Spiritual
Privileges, that have diftinguifhed it for Ages;
and what Requitals they deferve: think but,
how complicated a Bleffing this laft Deliverance
is : and labour to be induced, as much as you
can, by the Bounties of God to ferve him. But
let us be confcious alfo, that our Imperfection,
our Depravity, needs Awe, as well as Love, to

 ' Pfal. cxliv. 15.

move

move us; and ufe the joint Efforts of both, to produce in our Souls that filial Sorrow, and penitent Return to Duty, which will prove the Inlet, and is the only one, to all Manner of Confolation.

They, that thus *fow in Tears*, are intitled to *reap in Joy*[*]: their *Mouth may be filled with Laughter, and their Tongue with Singing*[t]: they may with Propriety, not only give, as they are bound, the more ferious Demonftrations of pious Gratitude, but indulge every lighter Expreffion of a chearful Heart, that Innocence and Prudence allows. Outward Rejoicings for Mercies, without inward Concern for Unworthinefs, and fixed Refolution of virtuous Improvement, is an abfurd and infolent, and will be a fhort-lived Triumph. *Praife is not feemly in the Mouth of a Sinner: for it was not fent him of the Lord*[u]. But when humble and hearty Devotion hath preceded, Gladnefs and Exultation, kept clear of Excefs and Riot, may and fhould follow, on Occafions like this. The Grief of our Offences fhould be loft, for the Time, in a thankful Senfe of God's Goodnefs: a chearing Hope be entertained, that *He who hath delivered, will deliver*[w]; and our Be-

[*] Pfal. cxxvi. 6.   [t] Ver. 2.   [u] Ecclus xv. 9.   [w] 2 Cor. i. 10.

haviour

haviour ſhew to all around us, what our Hearts feel. This was the Direction, immediately given to the *Jews*, when once they had been made ſenſible of their Tranſgreſſions, in their public Aſſembly for a Thankſgiving, on their Return from the Captivity : and I conclude with reciting it. *The Levites read in the Book, in the Law of God, and gave the Senſe, and cauſed them to underſtand the Reading. And all the People wept, when they heard the Words of the Law. Then Nehemiah the Governor, and Ezra the Prieſt, and the Levites, that taught the People, ſaid unto them, This Day is holy unto the Lord your God : mourn not, nor weep. Go your Way, eat the Fat, and drink the Sweet, and ſend Portions unto them, for whom nothing is prepared ; for this Day is holy unto our Lord : neither be ye ſorry, for the Joy of the Lord is your Strength. And all the People went their Way, to eat and to drink, and to ſend Portions, and to make great Mirth ; becauſe they had under-ſtood the Words, that were declared unto them* [x].

[x] Neh. viii. 7, 8, 9, 10, 12.

SER-

SERMON VIII.

(Preached on a General Fast.)

PSALM cxxii. 6.

O pray for the Peace of Jerusalem : *They shall prosper that love thee.*

GOD hath planted in the Hearts of Men, and it is a strong Proof of his Goodness to us, a Principle of tender mutual Benevolence ; which Reason enjoins us to exert on all Occasions: and Revelation both threatens our Transgression of this Rule with the severest Punishments, and encourages our Observance of it by Promises of the most effectual Assistance and noblest Rewards. But as all Mankind is an Object too large, for the Generality of Persons to embrace in their Affections, and for the rest to think of actually benefiting; the Scripture hath very justly appropriated our *Love* to *our Neighbour :* to every one, who is any

N   Way

Way brought near enough to us, to be capable of receiving any Service or Mark of Kindnefs from us: according to our Saviour's moft rational Explication of that Term[a]. And each Nation of the World being only a more extenfive Neighbourhood, of Perfons combined together, under one Head, for common Advantage: the Views of the feveral Members of it' may well reach thus far; but ordinarily fcarce farther. And therefore Love to our Country hath been ever confidered, not merely as an important and excellent Virtue, which it always is, when genuine and judicious; but as filling the whole Compafs of reciprocal Duty, which it ufually doth, provided we proportion it rightly to the various Relations, which we bear to each Perfon in the Society. Now this is the Affection, which the Pfalmift fo warmly recommends in the Text: *Peace* being well known to fignify, in Holy Writ, all Sorts of Profperity; and *Jerufalem* being the Centre of Unity of the *Jewifh* People, both in religious Affairs and Civil. *For thither the Tribes went up, to give Thanks unto the Name of the Lord: and there was the Seat of Judgment, even the Seat of the Houfe of* David[b].

[a] Luke x. 29, &c.   [b] Pfal. cxxii. 4, 5.

During

During the latter Part indeed of the Time, that their Government fubfifted, they had moft of them a Zeal for their Country, which excluded Charity towards the reft of Mankind. But this was a Corruption, not a Precept, of their Religion. For no Law of any other Nation ever enjoined fo ftrictly both Juftice and Mercy to Strangers as theirs: though it did provide againft needlefs Intercourfe with them, to prevent Imitation of their evil Cuftoms. It is true, they were commanded to extirpate the Inhabitants of *Canaan*. But thefe were grown to fuch a Height of monftrous Idolatry, unnatural Lufts, and fhocking Barbarities, as the Wifdom of God faw to be incurable. And he chofe the *Ifraelites* for *his Minifters, Revengers to execute Wrath upon them*[c], that they might learn to abhor what they had been employed to punifh. This done, their Commiffion expired: for it reached to no other Nation. And in fact, they were as quiet Neighbours to the Heathen round them, and as dutiful Subjects to their *Chaldean, Perfian* and *Grecian* Mafters, as any other People. Nor did the Text more plainly require them to *pray for the Peace of* Jerufalem, than the Prophet *Jeremiah* doth,

[c] Rom. xiii. 4.

to seek the Peace of the City, whither they were carried Captives, and pray unto the Lord for it [a].

We need not therefore fcruple to imbibe Love of our Country from the Sacred Writings of the *Jews:* and much lefs have we Caufe to imagine, as fome would perfuade us, that this is a Virtue not prefcribed to Chriftians. It is true, that as the *Romans* had long been ravaging the World, and the *Jews* in our Saviour's Days were evidently ruining themfelves; both of them prompted to what they did by a narrow-minded and unjuft Vehemence for their national Intereft and Honour: he earneftly recommended, as it was neceffary, not the particular Paffion, of which they had already too much; but the general Difpofition, which they wanted, of good Will to all Men. For that is the only fure Foundation of focial Behaviour: and while it reftrains Perfons effectually from doing any Thing wrong in favour of their Country, will incite them powerfully to do every Thing right. In teaching this Doctrine therefore, and indeed throughout his whole Conduct, he fhewed the kindeft and wifeft Regard to his undeferving Fellow-Citizens: for

[a] Jer. xxix. 7.

whom,

whom, ill as he was treated by them, he fully appears to have had the moſt affectionate Concern. Witneſs his Tears and pathetic Expoſtulations : *O Jeruſalem, Jeruſalem, thou that killeſt the Prophets, and ſtoneſt them that are ſent unto thee : how often would I have gathered thy Children together, even as a Hen gathereth her Chickens under her Wings, and ye would not*[e]. *If thou hadſt known*, or as it rather ſhould be tranſlated, *O that thou hadſt known, even thou, at leaſt in this thy Day, the Things, which belong unto thy Peace*[f]. Witneſs again his peremptory Command, even after he had been crucified there, *that Repentance and Remiſſion of Sin ſhould be preached in his Name to all Nations, beginning at* Jeruſalem[g]. The ſame heroic Sympathy his great Apoſtle St. *Paul* expreſſes, after the ſevereſt Uſage, in the ſtrongeſt Manner, *for his Brethren, his Kinſmen, according to the Fleſh*, declaring ſolemnly before *Chriſt and the Holy Ghoſt, that he had great and continual Sorrow and Heavineſs in his Heart* on their Account[h]. He hath not indeed exhorted the Chriſtians, whom he favoured with his Epiſtles, to the Love of their ſeveral Countries :

[e] Matt. xxiii. 37.   [f] Luke xix. 41, 42.   [g] Luke xxiv. 47.
[h] Rom. ix. 1, 2, 3.

for they were all under one Dominion, and defigned by Providence to remain fo. He hath
not exhorted Magiftrates to ftudy the Welfare
of thofe, over whom they prefided: for there
were no believing Magiftrates; and it might
have been deemed prefumptuous, and ill intended, if he had laid down Directions for
others; or foretold explicitly fo foon, that the
Gofpel would come to have Authority on its
Side. But he hath fufficiently, though ob-
liquely, intimated to Rulers, what their Office
requires of them: and urged private Subjects
moft convincingly and awfully to fuch Behaviour, as will render Communities quiet and
flourifhing.

Love of our Country therefore is an undoubt-
ed Chriftian Duty. And we fhall both be directed and encouraged in the Performance of it,
if we confider, as the Text leads us,

I. Wherein the Public Welfare confifts.

II. How we are to exprefs our Regard to it.

III. What Advantages will flow from expref-
    fing it as we ought.

I. Wherein it confifts. Now plainly the
Happinefs of any Society is that, which the

Perfons,

Perſons, who compoſe it, do or may enjoy in it. And therefore wide Extent of Dominion contributes nothing to the Happineſs of a State: for ſuch unwieldy Bodies are ſeldom or never kept long in good Health. Much leſs is military Glory the Point to be had in View, any farther than is needful to ſecure a peaceable Poſſeſſion of all important national Rights. For ſuch a Purpoſe, War is lawful: and they, who hazard their Lives in it, worthy of high Honour. But in all Caſes it is accompanied with dreadful Evils: of which we are apt to conſider the heavy Expence, as if it were the only one; and forget the Sufferings, and miſerable Deaths, of ſuch Multitudes of human Creatures, though every one of them is a Murder committed by the Authors of this Calamity; beſides the innumerable Diſtreſſes of Relations and Friends, the Devaſtations, Inhumanities, and Wickedneſſes of every Kind, which never fail to be its Attendants. Then if the Event of all ſhould turn, as God grant it always may, to the Diſadvantage of the Aggreſſors, here is much Miſchief brought on their Neighbours, only to bring more on themſelves. Or ſuppoſe their Succeſs be ever ſo great, the Injury done by them will be great in Pro-

                         portion;

portion : they will receive little real Good from it, and have paid very dear for that, even in this World : and in another, God will take effectual Care, that no one shall have Cause to rejoice in having broken his Laws, and used his Creatures ill.

The next Pre-eminence, commonly imagined to constitute the Prosperity of a State, is that of Wealth ; and its usual Source, Commerce. Now undoubtedly Riches are a valuable Instrument, both of common Defence, and separate Enjoyment. But then they are also a dangerous Incentive to Luxury and Debauchery : by which Persons grievously distress themselves, their Families, their Acquaintance, the Public, in many Ways, alas ! but too well known. And many, whom affluence doth not immediately seduce into gross Vices, it leads however to Indolence and Ignorance, to the Admiration of Trifles and Follies, and thence to the Neglect, and afterwards the Contempt and Ridicule, of virtuous and prudent Conduct. This wrong Taste being once formed, high Honours and Pompous Appearances are thought necessary by some ; the idlest Gratifications and Vanities, by others : the Means to procure and support them must be found : and when their Incomes

fail,

fail, as the largeft, with fuch Management, will fail; they muft fupply the Defect by any Bafe-nefs or Iniquity, that they can; at leaft any fuch, as general Practice, in a Time of general Corruption, makes a Shift to keep in tolerable Countenance. This Example in the upper Part of the World is followed of courfe by the lower: their Induftry leffens, their Expences increafe, their Principles are depraved, they and their Families ruined; they feek for Relief in Fraud, Violence, or Intemperance, and plunge them-felves by each deeper in Mifery. Even of the Regular and Diligent, the Home Labour is much of it employed on Things ufelefs or hurtful; the foreign Trade, in importing Superfluities. This Procedure muft as neceffarily empoverifh the Public, as it muft any fingle Perfon, or Number of Perfons: for the whole Number of them is the Public. And in fuch Circum-ftances, whatever prefent Show of Strength and Plenty there may be, is fallacious: like the over-full and florid Look of a difeafed Body, caufed by too indulgent Regimen; and under the fuperficial Appearance of redundant Health, betraying to the Skilful evident Symptoms of the moft fatal Diftempers, already begun, if not far advanced.

Another

Another Thing, conftantly and juftly mentioned, as a main Ingredient in political Happinefs, is Liberty: an invaluable Privilege; but
often mifunderftood, and ftill oftener abufed:
Abfolute Liberty, to do what we will, is abfolute Power. If one alone, or a few, have this,
the reft are in Slavery: if all have it, the whole
muft be in Confufion. Liberty therefore, in
order to preferve it, muft be reftrained by Law;
in whatever Cafes the Exercife of it may affect
others. And Regulations by Authority are neceffary, not only to prevent mutual Encroach-
ments, but to afcertain each Perfon's Claims
and Expectations; and to inftruct every one,
what he is to do, and what to avoid, for the
common Benefit. Now legal Provifions for
thefe Ends ought to be juft and equitable, fuit-
ed to the State of Things, known and fixed.
And thofe, which a Nation makes for itfelf by
its chofen Reprefentatives, are fo very much the
moft likely to have thefe Properties; that living,
as We do, under a Conftitution purpofely con-
trived for making, on every Occafion, fuch as
we want, is the greateft of civil Bleffings, provided we turn it not, by our Fault, into a
Curfe.

But

But to prevent this, befides Care and Impartiality in framing Laws, there muft be a general Obfervation of them: elfe they were enacted in vain. Even fuch, as are in their Nature the moft variable, muft be obferved while they laft. For not only the total Neglect of them will fruftrate their beneficial Intent, and open a Door to yet worfe Irregularities; but the partial, befides having this unhappy Effect in its Degree, will introduce a very dangerous Kind of Inequality: good Subjects muft be Lofers by their Obedience, and bad ones Gainers by their Tranfgreffion.

Still more effentially doth the common Welfare confift in the Practice of fuch Rules of Conduct, as are in themfelves, and therefore always, obligatory: in abftaining from Violence, Fraud, promifcuous Lewdnefs, Intemperance, Extravagance; in performing carefully the proper Bufinefs of our feveral Stations; in providing diligently what is needful for ourfelves, and thofe who belong to us; in relieving the Poor with prudent Bounty; in behaving with Refpect to Superiors, with Condefcenfion to Inferiors, with Friendlinefs to Equals, with peculiar Affection to thofe, whom either Nature or voluntary Ties have united to us more clofely:

Thefe

Thefe are the main Things, on which focial Happinefs depends. A Nation may be fmall and weak and poor; and yet the Perfons who compofe it, may enjoy their Beings very comfortably. But however great and powerful and rich it is, Folly and Wickednefs will bring Mifery on each Particular; which, put together, is general Mifery: and will befides gradually weaken and diffolve the whole. For the principal Supports of a State, confeffedly are, the Numbers, and Health, and Strength, and Induftry, and Probity, and Concord, of the feveral Members of it: all which good Morals promote, and bad undermine.

But as human Laws, in Multitudes of Inftances, cannot punifh, and much lefs prevent, the Breach of moral Obligations: the chief Security of Regard to them, in any Society, muft proceed from Reverence of the Divine Laws. And as the Precepts of Chriftianity are vaftly more determinate, accompanied with Communications of far greater moral Powers, and enforced by Sanctions of unfpeakably ftronger Terror to Sinners, and fweeter Confolation to pious Minds, than the Dictates of Nature, unaffifted by Revelation: eftablifhing a practical Belief of the Gofpel is fecuring and completing
the

the Provifion for National Felicity.   This will, in all Cafes, reftrain Men from what is wrong, animate them in what is right, make them eafy and happy under every Suffering.   Befides, Profeffion of the fame Faith and Hope, and Participation of the fame Worfhip and Sacraments, muft give fo peculiar a Sacrednefs and Endearment to the Bonds of civil Union, that Zeal in the common Caufe of our Country and our Religion, at once, will be intrepidly active, and indefatigably perfevering[h].   *For my Brethren and Companions Sakes, I will wifh thee Profperity: yea, becaufe of the Houfe of the Lord our God, I will feek to do thee Good[i].*   Then to all the Advantages, flowing naturally from Piety, we cannot doubt but God will fuperadd his Bleffing, and withhold it from the Profane; for his own Words are, *Them that honour me, I will honour: and they, that defpife me, fhall be lightly efteemed[k].*   Nor muft a further Confideration ever be omitted, for it is a very important one: that unlefs true Religion be cherifhed and practifed, falfe Religion will infinuate itfelf and prevail.   For the Mind of Man muft have fome: as the Experience of all Ages proves, and our own particularly; amongft

h Dion. Halic. Ant. Rom. l. ii. c. 23.   i Pfal. cxxii. 8, 9.   k 1 Sam. ii. 30.

whom

whom the Increaſe of Infidelity is accompanied with that of Popery: an Evil, which ought to be highly formidable to us; as it muſt of Courſe, if ever it gain Power enough, not only over-turn our preſent happy Eſtabliſhment, but in-troduce the crueleſt Tyranny over the Souls and Bodies and Eſtates of Men.

Having now ſeen, wherein the public Wel-fare coñſiſts, we ſhould all with great Seriouſ-neſs conſider,

II. How we are to expreſs our Regard to it. The Manner, preſcribed in the Text, accord-ing to our Tranſlation, is, *Praying for the Peace of* Jeruſalem : according to others, Aſking or inquiring concerning its Peace. Both imply, having it much at Heart. And whatever we have deſervedly at Heart, ought jointly to en-gage our watchful Solicitude, and our earneſt Petitions. I ſhall now begin with the firſt.

Pretences to public Spirit, if they are not ſincere, uſually cover hurtful Deſigns. There-fore we ſhould examine ourſelves cloſely, for Self-deceit is wonderfully frequent, *of what Spirit we* indeed *are* [1] *:* whether private Paſſions or Intereſts, concealed under ſpecious Appear-

***

[1] Luke ix. 55.

ances,

ances, do not influence our Difcourfe and Behaviour, perhaps our very Thoughts. And, fo far as we have Need to know, we fhould make the fame Inquiry concerning others alfo: forming our Opinions of them with Charity, yet with Caution. But, fuppofing the common Good be ever fo really Our Object and Theirs: unlefs we underftand well the Tendencies of Things, we may do it irreparable Harm, inftead of furthering it: and therefore fhould always be, according to St. *James's* admirable Direction, *Swift to hear, flow to fpeak, flow to Wrath*[m] : impartially diligent to learn the Truth, where it is our Bufinefs to judge and act; backward to meddle, where it is not; reafonable and moderate in all Matters. But let us confider our Duty more diftinctly, in Relation to the feveral Articles, that were fpecified under the preceding Head.

As Defence againft Enemies is an effential Ingredient in public Happinefs: Rulers are bound to provide for it with Vigilance, and Subjects to contribute to it with Chearfulnefs; far from repining at neceffary Burdens, though heavy ones. But we ought to oppofe with double Vigour, from Principle as well as Inte-

[m] James i. 19.

reft,

reſt, the deliberate, and habitual, and perfidious, and inſolent Diſturbers of Mankind: yet
always remembring, that the only lawful Aim,
even in the juſteſt War, is an equitable Concluſion of it. *The Lord give Strength unto his
People, the Lord give his People the Bleſſing of
Peace* [a] !

Again: as national Wealth, and private
Plenty of the Conveniencies of Life, are de-
ſirable in Communities, but Luxury and Extravagance deſtructive to them: all Perſons, in
their Stations, ought ſo to promote the former,
as to diſcourage the latter at the ſame Time:
which they will do moſt ſuccefsfully, by ſetting
Examples to others of decent Frugality, and
Attention to their own Affairs; by honouring
worthy Characters, though in mean Circumſtances; and expreſſing, in every proper Way,
Diſlike and Contempt of Baſeneſs, Debauchery,
Profuſion, Admiration of undeſerving Things,
Neglect of important ones; be they, who are
guilty of ſuch Faults, ever ſo diſtinguiſhed by
their Rank or Accompliſhments.

Further: as Liberty is a Bleſſing of ineſti-
mable Value in Society, it ought to be aſſerted
with the utmoſt Reſolution and Watchfulneſs,

[a] Pſal. xxix. 10.

not

not only againſt open Aſſaults, but every Practice, that may ſecretly and ſilently impair it;
yet with religious Care, neither to *uſe* it, nor
unwarily aſſiſt others to *uſe* it, *for a Cloke of
Malicioufneſs* *; nor ha'zard the Deſtruction of
it, by Attempts of improving it to a viſionary
Perfection.   Therefore Power, in a requiſite
Degree, muſt both be allowed and diligently
ſupported : They, in whoſe Hands it is placed,
muſt both be obeyed and humbly reſpected,
not only for Wrath, but alſo for Confcience Sake ᵖ;
even the Subordinate, much more the Supreme:
their whole Conduct muſt be viewed with Modeſty and Candour; their good Actions and Intentions acknowledged with due Thankfulneſs;
their Miſtakes and Failings, imagined or real,
borne with that Mildneſs, of which we have All
Need, to excuſe our own.   And the ſame equitable Temper ſhould always be preſerved between private Perſons, one towards another;
were their Differences about public Affairs of
ever ſuch Moment, whereas they are frequently
nominal or trifling; and were they ever ſo ſure
of being in the right, whereas poſſibly both of
them have Reaſon to diſtruſt it.   This is the
Method, and it is the only one, by which we

* ı Pet. ii. 16.   ᵖ Rom. xiii. 5.

can ever hope to fee *Jerufalem built as a City, that is at Unity in itfelf* [q].

Further yet: as good Laws, and the Obfervation of them, are neceffary to the public Welfare; all, who have a Share in Legiflature, ought to contrive or affent to fuch, and oppofe others, without fuffering any Confideration to bias them: all Magiftrates ought to execute them with Uprightnefs and Courage, yet with Humanity; and all Subjects, to obey them difintereftedly, and procure Obedience to them zealoufly.

But the Laws of Morality require peculiar Attention, for our Country's Good, as well as our own. Every Perfon who tranfgreffes thefe, *teaches* his Neighbour, *teaches* his Family, *an evil Leffon againft himfelf* [r], in Points of the greateft Confequence. And every Government, which connives at fuch Tranfgreffions, when it can fafely punifh them, connives at the Ruin of the People intrufted to its Care. But efpecially every free Government, guilty of fo culpable Remiffnefs, be it to court Popularity, be it to ferve what prefent Turn it will, undermines the only Ground it hath to ftand upon. For without Virtue, Liberty cannot fubfift.

<hr>

[q] Pfal. cxxii. 3.   [r] Ecclus ix. 1.

Nor

Nor indeed without Piety can Virtue subsist. For our good Affections are so weak, our bad Inclinations so vehement, and the Temptations of the World so numerous and inticing, that we need every possible Preservative. And evidently the Fear of God is the most awful Restraint from doing ill: and the Love of God the most delightful Inducement to do well. True Religion, therefore, must be established by the Authority of the Legislature, but with the tenderest Regard to scrupulous Consciences: and upheld in Reputation by the Countenance and Example of the Great. Its Ministers must be industrious, and their Superiors must see that they are, in teaching and defending it, and adorning their Doctrine by respectable and amiable Behaviour. Its Professors must be assiduous Attendants on its Exercises in the Congregation, and serious Practisers of its Injunctions at Home.

But particularly, in both Places, they must be earnest with God for their Country's Prosperity, and fervently *pray for the Peace of Jerusalem*. Many can do little else: but all can do so much for it. In some of our Endeavours to serve the Public we may err: in this we are sure to be right. Often we know not, what is best for it: Our heavenly Father always doth.

 Possibly

Possibly in Times of Difficulty and Danger we may be tempted to defpair of the Commonwealth : Praying for it will remind us, that its Fate is not in the Hands of Men, but of the Almighty.   In all Times, Refentments, Interefts, Prejudices, frequently blind and miflead us : devout Applications to Heaven will compofe our Paffions, purify our Intentions, obtain us Light to guide our Steps, and enlarge our Views.   Perhaps we have been diligent enough, or more than enough, in the Ufe of other Means, conducive, as we imagined, to public Good : but have never, humbly and heartily, ufed this.   And yet, if we believe a righteous Judge of the World, we muft furely believe, that he takes Notice of the Addreffes, which his poor Creatures, with pious Affections, offer up to him.   Or could we doubt it otherwife, we are fully affured of it in his Sacred Word. Not that naming our Wants informs him, or Acts of fervile Submiffion delight him, or unfit Importunities prevail on him : but that praying *in Spirit and in Truth* [*], while it feems intended to influence Him only, hath a powerful Influence on Us : and by ftrengthening the Senfe it expreffes, how dependent we are on his Mercy,

[*] John iv. 23.

and

and what Qualifications are needful to obtain it, fits us at the fame Time to receive it, and grow better by it: whereas beftowing his Favours on thofe who are too negligent of him to afk for them, might neither be fuitable to the Holinefs of his Nature, and the Honour of his Government, nor indeed contribute to their final Advantage.   Why then fhould not we addrefs ourfelves to the Lord of all, not in outward Form only, but inward Reality: not merely at diftant Seafons appointed for it, like this, but every Day of our Lives; that he would gracioufly protect the Community, of which we are Members, and inftruct and excite us to perform properly our Duty towards it? His own Declaration, even after he had promifed a Bleffing, is; *I will yet for this be inquired of by the Houfe of* Ifrael, *to do it for them* [t]. And the Direction of his Prophet is, *Ye that make mention of the Lord, keep not Silence, and give him no Reft, till he eftablifh, and till he make* Jerufalem *a Praife in the Earth* [u].

Affectionate Vigilance therefore to do each his Part for the Service of the Whole, and conftant Prayer, that God would *profper the* united *Work of his Hands* [w], are the genuine Demon-

<hr>

[t] Ezek. xxxvi. 37.   [u] If. lxii. 6, 7.   [w] Pfal. xc. 17.

O 3

ftrations

ftrations of that Regard, which we owe to the
public Welfare.   Let us now confider,

III. What Advantages will flow from expreffing it in this due Manner. *They fhall
profper that love thee.* Worldly Profperity is
defigned to partake of the Uncertainty of all
worldly Things : but, fo far as any Thing on
our Part can fecure it, a virtuous and pious
public Spirit muft.   Princes,   Magiftrates,
Teachers of. Religion, military Men, private
Perfons of all Ranks and Profeffions, who thus
exprefs the Love of their Country, will be
loved by it, and love one another. Such Union
will give them both the higheft Pleafure, and
the greateft poffible Strength: nothing will be
done to betray or thwart the general Intereft,
but every Thing imaginable to promote it : they
will be bold in Dangers, perfevere through Difficulties, furnifh mutual Affiftance at any Hazard : Allies will know they can truft them ;
Enemies will refpect and dread them.   Indeed
they will have no Enemies, but fuch as oppofe
Truth and Right : and therefore, when they
are driven to War, they will confider themfelves
as fighting the Battles of God. But ufually they
will enjoy Peace, at Home as well as Abroad,
and tafte the Comforts of it without Allay :
each

each delighting in the other's Good; each feeling the Tranquillity, the Wealth, the Honour of the Community, as his own; and rejoicing with humble Thankfulnefs, that His Share in the Production of it hath not been wanting. If fuch Happinefs be feldom feen, the Reafon is, that fuch Difpofitions towards it are feldom general. But let them be ever fo uncommon, and Affairs for Want of them ever fo unprofperous; whoever facredly preferves them in himfelf, and faithfully exerts them when he can, *his Soul fhall profper* [x], as St. *John* expreffes it: be filled with the Confolation, that he hath meant and endeavoured well, though furrounded with Examples and Temptations to the contrary; and that none of the Calamities, that have happened or may happen, can be laid to his Charge. Were he to be intirely deferted by other Men, he would fupport himfelf by our Saviour's Reflection: *Behold, the Hour cometh, yea, is now come, that ye fhall be fcattered, every Man to his own, and fhall leave me alone: and yet I am not alone, becaufe the Father is with me* [y]. Some, however, in the worft of Times, will probably bear Witnefs to him on Earth; but God will certainly look down upon him

[x] 3 John, ver. 2.   [y] John xvi. 32.

                    with

with Approbation from Heaven; and bless him
with a pleasing Consciousness of his Favour,
the Foretaste of future Reward.

Let us now, on the other Hand, contemplate
the Effects, I do not say of downright Ill-will
to the Public, which few perhaps can be wicked
enough to harbour knowingly, but of Indifference, and preferring other Considerations to its
Advantage. If Persons in Stations of Trust,
supreme or subordinate, regard Empire, absolute Power, Profit, Pleasure, Indolence, as their
Felicity: Inferiors will in Proportion be sacrificed, oppressed, exhausted, neglected. If these
Inferiors are principally intent on their own
private Gratifications of any Kind: even where
they have no Share in the Government, they
will hurt it by serving it remissly or unfaith-
fully, and be miserable by unwilling Subjection.
But where the Government is mixed, and divided between the Sovereign, the Nobles, and
the Representatives of the Commonalty; as it
cannot be carried on at all in that Form, without Professions, on every Side, of a patriot
Spirit: so in the Degree, in which these Professions are false, there will be a wide Door
open for supine Mismanagement, selfish Projects, Corruption, Treachery: the vilest of
Men

Men will fhelter themfelves under plaufible Appearances and favourite Names; and be fupported by Parties, which they have artfully
raifed or careffed. At the fame Time, they,
who think they have the tendereft Love for
their Country, perhaps will find on Reflection,
that in truth they love only the Faction, in
which they have lifted : or though it be their
Country; if they have not had Tendernefs
enough for it, to examine coolly what Conduct
its Interefts require, they may accelerate its
Ruin, by increafing the Fiercenefs of Conten-
tion, and lending the Reputation of their good
Meaning to colour over the bad Defigns of
others. Free Nations therefore, as they are
the happieft beyond Comparifon, if the general
Advantage be the general Object : fo they are
peculiarly uncomfortable, and expofed to Danger from within and without, if Divifions inflame men one againft another, or the Attention of each be confined to himfelf.

Still the *Wife in their Generation* ᶻ may imagine, that however impoffible it be for the
Whole to profper without the mutual Affection
of the Parts, they fhall profper the better for
throwing off a Principle, that will be always

------

* Luke xvi. 8.

interfering

interfering with their Interest or Inclinations.
But they cannot attempt to throw it off, or even
contradict it in a single Instance, without se-
verely condemning themselves in their Hours of
Recollection.   Or if they could, they will be
detected, in Spight of all Disguise, and abhor-
red by others, and most by the Worthiest:
which gives the hardest Hearts much greater
Uneasiness, than they are willing to own.   Besides, through the Mercy of Providence their
wicked Schemes often fail of answering their
Ends: and first to do wrong, and then be disappointed of their Aim in it, is double igno-
miny.   Punishment also not uncommonly over-
takes even the securest Criminal.   But supposing the selfish Wretch to succeed: that Success will tempt or provoke many more to imitate him in hurtful Designs and unfair Methods.
If they act in Opposition to him, he may suffer,
as he deserves, by the Example he hath set:
if they act in Conjunction with him, ere long
somewhat will disunite them.   Or however,
bad Precedents naturally produce worse, and so
they multiply continually; till at last the Authors and Encouragers of Mischief are in their
Turn involved in it.   But were they to escape
for Life, yet their Posterity, whose Advance-
ment

ment perhaps is the main Point, which they have in View, muft partake, it may be largely, in whatever the Commonwealth is brought to fuffer: befides the hereditary Difgrace of fpringing from fuch Anceftors. And, if ill People of every Rank would confider, what Figures their Predeceffors in Wickednefs make now in daily Talk; and are likely to make hereafter in Hiftory, if they be of Confequence enough; and in how very different a Light Men of Probity are feen, when the tranfient Mifts, that Artifice, Prepoffeffion and Refentment have raifed, are difperfed: furely it muft have a beneficial Influence on their Conduct.

Or if none of thefe Confiderations can affect them, there is yet another of infinite Moment. This Life, at beft, is fhort: and moft of the bufy Actors on the Stage of the World have probably but a fmall Part of it to come, before a ftrict Account of their Behaviour in it is demanded. And will it be well for us then, think we, that, for the Sake of Purpofes not to be owned, we have brought unjuft Reproach, Uneafinefs, Diftrefs on our Brethren; and difquieted, weakened, impoverifhed, undone our common Parent, whom Nature and Reafon and Revelation jointly require us to love and to ferve?

ferve? Or muſt it not be inexpreſſible Happineſs, for thoſe in low Stations to have diſcharged
the Duties of them with faithful Affection, both
to their Rulers and their Fellow-Subjects: and
for thoſe in the higheſt to be able to ſay, with
the excellent *Jewiſh* Governor, *Think upon me,
O my God, for Good, according to all that I have
done for this People* [*]?

If theſe be ſolid Motives, let us all be moved
by them: firſt, to uſe the utmoſt Caution, that
we do no Harm to our Country; next to try,
what Service we can do it; but eſpecially to
endeavour, for that we every one of us can, by
virtuous Lives, united Hearts, and fervent
Prayers, to call down the Divine Benediction
on our national Counſels and Undertakings. If
indeed we conſider worldly Appearances only,
we have great Cauſe to fear: if we reflect on
our many heinous Iniquities, we have ſtill much
greater Cauſe. But when we call to Mind,
what Deliverances God hath often and lately
beſtowed on us, what Warnings and what Time
he hath given us to repent, how ſlow and unwilling he appears to let our Enemies proceed
to our total Deſtruction, it cannot but kindle
in our Breaſts a moſt reviving Perſuaſion, indeed

[*] Neh. v. 19.

a full

a full Aſſurance of Hope [b], that would we but yet be unanimous and religious, we might yet by his Bleſſing be ſafe and proſperous. And may *the Lord ſo bleſs us, that we may ſee* Jeru-ſalem *in Proſperity all our life long* [c]: *but let* Them *be confounded and turned backward, as many as have evil Will at* Sion [d].

[b] Heb. vi. 11.   [c] Pſal. cxxviii. 6.   [d] Pſal. cxxix. 5.

SER-

SERMON IX.

(Preached *April* 25, 1749, on the Thankſgiving for the Peace.)

Psal. xxix. 10.

——*The Lord ſhall give his People the Bleſſing of Peace.*

WE are met this Day to thank God for a Mercy, that hath long been the Object of our earneſt Wiſhes, and ſolemn Prayers; that we have often had but ſmall Hope of obtaining, and yet now have poſſeſſed many Months, with an increaſing Proſpect of its Continuance: on which Account our Joy is ſtill more reaſonable, though it muſt, from the Conſtitution of our Nature, be leſs warmly felt, than it was at firſt. Accordingly we have juſt been expreſſing it in the Divine Preſence. And Inſtruction from this Place was not previ-
ouſly

oufly neceffary, to excite our Gratitude for a Benefit, fo vifible and fo important. But it may contribute, not a little, to fix in our Breafts a more durable Senfe of what we have acknow‑ledged: and, which is the End of all, direct us to fuch Behaviour, as will fecure and improve the Happinefs, we enjoy.

I fhall therefore at prefent,

I. Set before you the *Bleffing of Peace*.

II. Shew you, that it is the *Gift of God*.

III. Prefs you to remember, that only *his People* are intitled to it: and confequently to confider, whether We are fuch; and to labour that we may, in the higheft Degree.

I. I fhall fet before you the *Bleffing of Peace*.

Man appears, from the harmlefs Make of his Body, the converfable Difpofition of his Mind, the Tendernefs of his Affections, the Sovereignty of his reflecting Principle, the Neceffity of Af‑fiftance in his numerous Wants, and the Rules of Life prefcribed him by exprefs Revelation, to be formed for a focial inoffenfive Creature. Now the natural State of each Being is the happy one. And the Happinefs of Peace is like that of Health: it fpreads through the whole of the Civil, as that doth of the Animal Conftitution ; and furnifhes Vigour and Plea-fure to every Part, without being diftinctly per-ceived in one more than another : for which Reafon we are apt to overlook the Felicity of both, till the Lofs of them for a Time renews our Senfe of their Value ; and even fuch Expe-rience ufually doth not long preferve it in our Memory.   Therefore to difcern fufficiently the Advantages of Peace, we muft recollect the Miferies of War.

To thefe we feldom attend farther, than we immediately feel them.   And the Generality feel only the Expence: which indeed is a fore Evil, and hath been for many Years paft, and muft be for many to come, a heavy Burthen to us.   Perfons of low Degree are fadly ftraitned by it in their Enjoyment of the common Com-forts and Neceffaries of Life.   Their Superiors, it is true, need only undergo a Retrenchment of their Superfluities : which they might bear, if they would, without much Uneafinefs, or any Harm.   But as too many of them are pleafed to reckon their Grandeur and Luxury, their Follies and their Vices, the moft infepa-rable Privileges of their Rank ; they muft, by retaining thefe, be diftreffed equally with others,

P.   when

when the Demands of the State are larger than
ordinary.   And as their ufual Refource is the
very bad one, of fupplying a Fund for Extravagance and Immorality, by refufing Acts · of
Piety, Charity, and Juftice ; they force Multitudes round them to fuffer with them and for
them.   Frequently indeed the Load of Taxes
may not be the Caufe of this difhonourable Behaviour : but even then it is a plaufible Pretence and Excufe for it.   Nor doth the Mifchief ftop at particular Perfons: but the Public,
exhaufted by Payments, and funk under Debts,
becomes incapable of exerting itfelf, even for
its own Prefervation, when future Occafions
require.

Yet, melancholy as thefe Things are, an Article much more fhocking, and which ought
to be the firft in our Thoughts, is that of the
various and continual Toils and Hardfhips, that
muft be endured by fuch Numbers of poor
Creatures, expofing themfelves in Defence of
others, through fo long a Courfe of Time: the
Lofs of fo many Thoufands of Lives by Sicknefs
and in Battle ; the Grief of fo many Relations
and Friends, the Miferies of fo many deftitute
Families : Part of thefe, our Fellow-fubjects ;
not a few of them poffibly very dear to one or

other of us; a second Part, our Allies; the rest, called indeed Enemies: but it may be scarce any of them in Fault for that Enmity, how much soever their Rulers are; and all of them, in Truth, our Brethren; of the same Blood, and, in Essentials, the same Faith, though taught them with a Mixture of dangerous Errors.

Further still: War not only weakens and afflicts a Community in these Respects, but interrupts the Freedom of Commerce, retards the Propagation of Knowledge, prevents useful Improvements, takes off the public Attention from domestic Concerns, furnishes Occasion for Abuses, obstructs the Remedy of Inconveniencies, till they grow inveterate and hard to cure; in short, disorders and unhinges the whole System of Civil Affairs. Then besides, which is a vastly more alarming Consideration yet, all the Time that Hostilities last, who can tell how they may end? and had ours ended, as they easily might, in our being absolutely overcome, and obliged to accept the Victors Terms,——— what would they have been!

But War is also a State of no less Wickedness, than Calamity and Terror. Whenever it breaks out; one Side, at least, must have acted

P 2

grievously

grievoufly contrary to Humanity and Juftice.;
contrary too, in all Likelihood, to folemn
Treaties: and that from no better Motives,
than little Refentments, groundlefs or diftant
Fears, Eagernefs of gaining unneceffary Advantages, reftlefs Ambition, Falfe Glory, or Wan-
tonnefs of Power. To fuch deteftable Idols are
whole Armies and Nations deliberately facri-
ficed: though every Suffering, thus caufed, is
a heinous Crime; and every Death, a Murder.
Nor will the Side, which at firft is more innocent, fail in the Progrefs to be guilty of many
fhocking Tranfgreffions, in common with the
other. The whole Body of a People are apt
to grow uncharitable, unpitying, implacable;
and the Soldiery will plunge of Courfe into
Cruelty, Rapine, Profanenefs, Lewdnefs, Intemperance: not to add, that when the poor
Wretches have once changed the ordinary Employments of Life for this, they will be in great
Danger of never fettling honeftly and foberly to
them again. Some of thefe Things, to worldly
or inconfiderate Minds, may appear fmall
Matters. But every benevolent, or merely prudent Perfon, will efteem them very great ones:
and every pious Heart will moft ferioufly mourn,
that *the worthy Name, by which we are called,*

is

is blasphemed among the Gentiles[a], through the Sins, and peculiarly the Enmities, of those who profess the Gospel; instead of its producing that *Glory to God, Peace on Earth, and Good-will amongst Men*, which Angels proclaimed at our Saviour's Birth[b].

Still this dreadful Evil, big with so many more, becomes, by the obstinate Iniquity of Men, sometimes unavoidable. It must be the Will of the common Father of All, that Societies, as well as single Persons, be restrained from committing material Injuries: else destructive ones would be committed perpetually. Now certainly amicable Methods are to be tried in the first Place: but often the only effectual Method of Restraint is by Arms: and then, *the Minister of God*, the supreme Power, *must not bear the Sword in vain*[c]. Often again, Treaties made to support Allies, if unjustly attacked, are probable Means of preserving Peace: and when that proves otherwise, the Assistances promised must be given, in order to restore it. But above all, when a Nation is directly attacked itself, Defence is undeniably necessary. And our Case, in the late War, was compounded of

[a] James ii. 7. Rom. ii. 24.   [b] Luke ii. 14.
[c] Rom. xiii. 4.

all

all thefe. We have therefore the Comfort, that our undertaking it was juftifiable: and our Manner of carrying it on, I truft, no Way peculiarly blameable. But it could never be lawful to refufe any equitable, any tolerable Conditions of Agreement, for putting an End to fo much Guilt and Mifery. Whether thofe, which we have accepted, are defirable, is not a Queftion to be difcuffed here. You have decided it for yourfelves in the Affirmative, by joining in this Morning's Service: and the People in general have fhewn their joyful Concurrence in the fame Opinion. If fome well-meaning and able Perfons have thought otherwife, Diverfities of Judgments are always to be expected in fuch Matters: and if the Ill-wifhers to our happy Eftablifhment are forry and angry, we have the more Reafon to be glad. Let us therefore proceed to obferve,

II. That the *Bleſſing of Peace* is *God's Gift*.

This will need only a fhort Proof: but requires a much more ferious and practical Confideration, than we commonly allow it. Every Enjoyment is from His Bounty: every Suffering, His Infliction. The whole Series of Caufes and Effects, all the Connections of all Things,

were

were originally appointed, and are continually
fuperintended by Him.   He brings forth, in
each Generation, fuch Perfons, to act, according to their own free Choice, their various Parts
on the Theatre of Life, as he forefees will anfwer, fometimes by their great Abilities and
good Difpofitions, fometimes by the contrary,
his holy Purpofes of Judgment or of Mercy.
And the Influence of this one Arrangement on
the Reftoration of our prefent Tranquillity,
may have been, and probably hath been, unfpeakably great.   But be the Tempers, Qualifications, and Defigns of Men what they will:
He can, unperceived by themfelves, put Thoughts
into their Minds, to incite, withhold, divert
them to another Object, juft as he pleafes.
Then befides, the intire Frame of inanimate
Nature, as it was produced, is alfo actuated by
Him: and he could by its original Formation,
or can now by the flighteft Change in the fmalleft Part of it, occafion, obftruct, alter to any
Degree, the moft important Events.   And
laftly, the fame wife and gracious Motives,
which induced him to make the World, muft
certainly induce him to be attentive to it.   And
the Attention of an infinite Mind muft com-
prehend the Regulation of every Thing, even

P 4

the

the fmalleft: but Affairs of fuch momentous Confequence, as Peace and War, cannot fail to occupy a diftinguifhed Place in the Scheme of Providence.

Thefe Deductions of Reafon our Condition of late Years hath obliged me more than once to lay before you: but ftill they need to be inculcated. Paffages of Scripture too, confirming them, I have produced to you in great Numbers: but it is very eafy, and would God it were not neceffary, to add yet more. *I form the Light, and create Darknefs: I make Peace, and create Evil: I the Lord do all thefe Things*[a]. *The Heart of Kings is in the Hand of the Lord, as the Rivulets of Water: he turneth it whitherfoever he will*[e]. *The Lord is thy Keeper, the Lord is thy Defence upon thy right Hand*[f]. And on the contrary, *fhall there be Evil in the City, and the Lord hath not done it*[g]?

Frequently indeed we perceive no Marks of the Interpofition of God in what paffes. But we are both inadvertent and fhort fighted: ignorant, not only of the fecret Springs and material Circumftances of many human Actions, but yet more, beyond Comparifon, of principal

[a] If. xlv. 7.   [e] Prov. xxi. 1.   [f] Pfal. cxxi. 5.
[g] Amos iii. 6.

Purpofes

Purposes in the Divine Administration. Yet this however we know, that he is inceſſantly conducting the Affairs of the preſent World, towards a full Diſplay of his Wiſdom, Juſtice and Goodneſs, in the next: though often by Steps inviſible to our Eyes, and improbable to our Imaginations. *For his Judgments are unſearchable, and his Ways paſt finding out* [h]. Therefore in all Things we ſhould believe a Providence; but in many we may ſee it: and very plainly in our own Caſe: to whom 'true Religion and Liberty have been ſo wonderfully preſerved, in the Midſt of ſuch imminent Dangers; and Quiet and Safety ſo unexpectedly reſtored, when *the Help of Man was* confeſſedly *vain* [i]. Nor did God only beſtow the Bleſſing, but it is He who continues it : and every Day's Peace, as well as every Day's Bread, is a Gift from him.

Surely then we have Cauſe, not for Joy alone, but Thankfulneſs too, from the Bottom of our Hearts. And if we ungratefully diſown, or negligently forget, the Author of our Happineſs, what is it likelier, what is it fitter he ſhould do, than deprive us of it again? We may think perhaps, that we have fully diſcharged

[h] Rom. xi. 33.   [i] Pſal. cviii. 12.

our

our Confciences towards him by our Attendance on the prefent Solemnity. And God grant we may hear, it hath been every-where univerfally attended. But fuppofing that : outward Acknowledgments fingly are downright Pageantry and Mockery. Nay, inward Senfe of Obligation along with them, if it bring not forth fuitable and lafting Obedience, is imperfect, inefficacious, delufive Homage, which our Maker cannot accept. *Herein is my Father glorified,* faith our bleffed Saviour, *that ye bear much Fruit* [k]. And thus we are to underftand that awful Denunciation : *If ye will not hear, and if ye will not lay it to Heart, to give Glory unto my Name, faith the Lord of Hofts, I will fend a Curfe upon you, and I will even curfe your Bleffings* [l]. Accordingly the Text very clearly intimates,

III. That to entitle ourfelves to *the Bleffing of Peace,* we muft be *his People :* own his Authority by obferving his Laws.

The Practice of Religion and Virtue makes Nations induftrious, frugal, rich, healthy, populous, unanimous, public-fpirited, fearlefs; yet at the fame Time, juft, prudent, friendly :

[k] John xv. 8.   [l] Mal. ii. 2.

which

which are the very Qualities, that conftitute them formidable Enemies, defirable Confede-rates, inoffenfive Neighbours; and, fo far as any Thing can, will fecure them Peace. But Wickednefs impoverifhes, enfeebles, difpirits, depopulates, difunites; extinguifhes Concern for common Good, inflames felfifh Appetites and Paffions; renders Men rafh and provoking, yet indolent and defpicable. It feems hardly needful for Providence to interpofe, otherwife than it hath done in the Original Appointment of Things, to exalt a People of the former Charaffer, or deprefs one of the latter. But when it is, we may expeff it to be done. For God will reward what he loves, punifh what he hates. And though his Recompences are neither perfeff nor proportionable, they are real and confiderable, even here. Experience hath found it: Scripture hath foretold it. The *Jewifh* Nation indeed profpered or fuffered, ac-cording to their Doings, more conftantly and equally, than others. But ftill, not only *thefe Things happened to them for our Enfamples, and are written for our Admonition* [n] : but in the fame Ages, God vifited the Heathen alfo for their Iniquities; *and lengthened their Tranquil-*

[n] 1 Cor. x. 11.

lity,

lity, when they *broke off their Sins by Righteouf-
nefs* [a]. Chriftian States, we confefs, as they
were not in Being, are not mentioned, in the
Gofpels or Epiftles: but *Godlinefs hath the
Promife* there *of the Life that now is, as well as
that which is to come* [o]; and the *Revelation of
St. John*, a prophetical Work, defcribes whole
Kingdoms, and yet larger Portions of the
Earth, as undergoing the fevereft of temporal
Judgments, for the Abominations which they
had committed. We ought to be deeply affected therefore by every Declaration of God's Purpofes in this Refpect throughout his Word.
And the Sum of them is: *If ye be willing and
obedient, ye fhall eat the Good of the Land. But
if ye refufe and rebel, ye fhall be devoured with
the Sword: for the Mouth of the Lord hath
fpoken it* [p].

Which then is Our Cafe? Are we God's
People? Are we even fenfible what that Phrafe
implies? That we believe, not a prefumptuous
Scheme of falfely-called rational Religion, framed
by our Fancies, but the *Myftery of the Gofpel* [q]:
that we practife, not an arbitrary Syftem of
polite Morals, indulgently relaxed to fit eafy

[a] Dan. iv. 27.   [o] 1 Tim. iv. 8.   [p] If. i. 19, 20.
       [q] Eph. vi. 19.

upon

upon our Inclinations, but all thofe Duties, in their genuine Strictnefs, which *the Grace of God, that bringeth Salvation, came to teach: denying Ungodlinefs and worldly Lufts, living foberly, righteoufly and godly in this prefent World, and looking for that bleffed Hope, and the glorious Appearance of the great God and our Saviour Jefus Chrift; who gave himfelf for us, that he might redeem us from all Iniquity, and purify unto himfelf a peculiar People, zealous of good Works*.* Do we know ourfelves by this Picture? Or is not the very different one, which I have fo often been obliged to fet before you, ftill our true Refemblance? Are we not regardlefs in general, both of a prefent Providence and of future Rewards? Have not many of us caft off with Scorn, and moft of us contributed to loofen, thofe Ties of Faith and Worfhip, which in every Country elfe, and in this till of late, have always been held neceffary, even to civil Welfare? They, who have not rejected Religion, do they not however, Numbers of them, flight the Exercifes of it, wholly in private, and to a great Degree in public? Nay, fuch as appear pretty regular in them, and feem to have a real Senfe of Piety, have they any

* Tit. ii. 11—14.

Zeal

Zeal for it, any Sorrow for the Decay of. it?
Do they not feel and. exprefs more Diflike and
Contempt of thofe whom they think, and perhaps but think, *righteous overmuch* [1], than of
the moft thoughtlefs about their fpiritual State,
not to fay, the moft abandoned? Are we not
in common Life diffolute, expenfive, negligent
of our Affairs, our Families, our very Children,
at leaft in the moft important Point, their Principles ; overrun by an epidemical Rage for.
hourly Pleafures and Amufements, with an
utter Contempt of Confequences ; which, after
infecting almoft univerfally the upper, and next
to them the middle Part of the World, is yearly
fpreading wider among thofe, whofe Parfimony
and ufeful Induftry is the Wealth of the Nation ? Are we not alfo in our political Capacities, how irreconcileably foever we differ, lamentably alike : void of Reverence to Authority, fubordinate or fupreme ; attentive chiefly,
if not only, to felfifh or Party Confiderations,
varnifhed over with tranfparent Pretences of
Public Good ; vehement about difputable Matters, unconcerned about confeffedly neceffary
ones ; each Denomination, each Order and
Rank, bitterly accufing the other, and none

<hr>

[1] Eccl. vii. 16.

ever

ever thinking in earneſt to amend themſelves: extremely afraid of hurting Liberty by reſtraining Wickedneſs, but not at all of being undone by indulging it; wonderfully jealous of the Power of our own Church, which hath and deſires leſs, than ever any other in any Age; but perfectly eaſy about the daily Growth of Popery, the moſt tyrannical Empire over Soul and Body that can be, and the moſt peculiarly formidable to this Country? *My People is fooliſh, they have not known me: they are wiſe to do Evil, but to do Good they have no Underſtanding* [1].

Can ſuch a Nation hope for the Favour of Providence? Could it flouriſh, even were there no Providence? Evidently it is impoſſible. Sentiments of Religion and Virtue are the Seeds of all Happineſs, the Security in all Danger, the Support in all Affliction. Theſe are decaying apace, and wearing quite out. Habits of Prudence, formed by a careful Education, might in ſome poor Meaſure ſupply their Place. But we have them not. In Trifles indeed we are bred up to a ſtrict Obſervance of Rules and Forms and Faſhions: but in Points of Conſequence every one is left, from his early Youth,

[1] Jer. iv. 22.

to do as he pleafes; and They moft, whofe Example will be moft followed. General Diflike and Shame however might reftrain Perfons, when they come out into the World, from feveral Vices, againft which they had no Prefervative before. But with us, there are few Vices or none, of which any Body needs be afhamed: the moft notorioufly guilty of the worft, are as well received in all Places, if not better, than other Perfons. Yet, even in fuch a State, ftrict Laws, vigoroufly executed, might deter, at leaft from the more immediately mifchievous Crimes. But we are deftitute of this Guard alfo. A great Part of our Laws, from the univerfal Remiffnefs of the Times, are fcarce executed at all: and, from the Nature of our Conftitution, cannot be executed fo effectually, as where Power is lefs bounded. Still this Conftitution, with its many Defects, efpecially under a Prince, who, God be thanked, moft cordially wifhes the Continuance and Improvement of that and every Advantage to his Subjects, amply compenfates for many Inconveniencies; and preferves many valuable Privileges, not enjoyed elfewhere. But then fuch inward Diforders muft by Degrees impair and undermine it, till at length it will fall: poffibly the
fooner,

fooner, the more fafely we think we can follow our own Devices. Peace may be no Bleffing to fuch, as will abufe it: and the Scripture hath told us long ago, that *the Profperity of Fools fhall deftroy them*[a]. After all, it would be fomething, if when we had reduced ourfelves to the fame Condition with the reft of the World, in point of Freedom at Home, by our Unworthinefs and Incapacity of it, we had a Profpect remaining of Security from Abroad. Other Nations, neither free nor virtuous; though internally miferable on both Accounts, continue for a Time, perhaps a confiderable one, to an-fwer Purpofes of God's Wifdom, externally potent, courted and dreaded. But what Con-folation can We draw from hence: exhaufted and burthened as we are; with fo little to hope, as Experience hath fhewn us, even from the friendlier Part of our Neighbours; and fo much to apprehend from the neareft and moft powerful, who hath repeatedly attempted our Deftruction, whofe Strength in the only weak Article will be recruited with Zeal and Indig-nation, to whofe Defigns we have always been the chief Obftacle, and whofe Succefs in them

[a] Prov. i. 32.

Q muft

muſt be fatal both to our religious and civil
Intereſts ?

-Think not, that *I am become your Enemy, becauſe I tell you the Truth*[w]. Would God it would
permit me to ſay every Thing, that was pleaſ-
ing to you. Think not, that I delight, or even
mean, to foretel Evil : I mean only to caution
you againſt it. And who ſhall or will, if the
Miniſters of God's Word do not ? And what
muſt follow ? *I have ſeen,* ſaith He himſelf, *in
the Prophets of Jeruſalem, an horrible Thing :—
they ſtrengthen the Hands of evil Doers, that
none doth return from his Wickedneſs.—They ſay
unto them, that deſpiſe me, the Lord hath ſaid,
Ye ſhall have Peace ; unto every one, that walketh in the Imagination of his own Heart, no Evil
ſhall come upon you.—Behold a Whirlwind of
the Lord is gone forth in Fury : it ſhall fall
grievouſly on the Head of the Wicked.—But if
they had ſtood in my Council, and cauſed my People to hear my Words, then they ſhould have
turned them from their evil Way*[x]. Think not,
that, however, ſuch Language might be ſpared
on this Day of Rejoicing. It might ſo indeed,
had we either been hitherto innocent, or were
now duly penitent. But, being ſuch, as God

<hr>

[w] Gal. iv. 16.   [x] Jer. xxxiii. 14, 17, 19, 22.

knows

knȯws we are, Admonition of our Faults is in-
difpenfably neceffary, to excite our Thankfulnefs, that we are not punifhed in proportion to
them: and Warning of our Dangers, to remind
us of proving our Gratitude by that Obedience,
which alone will obtain us Protection.   Would
we but make this Ufe of the prefent Solemnity,
then it would be a Day of Gladnefs indeed: a
Day, *much to be obferved unto the Lord through
all our Generations* [y], for laying the only Ground-
work of public Happinefs.   And therefore I
muft repeat to you on the Conclufion of this
War, what I earneftly recommended to your
Confideration at the Beginning of it, that when
Afa King of *Judah*, was returning Home, both
with Peace and Victory, the Prophet *Azariah
went out to meet him, and faid: Hear ye me, Afa,
and all Judah and Benjamin.   The Lord is with
you, while ye be with Him; and if ye feek him,
he will be found of you: but if ye forfake him,
He will forfake you* [z].

Other Methods to fupport a tottering or raife
a finking State, without Reformation, frequently overturn it: and at beft are only Palliatives,
temporary Expedients, to delay a little its final
Ruin.   *Thus faith the Lord of Hofts,—They*

---

[y] Exod. xii. 42.   [z] 2 Chron. xv. 1, 2.

          have

*have healed the Hurt of the Daughter of my
People slightly, saying, Peace, Peace, when there
is no Peace*[a]. *There is no Peace, saith my God,
to the Wicked*[b]. And not only the sacred
Writings have said this: but Heathens have
said it who knew them not: Infidels have said
it, who regard them not: innumerable Facts
have proclaimed it in every Age. But above
all it holds in limited Governments, like ours.
There muſt be public Virtue, or they cannot
ſtand. There muſt be private Virtue, or there
cannot be public. There muſt be Religion, or
there can be neither. There muſt be true Religion, or their will be falſe. There muſt be
Attendance on God's Worſhip; or there will
be no Religion at all. Not four Years ago it
was univerſally doubted, whether we had Principle enough, of any Kind, left, to make an
Effort for the Preſervation of every Thing valuable to us. Moſt happily more appeared,
than was expected. Yet God knows how it
had proved, if the Trial had gone but a little
further. And for God's Sake let us provide,
as much as ever we can, againſt the next. How
ſoon it may happen, is beyond human Foreſight.
But in the mean While, we have ſome Leiſure,

[a] Jer. vi. 9, 14.   [b] Iſ. lvii. 21.

not

not only for perfonal Amendment, which is
equally poffible in all Seafons, but for concert-
ing Schemes, and executing, as well as framing,
Laws for public Reformation.   In War, many
Things, confeffed to be right and neceffary,
are put off, becaufe the Attention muft be confined to the immediate Danger. And if they
are put off in Peace too, becaufe there is no
immediate Danger, when they are to be mind-
ed; and what will be the Confequence, if they
never are?

I would by no means excite a rafh and ignorant Zeal, to be meddling where we fee not to
the Bottom of Things: much lefs a factious
one, to cramp and embarrafs, difquiet and inflame. Thefe Practices muft be hurtful: they
may be pernicious: and the firft Article in true
Patriotifm is confcientioufly abftaining from
them. Taking unwarrantable Steps, in Oppofition to fuch as we may think, whether too
haftily or not, bad Men and bad Meafures,
is only introducing additional Wickednefs of
our own, and giving others a Pretence for continuing, and even increafing theirs. Or fhould
we fucceed againft them: yet fuch, as act ill
to get Power to act well, feldom or never ufe

Q 3   it

it to that Purpofe, when they have it, whatever they may intend beforehand.

The Rule then is, that each perform his
own Duty fteadily and calmly; rejoice, and acknowledge it with Thankfulnefs, when others
perform theirs; and be very moderate, when
he apprehends they overlook or tranfgrefs it:
endeavour to rectify what is wrong, fo far as it
belongs to his Station; but *never exercife himfelf in Matters, which are too high for him*[e],
nor watch more folicitoufly over the Conduct
of the State, than over his own Heart and Life.
He, that neglects the latter, will feldom be
thoroughly in earneft, and feldomer yet impartial, about the former: or though he were,
will have much lefs Weight, than a better Man.
The one is incumbent on us all; the other on
very few: in the one we need never miftake or
fail; in the other we muft frequently. Therefore let us earneftly *pray for the Peace of Jerufalem*[d]: but remember that the fureft Way of
feeking to do it further *Good*[e], is firft to be at
Peace ourfelves with God and with Men.

Preffing you to general Reformation, as the
Means of general Happinefs, may feem a very
hopelefs Expedient. But it is the only one,

<hr>

[e] Pfal. cxxxi. 2.   [d] Pfal. cxxii. 6.   [e] Ver. 9.

which

which Heaven hath pointed out, or will blefs. Whether you will make Ufe of it, depends on yourfelves. We are *charged, before God, and the Lord Jefus Chrift, who fhall judge the Quick and the Dead at his Appearing and his Kingdom, to preach the Word; be inftant, in Seafon, out of Seafon; reprove, rebuke, exhort, with all Long-fuffering and Doctrine* [f]. We do accordingly, as *Ambaffadors for Chrift, as though God did befeech you by us, pray you in Chrift's Stead, Be ye reconciled to God* [g]: and when we have done fo, *we have delivered our Souls* [h]: but we beg you, think of your own. The fewer will amend, the more Need there is, that we fhould add to the Number. Our doing it may be of fome Benefit to others, we know not how great: but at leaft will be infinitely beneficial to ourfelves. We fhall be happy, whatever They be: happy, even at prefent; though lefs, than if all were fo. Probably, indeed, when Times of Trouble come, we fhall fuffer with them: but poffibly not, or however not fo much as we apprehend: *For the Lord knoweth how to deliver the Godly out of Temptation* [i]. Or if he determine otherwife, he will *enable us to bear it* [k]:

<hr>

[f] 2 Tim. iv. 1, 2.   [g] 2 Cor. v. 20.   [h] Ezek. xxxiii. 9.
[i] 2 Pet. ii. 9.   [k] 1 Cor. x. 13.

Q 4

and

and *suffering* now *according to his Will*[1], is a Title to more Enjoyment in a better Life. This World is not our main Concern. They, who take it for their Portion, will be every one anxiously providing for his own separate Advantage in it; and consequently every one injurious to his Neighbours, and uneasy in Himself: but let Felicity hereafter be the Point in View, and Tranquillity here will be the Result. *The Peace of God, which passeth all Understanding, shall keep our Hearts and Minds through Jesus Christ*[m]. Even if we suffer, not only in common with others, but more than others; if we are despised, hated, ill-treated, for what ought to procure us Honour and Friendship, our Piety, Integrity, Regularity: still the Spirit within us will support us; *we shall receive an hundredfold now in this Time, with Persecutions; and in the World to come, eternal Life*[n]. *Say ye to the Righteous, that it shall be well with Him: for they shall eat the Fruit of their Doings. Woe unto the Wicked, it shall be ill with Him: for the Reward of his Hands shall be given him*[o].

[1] 1 Pet. iv. 19.   [m] Phil. iv. 7.   [n] Mark x. 30.
[o] If. iii. 10, 11.

Doubtless

Doubtlefs good Perfons will be forry, as they have Caufe, for what the Public muft undergo, unlefs Reformation prevent it. But at the fame Time they will acquiefce, as they have Caufe, with entire Complacency, in the Juftice of Providence : and the more, as the fevereft Difpenfations of it are bringing forward continually, though by unfeen Ways, that bleffed State of Things, even on this Earth, of which, however elfe improbable in itfelf, the Attributes of God afford us Hope ; and his Prophets, Affurance. Nay, thofe Nations themfelves, whom by his Punifhments he makes miferable for being bad, may by that very Mifery be made good, and then happy. *I will leave in the Midft of thee*, faith God to *Jerufalem, an afflicted and poor People, and They fhall truft in the Name of the Lord. The Remnant of Ifrael fhall not do Iniquity, nor fpeak Lies.* It follows, *They fhall feed and lie down, and none fhall make them afraid* [r].

Such a Cure, though effected by fuch Difcipline, would be an unfpeakable Bleffing. But furely we are not refolved, that no other fhall do. God is trying at prefent milder Methods : and the Language of his Proceedings is, *How*

[r] Zeph. iii. 12, 13.

fhall

*shall I give thee up, Ephraim? How shall I de-
liver thee, Israel?—Mine Heart is turned within
me, my Repentings are kindled together*[q]. But
still in the Midst of his Mercies, his Threatnings
remain in full Force: and we have a solemn
Warning, that *if, when we hear the Words of his
Curse, we bless ourselves, and say, we shall have
Peace, though we walk in the Imagination of
our Hearts:—the Lord will not spare us, but
his Anger and his Jealousy shall smoke against
us; and all the Curses that are written in his
Book, shall lie upon us*[r]. For a long Time we
seemed to think, that we might securely trust
in our own Wealth and Strength, our own Policy and Bravery, let us behave to our Maker
as we would. He hath given us, through a
Course of Years, ample Conviction of our Mistake, if any Thing will convince us: and he
hath given us now Time to act upon that Conviction. Let us therefore at length intitle ourselves to trust in Him: turn our Minds *to fear
God, honour the King, love the Brotherhood*[s],
that is the Public: cease from our profane Dis-
course, our unbelieving Presumption, our uncharitable Contentions, our selfish Projects, our dif-
solute Pleasures, our idle Amusements, our

[q] Hof. xi. 8.　　[r] Deut. xxix. 19, 20.　　[s] 1 Pet. ii. 17.

fashionable

fafhionable Affectations, our deftructive Expences: beg Pardon of our Guilt, through Jefus Chrift; and Affiftance of our Weaknefs, through the Spirit of Grace: govern our Lives by the Rules of the Gofpel; and both awe and cheer ourfelves by continual Thoughts of that *Day, when God will judge the World in Righteoufnefs, by that Man, whom he hath ordained*[r]. All this is the indifpenfable Duty of every one, were he to be fingle in performing it: there are fome, God be thanked, who practife it now: the Addition of a few, that would be exemplary, might win many more: and were but the Imitation general, hear the Promife made to it. *Thus faith the Lord thy Redeemer, the Holy One of Ifrael: I am the Lord thy God, which teacheth thee to profit; which leadeth thee by the Way, that thou fhouldeft go. O that thou wouldeft hearken to my Commandments: then fhould thy Peace be as the River: and thy Righteoufnefs as the Waves of the Sea*[s].

[r] Acts xvii. 31.   [s] If. xlviii. 17, 18.

AN

quishing Affections, our customary Ex-
... they, I ... through Jesus
... and Assistance of our ... through the
... pline of Grace, govern our Lives by the
Rules of the Gospel; and have also that ...
... ourselves by rational Thoughts of that Day,
... and judge the World in Righteousness, in
that Day, when ... our ordained. All this
is the indispensable Duty of every one, were he
to be ... in persuading ... there are some,
God be thanked, who practise it now: the Addition ... that ... worthily, might
win many more; and ... have the ... present
... that the People ... to it. What
saith the Lord ... Relation, the High One of
Israel, I am the Lord thy God ...

AN

ANSWER

TO

Dr. *Mayhew's* Obſervations

ON THE

CHARTER AND CONDUCT

OF THE

SOCIETY

FOR THE

PROPAGATION of the GOSPEL
in FOREIGN PARTS.

AN ANSWER

to

Dr. Mayhew's Observations

ON THE

CHARTER AND CONDUCT

OF THE

SOCIETY

FOR THE

Propagation of the Gospel
in Foreign Parts.

AN

ANSWER

TO

Dr. *Mayhew*'s Obfervations.

DR. *Mayhew*'s [a] Book is written, partly againft the Church of *England* in gene-ral ; partly againft the Conduct of the Society for the Propagation of the Gofpel, in fettling Minifters of that Church in the *Maffa-chufetts* and *Connecticut* ; partly againft appointing Bifhops to refide in his Majefty's *American* Colonies. The firft, though not formally propofed by him as one Head of his Work, appears to be in his View throughout the whole of it. And if Satisfaction be previoufly given to candid Perfons on this Point, they will be better prepared for confidering the other two.

[a] The Quotations out of Dr. *Mayhew*'s Obfervations are taken from the *Englifh* Edition, which contains 147 Pages. The *American* hath 176.

He

He objects againſt the Conſtitution and Worſhip of the Church of *England*, as unſcriptual[b].
Now even had he attempted to bring Proof of
this, it would only lead into a long Diſpute,
very little connected with his profeſſed Subject,
and *into which*, he declares, *it was by no Means
his Deſign to enter* [c].   But inſtead of Proofs, he
contents himſelf with bold Aſſertions, reproachful Names, and ludicrous Repreſentations; a
likely Method indeed to pleaſe the Prejudiced,
and carry the Thoughtleſs along with him, but
not to perſuade the Conſiderate and Judicious.
Whatever the Doctor may think of our Church,
it hath ever been highly honoured by foreign
Proteſtants.   The *Lutherans* prefer it to the
Calviniſt Communion, the *Calviniſts* to the
Lutheran, the *Greeks* to both : which may ſufficiently juſtify the Expreſſion, underſtood in a
Latitude not uncommon, that all other Perſua-
ſions eſteem it next to their own[d].   And further, moſt, if not all of them, blame the *Engliſh*
Diſſenters for ſeparating from it.   The Doctor
ſeems to entertain the Worſe Opinion of it, becauſe the Members of the Church of *Rome* likewiſe eſteem it more than they do others[e]. But
we have to reply, that they hate it more alſo,

[b] Pag. 128.   [c] Pag. 126.   [d] Ibid.   [e] Page. 127.

as

as the moſt dangerous Enemy to their Cauſe, and ſtrongeſt Bulwark of the Reformation. If there be ſome Appointments in it, which the Scripture doth not require: ſo have there been from the firſt in the Church of *New England* too, as may be ſeen in the Appendix to the Hiſtory of that Country, written by Mr. *Neale,* a diſſenting Miniſter: and ſo there are in all the Churches of the World. Ours hath not many Things of this Kind, nor lays great Streſs upon them: and to think indifferent Things unlawful, is as unreaſonable and ſuperſtitious, as to think them neceſſary.

He ſpeaks with Horror of its *enormous Hierarchy, aſcending by various Gradations from the Dirt to the Skies*[r]: *and reſembling that of the* Romiſh *Church, in which one great Prelate preſides over the whole*[s]. What he means by the former Words, beſides indeterminate Abuſe, perhaps he could not eaſily explain. That there are different Ranks of Men in civil Government, was never held to be an Objection againſt it: and where is the Harm of it in Eccleſiaſtical? In the *Preſbyterian* Hierarchy, one is raiſed conſiderably above another, though the Preference uſually may be temporary: and their

[r] Pag. 128.   [s] Pag. 67.

R   Acts

Acts of Power have been as enormous, as those of the *English* Bishops formerly; and are much greater than those of the *English* Bishops now. In his favourite Comparison of our Church to the *Romish*, the Doctor quite mistakes the Matter. Not one, but two Prelates, preside over the Church of *England*; and four over her Sister Church of *Ireland:* which grievously spoils the Similitude, that he would make out. And all these *preside in Subordination to the King*, as he well knows; though he disingenuously hints a Doubt of it by his ironical Words, *I hope* [h]; at the same Time that, I believe, he would deny it to be in Subordination to the King, that He presides over *the West-Church in* Boston. As to *the Dirt*, which he mentions: If some Clergymen of our Church are very low in the World, so are some of every Church; nor do they deserve Scorn for it, but Compassion. And that any of ours are so high, as to do Harm, or cause Fear, by their Elevation, the Persons, amongst whom they live, find not: and he, who is placed so remote from them, had better judge by the Experience of others, than by his own heated Imagination.

[h] Pag. 64.

Bishops,

Biſhops, in his Language, are *the mitred lordly Succeſſors of the Fiſhermen of* Galilee[1]. Now if Mitres offend him, our Biſhops wear none. If they are ſtiled Lords, it is becauſe, by the ancient Conſtitution of our Country, they ſit in the upper Houſe of Parliament: where, I believe, they are thought as uſeful Members as the reſt. And I know not, whether the Doctor's Modeſty would propoſe, that our Conſtitution ſhould be altered in this Reſpect, or whether a much wiſer Man could foreſee the Conſequences of ſuch an Alteration. Men may be Lords, without being lordly: and they, who have profeſſed to abhor the Name, have carried the Diſpoſition of domineering to the Height; and lorded it over the Conſciences and the Liberties of others, as much as any who have worn higher Titles. What Intimation lies concealed under the Terms, *Fiſhermen of Galilee*; and whether, in the Doctor's Opinion, all Miniſters of Chriſt are to follow ſome Trade, he hath not explained, nor told us what his own is. But certainly reviling his Brethren is a very bad one.

He alſo charges the Church of *England* with Perſecution; and particularly with driving out

----

[1] Pag. 128.

                              the

the Anceftors of the prefent Inhabitants of *New England* into that Country [k]. Now it is a Matter of Notoriety, that the Lawfulnefs of Perfecution is no Doctrine of our Church: and there are few of its Members, if any, now, who approve it, or do not deteft it. But we muft acknowledge, that, when the Errors of the Church of *Rome* were caft off, this was not immediately perceived to be one by almoft any of the Proteftant Communions. The Church of *England* was but like others; and the Diffenters from it had not the leaft Degree more of a tolerating Spirit, perhaps not fo much. There were amongft them peaceable Men, and fo there were amongft us. But in general their avowed Aim was, not Exemption for themfelves, but the Deftruction of the Ecclefiaftical Eftablifhment [l]. On this they were treated too feverely, and they returned the Treatment to the full, as foon as they were able, in the total Overthrow of Church and State. Far from exaggerating, I chufe not to mention the Particulars of their Behaviour. Every good Man muft lament the Faults of both Sides; but to inveigh againft one with Bitternefs, and leave it

[k] Pag. 129.   [l] See this fully proved in *Maddox's* Vindication of the Church of *England.*

to be imagined that the other was innocent, which the Doctor doth, I hope he will ſee on Recollection is extremely unjuſt.

In the *Platform of Diſcipline, agreed upon in the Synod of* Cambridge *in* New England *in* 1648, and publiſhed by Mr. *Neale,* in his Hiſtory of that Country, it is declared, that *Hereſy is to be reſtrained and puniſhed by the Civil Magiſtrate; and that if any Churches grow ſchiſmatical, or walk contrary to the Rule of the Word, he is to put forth his coercive Power, as the Matter ſhall require* ᵐ. Accordingly Mr. *Neale* himſelf very honeſtly confeſſes, that *the Churches of* New England *were formerly very uncharitable to thoſe who differed from them, and had no Notions of Liberty of Conſcience, but were for forcing Men to their public Aſſemblies by Fines and Impriſonments* ⁿ. On their putting to Death ſeveral Quakers, as they did before and after the Reſtoration, till an Order from King *Charles* the Second prohibited them °, he hath theſe Words; *Now it appeared, that the* New England *Puritans were no better Friends to Liberty of Conſcience than their Adverſaries; and that the Queſtion between them was not, whether one Party of Chriſtians ſhould oppreſs another, but who*

ᵐ Vol. II. p. 306. ⁿ Vol. II. p. 248, 249. ° Vol. I. p. 334.

R 3

ſhould

should have that Power[p]. Nay, the Quakers affirm, that *they who had loudly cried out of the Tyranny and Oppression of the Bishops in Old England, from whom they fled, when settled in a Place, where they had Liberty to govern, made their little Finger of Cruelty bigger, than ever they found the Loins of the Bishops*[q]. Dr. *Mayhew* indeed saith, that *Severities are used against the Quakers, much less under the Notion of their being Dissenters from the* public *Mode of Worship, than of their being Disturbers of the Peace and religious Assemblies*[r]. But still Severities were used against them on the former Account; and they justly observe in Mr. *Neale*, that Offences of the latter Kind *have never been thought worthy of Death by any civilized Nation*[s]. But the Doctor asks, supposing the *New Englanders* to have persecuted the Quakers, *From whom did they learn this Practice? Episcopalians certainly should lay their Hands upon their Mouths*[t]. Now the plain Truth is, that all Protestants learnt this Practice from the Church of *Rome*, and all should lay their Hands upon their Mouths. But the Doctor hath no Right to open his as wide as he pleases, and require us to shut ours.

[p] Vol. I. p. 329. [q] *Grove*'s Preface to *Bishop*'s *New England* judged. [r] Pag. 79. [s] Vol. I. p. 331, 332. [t] Pag. 80.

God

God be thanked, the Members of our Church are grown wiser and milder; the Diſſenters in general, I am fully perſuaded, are ſo too: and it is high Time, that ſuch of both Parties, as are not, ſhould. But Performances, like the Doctor's, cannot ſurely contribute to this good End amongſt either. He aſſures us indeed at the Beginning, that he hath a *Regard to Truth and Juſtice*, with an *Averſion to Controverſy* ; and at the End, that *he honours candid and moderate Men of all Denominations, and would not unneceſſarily give Offence to any Perſon of the Epiſcopal Perſuaſion*. One muſt ſuppoſe, that he believes himſelf; and as far as is poſſible, I would believe him alſo. Some Perſons are ſtrangely ſubject to ſudden Guſts of Paſſion, and ſay and do Things in them, for which they are heartily ſorry the next Hour. But were this the Doctor's Caſe in Writing, he would blot out the injurious Expreſſions which had dropt from his Pen. Therefore his Malady hath a deeper Root in his Frame, and influences him more conſtantly, though it may be without his perceiving it. For I am exceedingly unwilling to think, that he inſerts his qualifying and healing Clauſes with an artful Deſign to procure

 ▪ Pag. 7.   ▾ Pag. 145.

R 4

himſelf

himfelf a Difpenfation for his Outrages. However that be, his Profeffions, that he doth not intend to do what he hath been doing juft before, and doth again foon after with all his Might, are Proteftations againft Fact which cannot be admitted.

But whatever Conceffions a Gentleman of this Turn makes to his Adverfaries, are to be received with great Regard, for one may be fure they are not too large. Let us therefore begin with thefe, in confidering his Remarks on the Charter and Conduct of the Society.

He owns, that *it hath a Right to plant Churches, to fupport Miffions and Schools,* &c. *in many of the* Britifh American *Colonies*; and adds, that *no one, who hath ever read the Charter, can poffibly imagine, that its Care and Charity ought to be confined to the Heathen Slaves in, or the Savages bordering on, the Plantations*[x]. Yet many have been led both to imagine and to affert this, merely from its Name. It is hoped, that for the future they will confefs and remember their Miftake. He owns likewife, that in three Diftricts of *New England,* i. e. New Hampfhire, Rhode-Ifland *and* Providence, *much lefs Care hath been taken for the Support of*

[x] Pag. 12, 13.

a pub—

a public Worſhip, than in the reſt [y] : and that
a few Miſſions from the Society *might be needed*
in theſe, *particularly in Rhode-Iſland* [z]. And he
blames them as unneceſſary, only in *the Maſſa-*
chuſetts and Connecticut. Nay, he declares,
that in theſe *it is by no Means his Intention to*
charge that venerable Body with any wilful known
Miſconduct, or improper Application of Monies,
even though any incautious Expreſſion ſhould at
firſt View have the Appearance of ſuch an Accu-
ſation [a]. Again he ſaith, *I would by no Means*
be underſtood, as charging ſo reſpectable a Body
with any wilful criminal Abuſe of Power [b]. Accordingly, after declaring *his Deſign to ſhew,*
that they have in ſome Reſpects counteracted the
Ends of their Inſtitution, he adds, *however con-*
trary to their Intention [c]. He hath alſo theſe
expreſs Words : *That the Society have chiefly*
ſent their Miſſionaries into thoſe Britiſh *Planta-*
tions, where they were much needed, according to
the true Deſign of their Inſtitution ; and that they
have hereby ſerved the Intereſt of Religion in them,
is by no Means denied : it were very criminal to
deny them the Praiſe, that is juſtly due to them
in this Reſpect. I honour the Doctor for theſe
Inſtances of Candor ; and if he had preſerved

<hr>

[y] Pag. 36.   [z] p. 46.   [a] p. 7.   [b] p. 93.   [c] p. 9.

the

the fame Temper throughout, fhould either have had no Controverfy with him, or have engaged in the friendly Debate with Pleafure: whereas now the frequent and copious Effufions of a bad Spirit in his Work make fuch Animadverfions upon him unavoidable, as I fhould otherwife gladly have fpared.

His Charge on the Society is, that they have *maintained Epifcopal Churches, where other Pro-teftant Churches were before fettled, and the Ad-miniftration of God's Word and Ordinances pro-vided for* [a], with a *formal Defign* which *they have long had, to root out* Prefbyterianifm, *&c. in the Colonies.* Now this Defign, *in Purfuance of which,* he faith, *they have in a great Meafure neglected the Ends of their Inftitution* [b], is falfely afcribed to them. They have never formed a Scheme *to root out* Prefbyterianifm, *&c.* in the Colonies, either by Force, which the Doctor could not mean, though the Word moft natu-rally fuggefts it, or even by Argument and Per-fuafion. Undoubtedly they would be very glad, if all the Inhabitants were of the Communion of the Church of *England:* as undoubtedly the Doctor would, if they were all of his Commu-nion. But they have fent no Perfons to effect

----

[a] Pag. 15.   [b] p. 86.

this.

this. He attempts to prove the contrary from the following Inſtruction, given by them to their Miſſionaries: *That they frequently viſit their reſpective Pariſhioners; thoſe of our own Communion, to keep them ſteady in the Profeſſion and Practice of Religion, as taught in the Church of England; thoſe that oppoſe us, or diſſent from us, to convince and reclaim them with a Spirit of Meekneſs and Gentleneſs*[r]. His Words on that Occaſion are: *This clearly ſhews, what they are after. It will alſo be obſerved here, that* WE *are conſidered as Pariſhioners of the Miſſionaries, no leſs than profeſſed Epiſcopalians. And we are often ſpoken of as ſuch by them in their Letters to the Society, as appears by the Abſtracts. How aſſuming is this*[s]! But ſurely it may be retorted, How unfair is this! The Inſtruction plainly relates, not to Miſſionaries ſettled in *Preſbyterian* or congregational Pariſhes, for there were none ſo ſettled when it was drawn up, but for Incumbents of epiſcopal Pariſhes, though with a Mixture of Diſſenters. And they would of Courſe underſtand, that endeavouring to *convince and reclaim* the latter was not to be their ſtated and principal Buſineſs, but occaſional

[r] Collection of Papers, printed by Order of the Society, p. 24.
[s] p. 89.

only

only and incidental. If the Doctor should happen to speak of the Episcopalians residing in his Parish, as Part of his Parishioners, and say, that he should endeavour *to reclaim them with a Spirit of Meekness;* would this be a Proof, that he was fixed there with a *formal Design to root out Episcopacy* in it? If there be Instances, in which Missionaries, who have no legal Parishes, have used the same Language; (for he quotes none, and I remember none) it only follows, that they have expressed themselves improperly, and should be set right when it is observed.

Another Evidence produced by the Doctor is, that *in the Account of the Society, published in 1706, after speaking of the independent Congregations in* New England, *they say:* " *Several* " *other Ways of Division and Separation did so* " *much obtain in other of our Colonies and Plan-* " *tations, that this made it more necessary to* " *think of providing for a regular and orthodox* " *Ministry,*——*to promote, as much as possible,* " *an Agreement in Faith and Worship.*" *This,* he saith, *can mean nothing, more or less, than Uniformity, or a general Conformity to the Doctrine, Discipline and Worship of the Church of* England [b]. I have not been able to procure

[b] Pag. 86, 87.

this

this *Account,* or to learn by whom, or whose Order, it was compiled. But the Passage quoted from it, expresly speaks, not of independent, or any Congregations in *New England,* but of other *Ways of Division and Separation in other Colonies,* and therefore is nothing to the Doctor's Purpose: besides that, *as much Agreement as possible in Faith and Worship* might be far less than a general Conformity to the Church of England; which it might be impossible to obtain, and yet as near an Approach to it as could be obtained, might even, in his Opinion, be more desirable, than letting them continue in their present Way. For how bad that was, appears not.

The real Conduct of the Society, with Respect to Provinces and Parishes not episcopal, hath been, to contribute towards supporting public Worship and Instruction amongst such Members of the Church of *England,* as cannot in Conscience comply with the Worship and Instruction of the other Congregations in their Neighbourhood, and yet cannot wholly maintain Ministers for themselves. The most of these will usually be in the more considerable Towns; and for that Reason it is, and not with a View of making Converts, as the Doctor pretends,

tends[i], that epifcopal Minifters are fettled in
fo many confiderable Towns of *New England.*
But they are fettled no where, till a competent
Number of our People inhabiting near, requeft
it, and fubfcribe what they are able.   Nay,
thefe Requefts have often, both formerly [k] and
lately, been rejected, or poftponed for many
Years together, when the Number did not appear to be fufficient, or the Society apprehended,
that too much of their Money was going this
Way.   And were it but known, as it feems to
be in fome Meafure to the Diffenters themfelves [l],
how continual and importunate the Calls and
Expoftulations of fuch Perfons are, the Impartial would wonder, how the Society could with-
ftand fo many of them, as it hath done.   Thefe
are plain Evidences, that Miffionaries are not
fent to *New England* for the Purpofe of making
Profelytes to Epifcopacy.   Accordingly, which
is a further Evidence, they have no Directions,
public or private, given them to make any, or
to preach at all upon difputable Points: but on
the contrary, one Rule laid down for them is,
that they keep always in View the great Defign
of their Undertaking; viz. to promote the Glory

---

[i] Pag. 46.   [k] See *Humphrey's* hiftorical Account, p. 61,
&c.   [l] See Mr. *Hobart's* ferious Addrefs, p. 133, 138.

of

of God, and the Salvation of Men, by propagating the Gospel of our Lord and Saviour [m] *; and another is, that the chief Subject of their Sermons be the great fundamental Principles of Christianity; and the Duties of a sober, righteous and godly Life, as resulting from those Principles* [n].

Nor can the Missionaries easily misapprehend the Intentions of the Society, thus manifested. Several of them have indeed spoken highly, sometimes perhaps, as it is but natural, too highly, of the Increase of their Churches; and have mentioned it with great Pleasure in their Letters, and no Wonder. But they have not ascribed that Increase to the Pains which they have taken to bring Persons over to it, but rather to the Satisfaction which our Service had given to Persons, who of their own Accord, from Curiosity or other Motives, attended it. Or if they now and then do mention themselves as making Converts, they do not ever, to the best of my Remembrance, mention this, as the End for which they were appointed. Dr. *Johnson*, one of the oldest of them, professes it not to be so, in these Words: *He* [Mr. *Hobart*] *is much mistaken in saying—we make it our chief and grand Business to proselyte Dissenters to the*

<hr>

[m] Collection of Papers, p. 20.   [n] Ibid. p. 23.

Church

Church of England.—*Our chief Bufinefs is, to minifter to thofe who are Church People; and if this proves the Occafion of increafing the Number, it is but what may naturally be expected, when they, by that Means, have Opportunity to fee how great the Advantage is on our Side*[*]. And Mr. *Beache*, one almoft, if not quite, as old, faith, *It is not the Defign of the Charter, that the Society fhould fend Miffionaries to convert* Prefbyterians *to the Church: and—it is a bafe Reflection to fay they do.—They never fend Miffionaries to convert Proteftants to the Church of* England, *but to minifter to Church People: and if Diffenters by that Means are added to the Church, they do not think by this any Evil is done. This is the Truth, and all the Truth*[*]. Accordingly a very refpectable Miffionary ufes the following Words, in a Paper not printed, which I have feen. " *I believe very few Inftances, if* " *any, can be produced of any Miffionary's begin-* " *ning with any Diffenter, with a View of re-* " *claiming him to the Church. I have long* " *known the Affairs of the Society, and know of* " *no fuch Inftance.*"

[*] Pref. to Mr. *Beache's* Vindication, or Addrefs, 1749, p. 5, 6.   [*] Second Vindication, or Addrefs, 1751, p. 67.

Therefore

Therefore Mr. *Apthorp* might well *aver,* as the Doctor tells us he is said to have done, *that he desires not to make one Proselyte from the congregational Church*[a]. The Doctor however thinks, that *there seems to be some Difficulty in reconciling this Declaration with the Hopes expressed in his Letter to the Society, of future Accessions to his Congregation.* But may there not be Accessions to it by the Settlement of more Members of the Church of *England* in those Parts, or by a Change of Sentiments in Persons of other Persuasions, without Mr. *Apthorp's* interfering? The Doctor, unable or unwilling to perceive so obvious a Solution, charitably helps him to come off, by supposing, that *perhaps it was from the College, not from the Church, that he flattered himself with such Accessions:* adding, *in which he is supposed to have been not a little disappointed.* But hath Mr. *Apthorp* attempted to make any Proselytes, either from the Church or the College? if not, why is a poor needless Evasion ascribed to him; and a Disappointment supposed of Hopes, which he doth not appear to have entertained? Why should not his Declaration, and suitable Behaviour, be rather deemed another Proof, that the Missionaries

[a] Ib. p. 63.

under-

underſtand their Buſineſs to be, not proſelyting Diſſenters, but officiating to our own People? The Doctor believes indeed what may ſeem a Preſumption of the contrary, *that ſcarce ten Families in the Town of* Cambridge *uſually attend the Service of the Church lately ſet up there*[r]. But it was repreſented to the Society, that 50 Families in the Town and Neighbourhood were deſirous to attend it. And ſhould they prove to be much fewer, yet ſeveral Members of the Church of *England* ſend their Children to *Harvard* College there : and ſuch a Place of Worſhip, as they and their Parents approve, may be reaſonably provided for them, without any Deſign of proſelyting others. There is indeed a College in *New England,* where Students have been forbidden to attend epiſcopal Service, and a young Man hath been fined for going to hear his own Father, an epiſcopal Miniſter, preach But in *Harvard* College, it ſeems, a better Spirit prevails : and it is more likely to flouriſh, both for that Moderation, and for the new Church built near it.

· The Doctor ſaith that in ſome other Places *the Supplicants* for Miſſionaries *have not exceeded* 8 *or* 10, *or* 12 *Heads of Families*[s]. But if this

[r] Pag. 48.   [s] Ib.

be

be true, they have petitioned in the Name of others, as well as their own. And suppoſing the Society to have been miſinformed about their Numbers, this may happen notwithſtanding good Care; and by no Means proves them to have a Deſign, which other Circumſtances prove they have not.

But the Doctor apprehends, that whatever the Number of theſe Petitioners any where may be, Conſcience is but ſeldom their Motive, and therefore they ſhould not be encouraged. Indeed, he ſcarcely ſeems to conceive how it can be their Motive: and wants to be told, *what there is that ſhould give Offence to good Proteſtants*[t] *in the Preſbyterian or congregational* Churches. We muſt not call them Independent, for he ſaith *the Epiſcopalians affect to reproach them under that Name*[u]: though Mr. *Neale*, himſelf an Independent, uſes it frequently, and it is more proper, and not reproachful at all. Nor muſt we call them Aſſemblies or Communions; for he hath rebuked Mr. *Apthorp* and the Archbiſhop of *Canterbury* for doing it[w], though he doth it himſelf. In theſe Churches therefore, he wants to know what there is that can give Offence: and ſo lets him-

[t] Pag. 66.   [u] P. 36.   [w] p. 67.

    ſelf

felf again into his darling Topic, of abufing the Church of *England* in Comparifon. However, he recollects that he hath heard fome Epifco-palians fay, and been told that others have faid, *that they fhould much prefer the Communion of the Church of* Rome[x] *to that of the Diffenters.* And indeed none are fo likely as he, and fuch as he, to provoke thofe into faying it, who would think very differently in their cooler Hours. But fuppofing this to be their fettled Judgment; would he have them left to turn Papifts, if they will, becaufe they are not fo good Proteftants as they fhould be? The Church of *Rome* and its Society *de propaganda,* would have Ground to thank him for eftablifhing this Notion. But if fome of his own Communion fhould fay that they had rather be Anabaptifts or Quakers than Churchmen, would that be a Reafon why they fhould have no Minifter of his Communion amongft them? I fhould ima-gine juft the contrary. Perfons of different Parties in Religion may think too ill of each other, without wifhing Ill to each other at all; and fo may mean very well, though they judge greatly amifs. Or even if they mean Ill, they

[x] Ibid.

have

have ſo much the more Need of ſuch Inſtructors as they eſteem, to ſet them right.

But the Doctor, *to do* the Epiſcopalians *Juſtice, doth not ſuppoſe that theſe Sentiments generally prevail amongſt them.* And he admits *that ſome of them may poſſibly, without going theſe Lengths, have conſcientious Scruples about the Means of Religion in* his *Communion* [r]. But he puts the Word *poſſibly* in *Italics:* which intimates, that he thinks it barely poſſible. And this Poſſibility he extends no further, in what follows, than to allow that there may be *ſome Things or Circumſtances which they cannot intirely acquieſce in, or approve of.* Now would he account us to be ſufficiently charitable, if we conceded only ſuch a Poſſibility of Conſcientiouſneſs to the Diſſenters from the Church of *England?* If not, why is he ſo exceedingly ſparing in his Conceſſions to us? We hold it to be probable, we hold it to be evident, that many Diſſenters who are far from thinking us worſe than Papiſts, yet cannot in Conſcience uſe the Means of Religion in our Communion. And ſurely we are intitled to as favourable an Opinion from them. Without maintaining that *they have no Goſpel Miniſters, or Sacraments, or Ordinances,*

[r] Pag. 68.

or

of Churches[z], we may apprehend, whether rightly or wrongly is not to be disputed now, but sincerely however, that Episcopacy is of Apostolical Institution, and that Scripture affords as good Proof of this, as of the Appointment of Infant Baptism and the Lord's Day. We may apprehend that after the ceasing of extraordinary spiritual Gifts, Forms of Prayer were always used, more or less, throughout the Church of Christ, and are needful for the Observance of the Scripture Rule, *Let all Things be done decently and in Order*[a]. Without *judging* those who reject both these, (for *to their own Master they stand or fall*[b]) we may judge it unlawful for us to join in the Rejection of either. Nay, were we only to think their Ministry, compared with that of our Church, to be unedifying, and make that our Plea for preserving a Separation from them, we should but follow the Pattern which many of the *English* Dissenters have set.

The Doctor indeed assigns very different Motives, for the Non-compliance of our People: *Levity, Petulance, Avarice, groundless Distrust at the stated Minister, Dissatisfaction about Pews and Rates, or at being under, or likely to come*

[z] Pag. 63.   [a] 1 Cor. xiv. 10.   [b] Rom. xiv. 4.

under

under Cenfure for immoral Practices. But *he doth not affirm pofitively that either* [he means any] *of thefe hath always been the Cafe without Exception*[c]. Here again he is remarkably careful, that his Conceffions to the poor Epifcopalians fhall not be too liberal. And to keep on even Terms with him, we do not affirm pofitively that none of thefe hath ever been the Cafe. But we muft infift, that the favourable Prefumption is the preferable one, and that Mens Profeffions, concerning their own Inducements, are to be credited, unlefs the contrary appears; which, according to the beft Intelligence that could be got, we believe it hath not ordinarily done, in the Matter now under Confideration. On one of thefe Heads, *Avarice,* the Doctor explains himfelf, by faying, that *till a Law was made, obliging the Epifcopalians to pay minifterial Rates in common with others,* but for *the Support of their own Clergy,* Epifcopacy made a great Progrefs; and that *if they had been exempted from all minifterial Taxes as the Quakers are; almoft all who loved their Money better than any Thing elfe, might in the Courfe of a few Years have adorned the Communion of the Church.* But what needed

[c] Pag. 47.   [d] P. 49.

                    they

they who loved their Money better than any
Thing elfe, turn Epifcopalians to fave it, when
turning Quakers would have ferved the fame
Purpofe more effectually ? And have any Epifcopalians turned Quakers, when they found
their former Change would fecure them no
longer ? If not, this Suggeftion is unauthorized
and unwarrantable. He declines giving *any
recent Inftances* of Mens acting upon the Motives which he alledges, becaufe if you will believe him to be fo tender, old ones, given by
another Perfon, may be lefs invidious. Of thefe
he produces two, from a Letter of Dr. *Colman*,
of *Bofton*, written above 50 Years ago to Dean,
afterwards Bifhop *Kennet*. And he obferves
rightly, that the Dean in his Anfwer expreffes
his Belief that they are true. But he plainly
believed it only on the Information of Dr. *Colman*, a perfect Stranger to him; nor can any
Inquiry into the real Truth be made now.
And I beg Leave to obferve in my Turn, that
according to Dr. *Mayhew*'s own Account, for
I have no other, the Dean thought the Society
was authorized to *plant epifcopal Churches,*
where, though there was *a fettled Miniftry,
there were* alfo *good Numbers; who could not in
Confcience conform to the Ways of Worfhip different*

rent *from the eſtabliſhed Church of* England[e]. Therefore aſſerting, that the true and only Deſign of the Society, in ſending Miſſionaries to the *Maſſachuſetts* and *Connecticutt* hath always been to provide for ſuch Perſons, is not a new Plea, ſet up to ſerve a Turn. The Dean had good Opportunities of knowing its real Purpoſes; and ſo worthy a Man as Dr. *Mayhew* allows him to be, would not have written as he hath done, if he had ſuſpected any further inſidious Scheme. Indeed the Society far from having formed a Project to epiſcopize (as the Doctor calls it) that Country, had but three Miſſionaries in it ſeven Years after; and the following ones went upon no other Errand than the firſt.

After ſaying that the abovementioned Cauſes produced Factions and Parties, and they produced epiſcopal Separations, the Doctor goes on to ſay, that *divers of the Miſſionaries have been much injured, (which there is no Reaſon to ſuppoſe) if they have not been very buſy in fomenting theſe Diviſions; yea, been at the Bottom of them*[f]. But I take the Liberty of maintaining, that there is *great* Reaſon to ſuppoſe they have been injured. For in all ſuch Diſ

[e] Pag. 50—55.　　[f] Pag. 57.

putes

putes it never fails, but each Side injures the other; and the Miffionaries would be very fure of having a double Load of Calumny thrown upon them. Still, that fome of them may have been to blame in this refpect, is not only pof- fible, but confidering human Nature, too like- ly. And if any where it can be proved that they have been *bufy Bodies in other Mens Mat- ters* [e], or ufed bad Arts to promote a good Caufe, they ought to be reprimanded, and if they amend not, removed. But the Doctor, confcious that Mifbehaviours of particular Per- fons would not come up to his Point, charges the Society itfelf with *manifefting a fufficient Forwardnefs to encourage and increafe fmall dif- affected Parties in Towns, upon an Application to them.* And this, he faith, *appears* [b]. But how it appears, he hath not faid, nor can I imagine. The Society hath never been made acquainted with any of the little Quarrels in the Towns of *New England*; and were they to know them, they are too remote to give Di- rections about them; unlefs the Doctor can make it *appear*, that they have given their Miffionaries a general Direction to inflame them all as much as they can.

[e] 1 Pet. iv. 15.   [b] Pag. 47.

Perhaps.

Perhaps he may think that no other Caufes can be alledged, than fuch as he hath produced, for the Increafe of Epifcopalians in thofe Parts. But this would be a great Miftake. Though the firft Planters of *New England* were Separatifts from our Church, many Conformifts to it came afterwards to fettle there; and fome of them, as I am credibly informed, were to be found fifty Years ago, in almoft every Town of confiderable Standing. Thefe new Comers were defpifed and reproached for their religious Principles by their Neighbours; moft of whom had been taught to think the Church of *England* nearly as bad as the Church of *Rome*. Thus attacked, it was natural that they fhould endeavour to defend themfelves, and procure fuch Books as would enable them to do it better. Some of the more candid and inquifitive amongft the *Prefbyterians* and Congregationalifts adventured to hear their Defences, and to read their Authors; were convinced by them, and became Churchmen. As their Number grew, it was natural that they fhould endeavour to procure themfelves Minifters, and on their Requeft the Society helped them. This occafioned a further Augmentation, to which alfo contributed greatly the wild Enthufiafm that prevailed in feveral of

the

the *New England* Churches, even before Mr.
Whitefield came amongst them, but was mightily
increased by him and the strolling Teachers
that followed him; as did likewise their extend-
ing spiritual Censures to mere Trifles, with
their endless Contentions and Confusions on the
settling of Ministers, and on various Occurren-
ces besides; all which Things disgusted and
wearied out many of their People, and induced
them to seek a peaceable Refuge in our Communion.   If these are known Facts, as I am
assured they are, they will go a very great Way
towards accounting for the Growth of the epifcopal Party; and the Doctor should not have
suppressed them, and ascribed it wholly to such
bad and such low Motives as he hath done, in
order to throw an Odium upon the Society, as
encouraging what it abhors, for the Attainment
of a Design which it never framed.

But the Doctor seems to intimate, that *even
upon Suppofition*, that the Episcopalians in *New
England*, who pleaded that they had no Minifters whom they could attend, were *confcientious
People*, yet they were not *much to be pitied*, or
really Objects of Charity [1].   Surely he could not
mean this.   At least, I should have great Com-

[1] Pag. 69.

passion

paſſion for a Number of Diſſenters in the ſame State. Thus much however he allows, that *if any Perſons in* England, *in their private Capacity, ſhould think it,* which again rather implies that he in their Condition ſhould not think it, *a Deed of Charity to ſupport epiſcopal Churches in* New England, *for the Sake of thoſe comparatively few conſcientious People, to whom the Means of Religion, to be had in the Proteſtant Diſſenting Communion, are no Means—they have a Right to do it.* But he inſiſts that the Society hath not, *their whole Fund and Revenue being otherwiſe appropriated;* which he undertakes to prove from their Charter.

Now I acknowledge that the Caſe of the *New England* Epiſcopalians, is not particularly deſcribed and provided for in the Charter. But ſo neither is the Caſe of any other *Indians,* than ſuch as are the King's *Subjects, and People* living *in his Plantations and Colonies,* for to theſe only the Letter of the Charter extends; and in reſpect of others, Mr. *Apthorp* might juſtly ſay, that *Indian Converſions are undertaken by the Society, as it were, ex abundanti.* Yet Dr. *Mayhew* is ſo far from blaming the Society for applying Part of their Benefactions to the Inſtruction of ſuch *Indians* as only border on his Ma-

jeſty's

jefty's Dominions, that he blames them greatly
for not applying more of it to that Ufe.   Now
if their Cafe, which exifted when the Charter
was granted, and yet is not named in it, may
however be looked on as comprehended within
its Intention, and obtain Relief by Means of it
in Confequence of the general Principle on
which it is founded, much more may that of
the Epifcopalians, which did not exift, and was
not forefeen, and therefore no Wonder it was
not named.   Though it was not exprefsly mentioned before it was in Being, ftill if, when it
came into Being, it was included under the
Reafon and Equity of the Purpofes which are
exprefsly mentioned; paying Regard to it muft
be underftood to be allowed by the Charter,
and virtually directed in it.   For the Rules of
Law require that Grants of Princes, and particularly Grants in Favour of Religion, be interpreted as liberally as may be [k].   And thus far,
I conceive, Mr. *Apthorp* rightly afferts, that
*the Society have a difcretionary Power of making
Alterations in their Inftitution;* nor do I believe
that he meant to carry it further, however un-

---

[k] See thofe Rules in *Wood's Inftitutes of Civil Law,* Introd,
c. 13. §. 3. No 13. 17.

mercifully

mercifully Dr. *Mayhew* hath treated him [1] on the Suppofition that he did.

If it be doubted, notwithſtanding the above-mentioned Argument *à fortiori*, whether the Caſe of the *New England* Epiſcopalians comes within the Charter or not, I beg the Reader's Attention to the following additional Conſiderations. The King ſets forth in it as a principal Reaſon of granting it, that *for Lack of Support for Miniſters, many of his loving Subjeĉts want the Adminiſtration of God's Word and Sacraments.* Now muſt not they who lack Support for ſuch Miniſters, as they can with a good Conſcience attend, want the Adminiſtration of God's Word and Sacraments? Would not the Generality of the *Preſbyterians* and Congregationaliſts in *New England* think they wanted it, if there were no other than epiſcopal Churches there? and why may not Epiſcopalians think in a like Manner? And can one imagine, that when the King's Subjeĉts abroad, Conformiſts to the Church eſtabliſhed in *England* by Law, were, without their own Fault, and merely through their Situation and their Poverty, unprovided of ſuch public Means of Religion as their inward Perſuaſion required, it could be

[1] Pag. 110—116.

agreeable

agreeable to his Royal Will that they should be excluded from the Benefit of this Charter? But further, the King recites that Part of his People, through the forementioned unhappy Circumstances, *seem to be abandoned to Atheism and Infidelity,* and others are in Danger of being *perverted to Popish Superstition and Idolatry;* and both these Things he was desirous to prevent. Now doth not the Doctor think the Episcopalians, when they have no Ministers in whose Ministrations they can acquiesce, must be grievously liable to the one or the other? Particularly, must not those of them be in great Danger of Popery, who, as he tells us, prefer that to the Worship of the prevailing Party in *New England?* And must it not be presumed that the Charter would have guarded explicitly against these Evils, had they been foreseen? But further still, the King declares, that *he thinks it is his Duty as much as in him lies, to promote the Glory of God by the Instruction of his People in the Christian Religion.* Now will not this be more fully effected if the Episcopalians in *New England* are instructed, than if they are not instructed? And lastly, the King proposes, that *for accomplishing the Ends* intended by the Charter, *a sufficient Maintenance be provided for*

an

an orthodox Clergy to live amongst his Subjects in thefe Parts. I do not lay the greateft Strefs on this laft Claufe, becaufe it fpecifies only what Sort of Clergy fhould be fent, not to whom they fhould minifter. And yet, if the Intention was that only Clergymen of the Church of *England* fhould be employed, (and public Authority, I believe, hath never directed others to be employed) it muft furely be intended likewife, that all the Laity of the Church of *England,* who could be benefited by them, fhould.

Here indeed the Doctor objects, that *Orthodoxy, in its moft common Ufe, hath no Reference to ecclefiaftical Polity*[m]. But fuppofing that, why may not the Charter ufe it in its original and not uncommon Signification, of right Notions in religious Matters, whether they relate to Faith, or Morals, or Worfhip, or Church Government? The Head of an epifcopal Church cannot be deemed indifferent about any of thefe; efpecially in forming a Corporation, into which, I believe, no one Diffenter was by the Charter admitted. But he objects again, that *King* William, *though as Head of the Church of* Eng-land, *there was a Neceffity of his externally con-*

[m] Pag. 60.

T   *forming*

forming to its Rules and Discipline, cannot be supposed by orthodox Ministers to have intended those of the Church of England *in Distinction from others* [u]. Thus he is pleased to represent, for the Sake of his Hypothesis, our glorious Deliverer as a mere *external,* and consequently hypocritical Conformist : though it is well known, that on his Death-Bed he was attended by Ministers of our Church and no other, and received the Sacrament from a Bishop's Hands. Nor, I presume, is the Doctor ignorant, that he settled 100*l.* a Year on an episcopal Church at *Boston* [o] ; which clearly shews, that he thought episcopal Churches proper Objects of Royal Bounty, even in Places where there was a settled Ministry of another Sort before. And his Successors to this Day have thought in the same Manner. But had he been ever so rigid a Nonconformist, every Word of his Charter must have been interpreted, not by his private Opinion, but by the Spirit of the Laws and the Constitution.

The Doctor pleads also, that *divers* of the *New England Laws,* relative to Ministers, *in which they are designed as orthodox, have had the Allowance of the King* [p]. And had the Intent of these Laws been to enact, that they were or-

[u] Pag. 20.   [o] *Humphreys's* Account, p. 7, 313.   [p] p. 61.

thodox,

thodox, the Plea would have been of ſome Weight. But where the King only aſſents to a Bill, framed for another Purpoſe, in which this Word, uſed by them concerning themſelves, is to be found, his Connivance at their Uſe of it, againſt which it might have been hurtful to object, can never ſhew, in what Senſe he uſes it of his own Accord in an *Engliſh* Charter. He ſaith likewiſe from Mr. *Hobart*, that *if we think none but the Clergy of the Church of* England *are in a legal Senſe orthodox Miniſters, we may be informed how that Matter was determined by the King in Council, in the Cauſe between Mr.* Macſparran *and Mr.* Torrey[*]. But the Council did not declare the Diſſenting Miniſters to be orthodox in the legal Senſe, but in the Senſe of the Donors of the Land in Diſpute. And this Anſwer Mr. *Beache* gave long ago to Mr. *Hobart*[*]. But the Doctor hath choſen to repeat the Objection, without taking Notice of the Anſwer.

He urges alſo, that if *we deny the* New England *Miniſters the Title of orthodox, we muſt deny it to the Miniſters of all other Churches, except perhaps that of* Rome[*], *and engroſs the*

[*] Pag. 62, 63. [*] Second Vindication or Addreſs, p. 69. [*] p. 61.

whole

whole of that precious Commodity, as he fcornfully calls it, *to our own Party* '. Now he knows in his Heart, that we think the Church of *Rome* far more heterodox than we do any of the Proteftant Churches, yet he could not refift the Temptation of infinuating the contrary. I hope his Confcience will do him the kind Office of putting him to the Blufh in private, for this and many like Inftances of Difingenuity. As to other Churches, fo far as their Opinions differ from ours, be it in Points more or lefs material, we do indeed think them miftaken, or, if the Doctor pleafes, heterodox; but without the leaft Contempt of them, or Breach of brotherly Love towards them : and we allow them to think us fo, without taking it amifs. But he hath thought fit to acquaint us, that Heterodoxy and Herefy are the fame Thing ". So that whoever diffents from Dr. *Maybew* in any Point relative to Chriftian Faith, it feems, is accounted by him an Heretic. His *New England* Brethren, if indeed they acknowledge him for a Brother, are defired to confider the Confequences of this Way of thinking. *We have not fo learned Chrift* ".

' Pag. 59.   " p. 20, 58, 61.   " Eph. iv. 20.

But

But the Doctor hath not yet done with Orthodoxy. *That precious Commodity,* he fancies, will afford him ſtill further Advantages. And therefore he tells us, it is known, or at leaſt generally ſuppoſed amongſt them, that their *New England Miniſters adhere much more cloſely both to the Letter and the Spirit of the doctrinal Articles* of our Church, than *moſt of the epiſcopal Clergy themſelves*[x]. Thus imaginary Notorieties and vague Suppoſitions, anſwer equally the Doctor's End of blackening the Epiſcopalians in the Eſteem of his Neighbours, by imputing to them Deviations from the eſtabliſhed Faith, for which, if they were real, he would, *unleſs* (to uſe his own Words) *he is much injured,* like them the better. We can only deny the Charge and put him on the Proof, which we do. And he would ſeem to attempt a Proof in Reſpect of Mr. *Apthorp,* ſetting ſome Paſſages in a Sermon of his, and ſome of the 39 Articles, in a pretended Oppoſition[y]: though it is viſible at firſt Sight, that Mr. *Apthorp* ſpeaks only againſt the Doctrine of unconditional Reprobation, and the Extravagancies of the *Antinomians,* and that the Articles quoted aſſert neither of them. But this Accuſation ſerved a double

[x] Pag. 60.　　　[y] p. 76, 77.

T 3

Purpoſe;

Purpose; of intimating firſt, that Mr. *Apthorp* ſubſcribed the Articles inſincerely, and then af‑ fecting to bring him off by a Subterfuge, of which he hath no Need, that *poſſibly he hath altered his Opinion ſince.*

I have dwelt too long, in Complaiſance to the Doctor, on the Term *orthodox.* Now I proceed with his Proofs of the Society's Miſ‑ conduct.   He alledges, that *Dr.* Bray *took great Pains to inform himſelf of the State of Religion in the Colonies; and deliver'd it, as the Reſult of his Inquiries, that he found no Need at all of Miſſionaries in* Connecticut *and the* Maſſachu‑ ſetts[z].   This again he quotes from Mr. *Ho‑ bart*; and again omits to take Notice of the full Anſwer which Mr. *Beache* had given to it fourteen Years ago, in theſe Words: " I grant " there was a Time, when, as Dr. *Bray* ſaith, " there was little or no Occaſion of ſending " Miſſionaries to the *Maſſachuſetts* or *Connec‑* " *ticut*, becauſe there were then few or no " Church People who wanted a Miniſter. Yet " now the Caſe is very much alter'd; and as " there are ſome thouſands, ſo they are like to " increaſe[a]." Had the Deſign of the Society,

* Pag. 41, 42.   * Second Vindication or Addreſs, p. 67, 68.

in

in fending Miffionaries to thofe two Governments, been to make Profelytes, they would
have thought there was moft Need, inftead of
no Need, to fend, when there were feweft
Church People in them. But they fent none
for eight or nine Years, as Dr. *Mayhew* himfelf obferves [b] : and they have fent them afterwards, juft as the Neceffities of the People required : not to propagate the Peculiarities of the
Church of *England*, as he pretends [c], but to
preferve a due Senfe of Chriftianity, and perform religious Offices amongft its Members.

The Doctor alledges alfo, that *in fome Churches,
which according to the Abftracts have been reprefented as growing, flourifhing, and increafing
in Reputation, for near half a Century, the Number of ftated Worfhippers at this Day, very little,
if any Thing, exceeds ten or twelve Families* [d].
Yet he tells us himfelf, that in 1718, which is
not half a Century ago, there were but *three
Miffions in all New England* [e] : and every one
of thefe far exceeds that Number of Families; ·
as do the latter alfo, if we may believe Accounts, as credible as the Doctor's, who, though
he denies thofe of the Miffionaries to be true,
confeffes, that *the direct Proof of a Negative,*

[b] Pag. 44. .   [c] p. 43.   [d] p. 48.   [e] p. 44.

n *such Cases, is no easy Matter*[f].   The Society
wish, and endeavour to be well informed, concerning the Number of Families in every Mif-
sion.   If they are misinformed only in some few
Instances, it is neither a great Marvel nor a
great Objection.   And if they apprehend many
Missions to be more confiderable than they are,
since Episcopacy thrives so poorly, the Doctor
hath no Reason to be alarmed about it.   For
supposing them to have engaged in the Enter-
prize which he imagines, they will certainly
grow sick of it and abandon it.   But indeed I
doubt whether any one of them ever dreamt
of what he is pleased to say *hath long been their
formal Defign, the true Plan and grand Myftery
of their Operations in* New England[s].

Another Thing, afferted by him, is, that
after episcopal Congregations *in fome Places have
become well able to fupport their own Minifters,
the Society have ftill continued to pay thefe:* to
which he adds, that *the only Reafon, why he
doth not come to Particulars, is, left it fhould
feem too invidious;* and that *this Conduct of the
Society for fome Years, proved no inconfiderable
Means of increafing the Church Party*[h].   Now
the Society hath always been desirous to know,

<hr>

[f] Pag. 83.   [s] p. 49.   [h] Ibid.

4   when

when any Congregation became able to support itself without their Help; and have never continued their Contribution, when they have understood that to be the Case. If their Friends have been too slow in giving them Intelligence, which may have happened, and the Doctor will favour them with any, which on Inquiry shall appear to be well grounded, they will both be thankful to him, and shew the World that they are far from wishing to increase the Church Party by profuse Liberalities.

The Doctor exaggerates the Fault, with which he charges the Society, of misapplying their Money, by alledging further, that they have done no Good by it. He declares, that *he never knew an Example of any Proselyte from their Churches to ours, being brought back to a Christian Life:* but that there *are numerous ones of Persons, whose Morals, though exceptionable before, were much worse afterwards;* that *they often become loose, profligate, vain and censorious, seemingly placing no small Part of their Religion in railing at their congregrational and Presbyterian Neighbours*[1]. Now in Answer to an Accusation of the same Nature, brought by Mr. *Hobart,* Mr. *Beache* hath *seriously declared,*

[1] Pag. 82.

that

that he hath known many Perfons who have greatly improved in Virtue by the Change[k]. And other worthy Miffionaries have declared the fame Thing. The Doctor indeed will perhaps treat me for producing Miffionaries, as he hath Mr. *Apthorp* for producing Members of the Society, as *Witneffes in* what he calls *their own Caufe*[l]. But the Teftimony of its Accufer is not more admiffible. The Zealots of all Parties, and thofe of his own at leaft as much as others, are mighty apt to fpeak with overgreat Severity of fuch as forfake them. And if the Doctor himfelf doth not place fome Part of his Religion in railing at the Epifcopalians, it is very hard to account for his practifing it fo much. But befides, the Queftion is not, whether Profelytes to the Church of *England* grow better, but whether the Members of the Church of *England* would not grow worfe, if they had no ftated Miniftry to prevent it.

Inattentive to this, he urges further, that fwearing, gaming, &c. *are beyond all Comparifon more frequent, fince the Church of* England *prevailed there, than before*[m]. Yet Mr. *Beache* faith, *he is perfuaded, that folid Chriftian Virtue,*

[k] Firft Vindication or Addrefs, p. 43.   [l] Pag. 9. 70.
[m] Pag. 75.

as well as *Knowledge,* increases, as the Church gains Ground in the Country, and thousands of People are really better'd by it in their moral *Character*; But suppofing the abovementioned Vices are more frequent fince that Time, fo I fear thefe and others are in *England* fince the Revolution and the Toleration. But would it not be very wicked to afcribe the Increafe of them to either of thefe? Are the Miffionaries Examples of Vice? The Doctor hath not dared to fay it. Do they preach in Favour of Vice? Are they not as diligent and zealous to the full, in teaching moral Duties, as the Minifters of his Communion, if not more fo? And why then are the Immoralities, of which he fpeaks, to be imputed to them, or the Society, or the Church of *England,* when perhaps his own Friends are as much degenerated as any? He declares indeed, that *he will not affirm that this is greatly the Work of the Society.* But he hath done his utmoft to make others think it; and, I fuppofe, imagines that Epifcopalians deferve no better Treatment. In one Thing however he hath dealt very fairly. After expreffing his Perfuafion, that *there is lefs real Religion in thofe Parts of* New England, *where* the Society's

* Second Vindication or Addrefs, p. 65.

Money

Money *hath been expended, than there would have been, had it been sunk in the Ocean,* he adds, *'tis not to be supposed that any Episcopalians can be of this Opinion; neither is any Stress laid upon it in the present Argument*[o].

Mr. *Apthorp* asserts that, instead of Harm, the *New England* Missionaries have done great Good there; *that the religious State of the Country is manifestly improved,*—though *much indeed remains to be done in Manners and Piety.* And here the Doctor, with his usual Charity, represents him as making a *Concession, that this boasted Reformation very little, if at all, consists in the Improvement of Piety and Morals*[p]. Then he proceeds, without any Occasion given him, to a mock Defence of the *formal Air,* which he admits the old Divines of that Country had, compared with the *jovial Countenances* which he ascribes to the Missionaries[q]. What the Doctor's Countenance is, I know not; but I wish he gave as good Proofs of a serious Heart, as the Missionaries in general do. That Religion wore a gloomy and uninviting Appearance amongst the Puritans there formerly, and now wears a more pleasing one amongst their Descendants, and that in Part they have learnt

[o] Pag. 96, 97. [p] p. 73. [q] p. 74.

this Alteration for the better from the Members of the Church of *England,* the Doctor, I prefume, will not deny, though he will not permit an Epifcopalian to fay it; and Mr. *Apthorp* did not mean to fay more on this Head.

What he faith in the next Place, of the Improvements lately made there in the fpeculative Doctrines of Religion, the Doctor endeavours to conftrue into the licentious Infult on their *Fathers* and Teachers, *living and dead*[r]; of which Mr. *Apthorp* had evidently no Intention, though he doth ufe a ftrong Expreffion or two, which probably were not meant even of the dead Teachers at large, but of the wild Sectaries with which that Country abounded[s]. At leaft they cannot be meant of the living Fathers, becaufe he both owns and pleads, that the Faults, which he blames, are amended. And after abufing him for fome Time, the Doctor himfelf allows, *it was too common a Thing for People in* New England *to exprefs themfelves in a Manner juftly exceptionable upon thefe Points;* and that they may be *indebted to the Society* or their *Miffionaries* in fome *Degree,* for their doing otherwife now[t]. So that in the

---

[r] Pag. 75.   [s] See *Humphreys's* Account, p. 36, 37, 38.
       [t] Pag. 78.

main

main he agrees with Mr. *Apthorp*, at the fame
Time that he inveighs againft him ; and probably wifhes that far greater Changes were
made in the fpeculative Doctrines of his Brethren, than the Society and its Miffionaries
would approve.

Mr. *Apthorp* adds, that *Hypocrify hath worn
off, in Proportion as Men have feen the Beauty
of Holinefs :* that is, in Proportion as the Face
of Religion hath become amiable, and its Doctrines have been rationally explained.; the two
Things which he had mentioned immediately
before. But the Doctor chufes to mifunderftand
him of the Beauty *of Rites, and Modes, and Forms,*
in order to get an Opportunity of reproaching
the Church of *England* again, as placing Holinefs *in a Zeal for thefe*[u], which it notorioufly
doth not. I wifh others were as far from
placing it in a Zeal againft them.

The laft Inftance of religious Improvement,
in which Mr. *Apthorp* thinks the Miffionaries
have been inftrumental, is the *exterminating of
Perfecution.* On this the Doctor obferves, that
no Acts of Uniformity ever took Place in New
England[w]. Very true, for they could not obtain them : elfe there was a Time when they

[u] Pag. 79.　　　　[w] Ib.

certainly

certainly would. But they made a Shift to per-
secute pretty effectually without them. He
adds, that no Persecution *had been known amongst
them for many Years before the Society was in
Being* [x]. But can he prove that they held it
unlawful before that Time? He represents it
as incredible, that *the Posterity of those who had
persecuted their Fathers into* America, should
teach the present Generation their *Charity and
Moderation.* But why more incredible, than
that the Posterity of those who had persecuted
the Quakers in *America*, should now be Enemies to Persecution? The Act of Toleration
was passed by Members of the Church of *England.* Mr. *Locke*, a Member of the same
Church, was, of all *English* Writers, the
greatest Advocate for Toleration. The Esteem
of it increased continually. The Generality of
our Missionaries, I hope, carried that Esteem
with them into *New England.* Their Need of
Toleration there, must recommend it still more
to their good Opinion; the Necessity of allowing it to them must gradually reconcile others
to an Approbation of that Allowance; and
better Motives, I doubt not, co-operated with
these; which had the strongest Influence, I do

[x] Pag. 80.

not

not undertake to determine. But furely the Doctor goes too far, when he faith, *Wherever we learnt Chriftian Charity towards thofe who differ from us, we did not learn it of the Church of* England. Where elfe they learnt it, he doth not fay; and they certainly might learn it from her, unlefs they difdained to learn any Thing from her. Where he learnt it indeed will be very needlefs to enquire, till he gives better Proofs of his having learnt it at all. For one who ufes his Pen in fuch a Manner, feems but too likely, notwithftanding a few Expref-fions of gentler Import here and there, to ufe other Weapons, if he had the Command of them. Yet I do not fufpect him of *hoping to fhoot* Epifcopalians *as freely as Pigeons;* though he faith it is credibly reported, that *fome of the warm Epifcopalians hope for the Time when they may* treat *Diffenters* fo [y]. Mr. *Beache* on the other Hand, had actually *heard fome of the* Prefbyterians *fay, it was Pity that all thofe, who firft fet up the Worfhip of God according to the Church of* England *in that Country, had not been hanged, as the Quakers were formerly at* Bofton [z]. Such hot headed Creatures, I am perfuaded, fay much more than they deliberately

[y] Pag. 81.   [z] Vindication or Addrefs, p. 28.

think;

think; and are too few, on either Side, to deſerve the Notice of the other. The *New England* Epiſcopalians in general, ſo far as I can learn, ſincerely deſire to live amicably with their Neighbours. And amongſt the *Engliſh*, with whom my Acquaintance hath been pretty extenſive, and without whom the others cannot be formidable, I know not a Man of the Clergy or Laity, and do not believe there is one in a hundred, perhaps I might ſay a thouſand, who wiſhes to overturn the preſent Toleration of the Diſſenters. I ſhould be glad of an Aſſurance, that They wiſh no worſe to the Church Eſtabliſhment. The Doctor ſaith, *they do not in all Reſpects find the kindeſt Uſage from* us, *being ſubject to divers temporal Inconveniencies*[*]. I ſuppoſe he hath principally in View the Teſt Act. Now without digreſſing to enquire whether this be juſtifiable or not, they who approve of reſtraining them ſo far, may heartily diſapprove any further Reſtraints; nay, many of them have given the ſtrongeſt Evidence that they do. And perhaps as many Epiſcopalians in *New England* are excluded from Offices without Law, as Diſſenters here by Law, on Account of their Religion. But enough of this.

[*] Pag. 80.

U   The

. . The Doctor argues moreover, that even fuppofing the Miffionaries in *New England* to have
done Good there, *though it may be fome Apo-
logy, it will not juftify the Society, if it hath occafioned the Neglect of a much greater Good to the
Heathens, or* unprovided *Colonies*[b], *who had an
exclufive Right to the Money which hath been funk
in the epifcopal Gulph*[c]. But the exclufive Right
hath been difproved, and there hath been no
defigned Neglect. The Heathens meant muft
be either the *Indians* or the *Negroes*. Now the
Doctor owns, that *as to the* Indians, *there have
been, and ftill are, fome great Difcouragements in
attempting to chriftianize them.* But he faith
that *according to divers Appearances, the Society
have had this Work lefs at Heart than that of
propagating Epifcopacy in* New England[d]. I
hope he would not have the Complaint made
by the *Indian Sachem* in June 1700[e], reckoned
amongft thefe Appearances, for the Society was
not incorporated till a Year after. But he faith,
that *the Accufation of neglecting the Natives in*
America, *hath been in fome Sort allowed to be
juft by* the Society *themfelves*; and brings for
Proof of it, Bifhop *Williams*'s Sermon before

[b] Pag. 72.		[c] p. 91.		[d] p. 98.		[e] p. 107.

them

them in 1705[f]. Now, unhappily for the Doctor, Bishop *Williams* doth not speak of the Society, in the Words which he quotes, but of the *English* Nation. Nor could he speak of the Society, as neglecting the *Indians,* and yet less as neglecting them to propagate Episcopacy in *New England;* for the Society had not subsisted five Years, and had but one, if any, Missionary in that whole Province. But the Bishop's Words sounded so plausibly for a Charge upon the Episcopalians, that he could not forbear misapplying them. He affirms, that *it would not be difficult to justify this Complaint by an Appeal to any of the later Sermons before the Society.* I conceive it would, and he hath not attempted it. In one Place he expresses a Doubt, whether the Society have so much as *begun to use Methods of converting either the* Negroes *or the* Indians. But in another he owns, that *they have made some Essays from Time to Time towards the Conversion of the Savages; but very feeble and sparing* ones; *compared with the Zeal of the* French *to popize the* Indians, *or with their own Zeal to episcopize* New England[g]. Now indeed they have shewn no Zeal to episcopize *New England;* and it is much easier (I go on

[f] Pag. 98.   [g] P. 134, 125.

                                        with

with the Doctor's Language) to popize than to chriftianize the *Indians.* Teaching them a few Words and Ceremonies, of which they know not the Meaning; giving them a few Trinkets, and infpiring them with a mortal Hatred againft the *Englifh,* makes them good Chriftians enough to ferve the Purpofes of the *French;* and no Wonder that fuch Converfions are effected with Eafe. Our Society cannot undertake to make Profelytes in this Manner. Befides, it hath not fuch Numbers to employ, fuch Funds to maintain them, or fuch Authority to require their Perfeverance in the Work. Many of their Miffionaries are under Vows of abfolute Obedience, none of ours are; and therefore they will engage to go only where they chufe, and will ftay no longer than they chufe. Reafonable Perfons will be moderate in blaming them, if they confider the manifold Difagreeablenefs and Danger of fuch an Employment; but at leaft they will be far from blaming the Society for not fending Miffionaries, when they cannot procure them. And that they have failed to ufe their beft Endeavours for procuring them, the Doctor doth not affert.

Inftead of this, he firft infinuates without Proof, what would be nothing to his Purpofe

if

if true, that *the Missionaries have frequently given the World too pompous Accounts of their Efforts, and spoken hyperbolically of their Difficulties, and been too soon discouraged* [g]; then goes on to make Remarks on Mr. now Dr. *Barclay's* Mission about 25 Years ago, as if nothing worth Notice had been attempted before. He is careful indeed to tell us, that an Order of Council was made very early [in 1702] for sending two Protestant Ministers to the *Indians* of the Five Nations; that this Order was communicated to the Society, and referred to a Committee [h]. But that any Thing was done, or tried upon it, or about the same Time with it, he hath not given the least Hint. Yet he might have known, and probably did know, from Dr. *Humphreys,* to whom Mr. *Apthorp* refers his Readers, not only that the Society sent a Missionary that very Year, the first after it was formed, to endeavour the Conversion of the *Indians* bordering on *South Carolina,* and that *the Governor and other Gentlemen there, thinking it not to be a proper Season,* disposed of him another Way [i]: but that in Pursuance of the above Order, the Society, after inviting unsuccessfully a *Dutch* and an *English* Minister,

g Pag. 99.　　　h p. 108.　　　i Ib.

U 3　　　　　　who

who lived in the Neighbourhood of thofe Nations, to undertake their Converfion, prevailed
on the Rev. Mr. *Thoroughgood Moor* to go upon
this Defign in 1704, who applied to the *Mo-
hocks,* and acquainted them, *that another Minifter was daily expected for the* Oneydes, *and
one for every other Nation, as foon as proper
and willing Perfons could be found*; that they
feemed at firft highly pleafed with the Care
thus taken of them; but would give no determinate Anfwers to his Offers of inftructing
them, nor at laft any Anfwers at all, *though he
ufed all the Means he could think of to get their
Good-will:* fo after near a Twelvemonth's Trial
he left them, and was foon after loft at Sea[k].
The Doctor might alfo have known, if he did
not, that Mr. *Barclay,* a different Perfon from
the abovementioned, being fent Miffionary to
the fame *Indians* in or before 1709, *tried all
the Methods he could, to engage them to be inftructed in our Language and Religion, but with
very fmall Succefs;* that *feveral indeed would
feem for a Time to be converted, but foon after
they would return again to their firft favage
Life*[l].

[k] Pag. 286—291.   [l] Ibid. p. 215, 216.

His

I

" His paffing over in Silence the following Account is yet more obfervable. In 1710, the Requeft of the four *Sachems,* who came over to *England* that their Subjects might be inftructed in Chriftianity by refident Minifters, being thought to favour a new Attempt, *the Society agreed to fend two Miffionaries to the* Mohock *and* Oneydes Indians, *with a Salary of* 150l. *Sterling each, together with an Interpreter and Schoolmafter to teach the young* Indians. Accordingly Mr. *Andrews* was fent as Miffionary, and an Interpreter and Schoolmafter were affigned him. He was prefented to the *Indians* with great Solemnity, and received by them with great Marks of Joy; but the Parents obftinately refufed to let their Children learn *Englifh.* Therefore both Parents and Children were inftructed in the *Indian* Tongue, as well as the Nature of it would permit. But in 'a fhort Time they grew weary of being taught. Their Fathers would not fuffer their Boys to be corrected or difpleafed, in Order to their learning any Thing. As they grew up, they took them along with them, when they went out in Bodies to hunt, for feveral Months together, and they could not be brought to a fettled Life. They took and difmiffed Wives at their

Plea-

Pleafure; were continually making Expeditions, and practifing Cruelties one upon another; left their aged Men and Women to perifh; got drunk whenever they could, and in their Drunkennefs were mad and mifchievous to the higheft Degree. They who had learnt fomething, fhewed in their Lives no Regard to it; and even the four *Sachems* became Savages again. *French* Jefuits from *Canada* inftilled into them Jealoufies by falfe Affertions, which Popifh Miffionaries never fcruple; and fome of the *Jufcararo Indians*, driven from *North Carolina*, which they had perfidioufly attacked, filled them with fuch groundlefs Refentments by unjuft Reprefentations of what had paffed there, that they forbad Mr. *Andrews* to vifit them at their Habitations, would no longer come to the Chapel or the School, nor fuffer him to fpeak of Religion to them when he met them occafionally; but infulted and threatened him and his Companions, who were in Danger of their Lives whenever they ventured out of the Fort, where they dwelt. At length therefore he reprefented to the Society, that he defpaired of any further Succefs. Yet they would not hearken to his fingle Narration and Opinion, but requefted Mr. *Hunter*, Governor of *New York*,

to

to make Enquiry, whether continuing his Miſſion was likely to be of Uſe. And on the Governor's confirming the Accounts which Mr.
Andrews had given, they recalled him, after a
Trial of ſix Years[m].

I beg the Reader to compare theſe Relations,
taken from authentic Papers, with the Doctor's
unauthorized Suggeſtions, that the Miſſionaries
told what Stories they would, and the Society
believed them without Examination, or wilfully neglected this Part of their Buſineſs.
Without entering into the ſubſequent Particulars of this *Indian* Undertaking, I ſhall only ſay,
in general, that other Miſſionaries were ſent
afterwards, and with ſome Effect, down to the
Year 1735, when the firſt mentioned Mr.
Barclay went, of whoſe Miſſion alone the Doctor is pleaſed to take Notice, becauſe he thinks
it will afford Matter of Objection.

Accordingly he alledges, that Mr. *Barclay*
had not *half a proper Support*, but *the Miſſion
was ſtarved*. For Mr. *Sergeant*, a Miſſionary
from the Society incorporated in 1661, reports
from a Letter of Mr. *Barclay*, that *he had but
a ſcanty Allowance*, (i. e. from the Society) *and
could obtain no Salary for an Interpreter or*

[m] Ib. p. 295.—311.

School-

Schoolmafter ". And Mr. *Barclay* himfelf faith in a Letter, *June* 11, 1736, that *he laboured under great Difadvantage for Want of an Inter-preter, which could he but enjoy for two or three Years, he fhould be Mafter of the* Indian *Language* ". Now when Mr. *Barclay* wrote thefe Letters, of which I know nothing but from the Doctor, he was not a Miffionary but a Cate-chift only. And though he had; as he faith, but a fcanty Allowance, *i. e.* 30*l.* a Year from the Society, yet he expected *further Encou-ragement* from them; and the Affembly of *New York* had alfo voted him 30*l.* a Year, which may account for the Smallnefs of the Society's Allowance. Only he had not received either of the Salaries ". But before the End of the fame Year, he wrote to the Society, that he had made himfelf Mafter of the *Mohock* Lan-guage, which probably induced them to think an Interpreter unneceffary. The next Year they raifed his Salary to 50*l.* Why he defired in 1740 an Interpreter, as well as a Schoolmaf-ter, appears not; but in the fame Year a School-mafter was allowed him. That the Society fhould be cautious and frugal in the firft Trial of a young Man, after fo many Difappoint-

---

" Pag. 101. ° p. 102. ᵖ p. 102, 103.

ments,

ments, is far from being ſtrange. And the Expence of an Interpreter for two or three Years, which is all that Mr. *Barclay* wiſhed, could not poſſibly be grudged, in Order to ſave ſo trifling a Sum towards a more favourite Purpoſe, as the Doctor would have it believed. Nor did the Miſſion miſcarry for Want of due Support, as he leads his Readers to imagine it did. What he quotes from Mr. *Apthorp*, that *from the lateſt Accounts we find this Miſſion much dwindled, or greatly interrupted*, relates to the State of Things brought on 18 Years afterwards by the late War. Mr. *Barclay*'s Miſſion was carried on with ſeeming Succeſs till about the Year 1745, by which Time the *French* had infuſed ſuch dreadful Imaginations into our *Indians*, and incited their own to ſuch Violences, that it was no longer ſafe for Mr. *Barclay* to ſtay amongſt them. There is therefore not the leaſt Ground for the Doctor's Pretence, that the *Indians* did not think the *Engliſh* in Earneſt, or that the *French* made their Advantage of any Negligence of the Society. Inſtead of deſpiſing what the Society was doing, they were alarmed at it, and employed both all their uſual Arts and open Force to defeat it. However, Mr. *Oel, a German* Clergyman appointed

by

by the Society, ftaid with the *Indians* during the
War, in which they were faithful to this Country.   And he, and *Paulus,* a *Mohock,* whom the
Society made School-mafter, were ftill doing the
beft they could there when the laft Accounts
came.   Mr. *Barclay* being fettled at *New York*
in 1746, Mr. *Ogilvie* was fent in his Stead to
the *Indians* in 1748, who found that many of
them were removed into the *French* Territory,
and the reft fo much addicted to Drunkennefs,
which hath fince deftroyed a great Part of them,
that he had little Hopes, excepting from the
Children, and not much from them, unlefs they
were maintained in Houfes appropriated to their
Inftruction.   Now this Undertaking would not
only be exceffively expenfive, particularly becaufe the Parents muft be well entertained as
often as they pleafed to vifit their Children, but
in all Likelihood fruitlefs, confidering their Difpofitions with Refpect to their Children already
mentioned.   Mr. *Ogilvie* took one by Way of
Trial, cloathed, maintained and inftructed him.
But his Friends fetched him away, left he fhould
learn to defpife his own Nation.   Notwithftanding all this, Mr. *Ogilvie* continued his
Endeavours there, till he was carried off in
1758 for his Majefty's Service, by the Com-
mander

mander in Chief of his Forces in thofe Parts. There are ftill, or lately were, Hopes of his Return; in the mean Time, the Rev. Mr. *Brown* fupplies his Place.

Befides thefe Attempts, and feveral other occafional ones by feveral Miffionaries, one of which, by Mr. *Beach*, he faith, was fruftrated by the Diffenters prejudicing the *Indians* againft him [q]; there was a Refolution taken by the Society in 1743, to effay the Converfion of the *Mofkito Indians*, which Mr. *Hobart* hath mifreprefented. He faith, *the Society fpent fo much Time in endeavouring to perfuade either the* Indians *themfelves, or the Government of* Jamaica, *to fupport the Miffionary, that though the Letter from the* Indians *requefting Affiftance, bears Date* May 19, 1739, *yet Mr.* Prince *at the Time of his Death,* July 25, 1748, *had not reached the Place of his Miffion* [r]. Any Reader would conclude from hence, that the Letter from the *Indians* was either written to the Society, or inftantly communicated to them, and that the Delay arofe wholly from their Unwillingnefs to part with their Money on the Occafion. But the Truth is, that the *Indians* applied in 1739

[q] Second Vindication or Addrefs, p. 70. [r] *Hobart*'s fecond Addrefs, p. 141.

to Mr. *Trelawney*, Governor of *Jamaica*, without naming the Society, whofe firft Knowledge of their Application was in the latter End of the Year 1742 : that on this they wrote immediately to the Governor, not to perfuade any Perfons to contribute, but folely to enquire whether the *Indians* were able or the *Jamaicans* willing, which was furely a juftifiable Piece of Prudence : that as foon as they had his Anfwer, giving no Ground to hope for pecuniary Affiftance, which was in a few Months, they agreed to fend a Miffionary and Schoolmafter ; that Mr. *Prince*, then in *America*, being recommended to them for this Work fhortly after, they agreed without Delay to accept him, if he brought proper Teftimonials ; but that Objections were made to him from thence, which could not be fully difcuffed under a confiderable Time : that when his Character was cleared, he was directed to come over, and ordained : that he returned as foon as he could, but died on his Way from *Jamaica* to the Place of his Deftination : that on hearing this, the Society ordered another Miffionary to be provided, but no one could be got.   Evidently there was no Backwardnefs in this Cafe ; but Affiftance was moft readily fent to *Indians* not comprehended

within

within the Letter of the Charter, not being in any of his Majeſty's Colonies; on which Account the Treaſury refuſed Mr. *Prince* the uſual Bounty granted to Miſſionaries, and it was made up to him by the Society, who might eaſily and plauſibly have excuſed themſelves from engaging in this Matter, if they had not really had it at Heart.

From theſe various Attempts it appears, that the Society have always been deſirous, always endeavouring, to make Impreſſions on the *Indians*. And from their bad Succeſs with thoſe on whom they beſtowed the moſt Pains, it appears, that notwithſtanding their ſeeming good Inclinations towards Chriſtianity, and their Petitions to be inſtructed in it, on which the Doctor lays ſo much Weight[*], they were either inſincere, or quickly changed their Minds and grew intractable; ſo that appointing more Miſſionaries, if the Society could have found them, would probably have been little elſe than *ſinking more Money,* if I may preſume to imitate his Style, *in the* Indian *Gulph*[†], inſtead of making *thoſe Tribes in general profeſſed Chriſtians,* which he deſires to have it thought would have been the Conſequence. His Preſbyterian and

[*] Pag. 100, 106.　　　[†] p. 109.

con-

congregational Friends have had a much longer
Space of Time for this Work than the Society;
they have also lived in great Numbers amongst
the *Indians*, which is another Advantage. Yet I
fear the Fact is rather, that few *Indians* are left
in *New England*, than that many are Christians.
And though the Doctor tells us, that two Miffionaries, lately fent from *Boston* to the Five,
otherwife Six Nations, give *very encouraging
Accounts of their Difpofition* [u], one cannot help
doubting, whether thefe Accounts will end in
any Thing better, than the abovementioned
like Accounts given to the Society. I heartily
wifh they may. But furely as yet, it is too early
to infult us with the Superiority of their Succefs to ours.

The Doctor faith, Mr. *Barclay*'s *Miſſion was
ſtarved* [w] : I hope the contrary hath appeared.
Much lefs was it ftarved to propagate Epifcopacy in *New England*, for at that Time the Society had fcarce any Miffionaries there; yet in
a great Meafure it failed like the reft. And
therefore it is very unjuft to impute the Failure
of any to that Caufe, when it may be fo naturally imputed to thofe which produced the fame
Effect before; and are likely, though not fo

[u] Pag. 105.   [w] p. 104.

likely,

likely, to do it again. However in the Beginning of the Year 1756, the Society confulted fome of their *American* Friends, whether a few *Indian* Boys might not be procured, and taught in the Colleges of *New York* and *Philadelphia,* and fent from thence to inftruct their Countrymen. The Anfwers to them reprefented great Difficulties of obtaining Children, greater ftill of keeping them long enough; and no fmall Danger of national Refentment, if any Accident fhould happen to any of them. The Society notwithftanding, the College of *New York* being not as yet in a Condition to receive any fuch Children, refolved to give 100*l.* a Year towards educating fome in that of *Philadelphia,* in which they had Hope alfo of further Affiftance. But a frefh War foon broke out. Now in a Time of War, and it fhould be remembered, that there have been very frequent ones fince the Incorporation of the Society, fome taking their Rife in *Europe,* fome only in *America,* little or nothing can be done, even with the friendly *Indians,* in Favour of Religion. On the late Peace with *France,* another *Indian* War hath unexpectedly followed. When God in his Mercy fhall permit thofe Regions to enjoy Tranquillity again, it will be a proper Seafon to refume this Project.

X In

In the mean while, our Society hath agreed
with that of 1661, to fend jointly a Lay In-
ftructor to the Six Nations, as foon as it is fafe,
and to bear much the greateft Part of the Expence. The Doctor, it is hoped, will, on confidering thefe Things, retract his Affertion, that
little more can be faid, than that the Indians *have
not been wholly neglected by the Society* [x]. At
leaft, as it hath never been charged with Remiffnefs in this Article, either by the Government at Home, or by any of the fucceffive Governors Abroad, this may furely be accounted
as confiderable a Prefumption in its Behalf, as
his Opinion is againft it. And I dare fay the
Promifes, which it voluntarily and freely made
to the King on his Acceffion, will be faithfully
kept, as far as the Means of fulfilling them can
be found.

With refpect to the Negroes, the Doctor is
not particular in his Accufation of the Society,
and therefore a general Anfwer will fuffice.
He obferves juftly, that *our* Weft India *Iflands
abounds with them* [y], and fo do fome of our Plantations on the Continent. But in both they
live under the abfolute Government, chiefly of
hard Mafters; too many of whom forbid them

[x] Pag. 109.   [y] P. 95.

to be inftructed in Religion, and others deprive them of Time for it, by making it neceffary that on *Sundays* they fhould work for themfelves. Where they are allowed to attend the Minifter of the Parifh, they are properly under his Care; and where Negroes abound moft, the Parifhes are in general fo well endowed, that the Society have not, and need not have, Miffionaries in them; but Provifion, even for the loweft of the People, may be eafily made without them. Where they have Miffionaries, the Negroes are underftood to be Part of their Flock, whom they have been ftrictly charged not to neglect. In thofe Places where there are no Minifters, it is impoffible to appoint a feparate Miffionary or Catechift for the Negroes of each Family, and almoft impoffible to affemble thofe of diftant Families together. The Proprietors of large Numbers of them are ufually well able to get them inftructed by fome of their upper Servants, or a neighbouring Schoolmafter; and if they are unwilling, would be very apt to defeat the Endeavours of Perfons appointed by the Society. If fuch in any Place, as are well difpofed, will form any reafonable Plan for the Inftruction of the Negroes belonging to them, or near them, which they may contrive much

better

better on the Spot than the Society can at a Diftance, they will be fure to receive as much Help from it, as they can expect. The Society hath for many Years maintained Catechifts for the Negroes in the two great Cities of *New York* and *Philadelphia,* with very good Effect. And of late they have been blamed for it, as overdoing, becaufe the Inhabitants may well bear that Burthen themfelves. However this may be, they can truly anfwer to the Doctor's Charge, that they have refufed no Affiftance towards the Converfion of the Negroes, which they have been afked, or faw how to give; and particularly, that they have withdrawn none fince the Increafe of their Miffions in *New Eng-land.* On the contrary, they have extended their Care far beyond the literal Bounds of their Charter, and in 1751 appointed a very worthy Miffionary, with a Salary of 70*l.* a Year, to in-ftruct the Negroes in *Africa:* where he con-tinued five Years, and then returned to *England* on Account of his Health; having firft fent over to the Society three Boys of good Families, to be educated here under their Direction. One of thefe is dead; the other two have been main-tained, though as frugally as was proper, yet at no fmall Expence, and taught whatever would

fit

fit them to propagate Chriſtianity in their na-
tive Country, to which they are now on the
Point of going back.   The greateſt Part of this
the Doctor muſt have known from the Abſtracts, but hath mentioned nothing of it.   For
it would have been hard to reconcile with his
Accuſation of the Society, that they have difregarded every Thing elſe, to propagate Epiſ-
copacy.

The laſt Head of his Charge of Neglect relates to the Colonies, unprovided of a competent
Number of Miniſters.   Here he ſaith, that
*though he will not affirm it for Truth, yet he hath
been very credibly informed, that the People in
ſome of the Southern Colonies, and particularly in
thoſe Parts of* North Carolina, *which were entirely deſtitute of Miniſters, had made earneſt and
repeated Applications to the Society for Miſſionaries, ſometimes without any Anſwer for Years
together, and at laſt without Succeſs:* and that
*ſome ſenſible and ſerious Perſons from that Coun-
try, ſeveral Years ago, he thinks, gave him the
ſame Account; but that whether they did or not,
they made ſuch a Repreſentation of their ſad State
for Want of Miniſters, that at the Moment* of
his Writing, *it was not in his Power to refrain
from Tears in reflecting on it.*   And then he

X 3

makes

makes his ufual charitable Addition, that *per-haps* the Society *had it not in their Power to comply with thefe Solicitations, by Reafon of their large Expence in the noble Defign of fupporting and increafing little epifcopal Parties, or Factions, in* New England [z]. So the Doctor's credible Information of what he will not affirm for Truth, and his thinking he remembers what he is not fure he ever heard, is produced againft the Society, to juftify a Conjecture about their Motive for acting as they never did act. Indeed, that the poor People, over whofe Cafe he hath wept fo long after, would have accepted Minifters from the Society, is far from certain; nor is it likely from feveral Parts of his Book, that he would have reckoned the Want of epifcopal Minifters any great Calamity. At leaft, I cannot learn from the Books of the Society, which have been confulted on this Occafion, that any Applications, made to them from *North Carolina,* have been rejected or poftponed. But it appears, that they fent a Miffionary thither in 1703, who was difcouraged by the Inconveniencies of the Climate and Country, by the inteftine Feuds of the People, by the Profanenefs of many of them, and the Indifference of others to all Re-

[z] Pag. 97, 98.

ligion;

ligion; that on his Return they ſent two more in 1707, who after a few Years were alſo wearied out; and again two in 1711, who uſed their beſt Endeavours for ſeveral Years, but ſucceeded no better, and at laſt quitted the Undertaking. Yet all of them were Men of very good Characters, as the Inhabitants acknowledged. On a freſh Application, a ſixth Miſſionary was appointed in 1722, who died the next Year, and a ſeventh in 1725, who ſeems to have deſpaired like his Predeceſſors[*]. Then the Inhabitants, I believe, were for a Time left to themſelves, and very inſenſible of the Unhappineſs of their Condition. But gradually the Society ſupplied them a-new; and for ſome Years paſt they have had more Clergymen amongſt them, though at moſt perhaps but ſeven at once, than ever they had before; and therefore they have not been neglected for the Sake of epiſcopizing *New England,* as the Doctor ſuggeſts. The Society hath acquainted them long ago, that if they were willing to do what they were well able towards maintaining more Miſſionaries, it would be glad to aſſiſt them. But inſtead of this, they have uſed thoſe ill, in many Ways, whom they have had already.

---

[*] See *Humphreys,* p. 128—143.

Par-

Particularly, though they have made Laws, both formerly and lately, for Salaries to Mini-sters, they have been temporary, and insuffi-cient, and ill executed. And when the prefent Governor once thought he had put Things on fuch a Footing that the People might maintain their cwn Minifters entirely, the Society could not find Minifters to fend over to him; which Dr. *Mayhew* himfelf will allow they would have done readily in this Cafe, if they had been able, becaufe it would have coft them nothing. In-deed we have not Perfons enough in Orders to ferve the Parifhes of *England* properly, and therefore it muft be difficult to engage a fuffi-cient Number for the Plantations. But the Difficulty is much greater to provide them for the Southern ones, than for *New England*, where many are content to come over and be ordained, provided they may return to officiate amongft their Relations and Friends. And this is one confiderable Reafon of the larger Pro-portion of Miffions in that Province, which the Doctor afcribes entirely to a quite different Caufe.

Relying on his Proofs, that the Society have mifapplied a Part of the Money intrufted with them, he endeavours to compute how much it

is,

is, and shews the same Inclination to exaggerate in this, as in every Thing. Having confuted those Proofs, I shall not follow him through the Dark into the random Calculations built upon them. He would have it thought, that in 25 Years the Sum hath amounted to 35,000*l.* *with which,* he saith, *forty or fifty Millions might have been comfortably maintained amongst the Heathens and in heathenish Places, every Year, for more than 30 Years past*[b]. Now if fifty Missionaries are to be paid for 32 Years out of 35,000*l.* they will not have each 22*l.* a Year. And if only forty Missionaries were to be paid out of it for only 30 Years, they would have but 29*l.* a Year. The Doctor, I believe, would not undertake such a Mission with such a Salary. He saith, the 30*l.* a Year given to Mr. *Barclay,* was *not half a proper Support* for him, though he was only a young Catechist, and had 30*l.* more from the Assembly of *New York*[c]. But no Matter how inconsistent the Reckonings are, provided each in its Turn will bear hard on the Society.

An additional Charge, brought by him, is, that the Society hath obtained Contributions by Sermons, representing the Work in which they

[b] Pag. 95.   [c] p. 104.

are

are engaged, to be merely the Propagation of
Chriftianity, though a confiderable Part of it
hath been the Propagation of the Church of
England; that in this they have imitated the
Practice of the *Romiſh* Society *de propaganda
fide,* though the Preachers before them have
condemned it as unfair; that thus the Diffenters
in *England* have been mifled to encourage Defigns againſt Churches of their own Communion in *New England,* and *fome thoufands of
Pounds* have been *drawn from them,* which
have in Part been applied to that Purpofe [d].
Now in Truth, the Society have made it their
Bufinefs to do juſt what their Preachers reprefent them to have been doing, excepting that
they have not been able to do fo much towards
the Converfion of the *Indians* and *Negroes.*
Whilſt there were but few Perfons in the *Maffachufetts* and *Connecticut,* deftitute of fuch
Modes of public Worſhip as they could attend,
few or no Miffionaries were fent thither, and
the earlier Sermons took no Notice of this
Cafe. When they increafed, Provifion was
gradually made for them; the Preachers mentioned it in general Terms; the prefent Archbiſhop of *Canterbury* mentioned it very expli-

[d] Pag. 26—33.

citly

citly above twenty Years ago: and at the End of the Sermons, both before aud fince, Lifts of the Miffionaries, their Places of Refidence and their Salaries, with Accounts of the State of their feveral Congregations, have been publifhed annually. Surely this is far remote from fraudulent Dealing. And no one, that was at all attentive to the Proceedings of the Society, could be ignorant of this Part of them; though Dr. *Mayhew* thinks Bifhop *Butler* was, when he preached before it, which is incredible in the Nature of the Thing, and falfe in Fact. The Popifh Society *de propaganda* never was blamed in Sermons before ours, for fupplying thofe of their own Communion with the Means of their own Worfhip; but for making it their principal Employment to bring over other Chriftians to that Worfhip, which ours hath not done. And if the Diffenters have contributed any Thing confiderable to the Support of our Miffionaries, they muft be prefumed to have done it with their Eyes open, and either to have chofen rather to affift Epifcopalians in that Mode of public Worfhip, than let them be without any; or to have liked the general Defign of the Society fo well, as not to be influenced by their Diflike of its Management in this Particular. But I believe the Truth is, that

the

the Diſſenters, at leaſt for many Years paſt, have contributed little or nothing. I know not that any one of them is, or lately hath been, a Member and Subſcriber, or hath made any Preſent, or left any Legacy to the Society. Nor have they been called upon, when the Crown hath appointed Collections for it. But ſome, if not many of them, have taken great Pains to diſſuade Members of the Church of *England* from giving on ſuch Occaſions. And though I ſhould miſtake in any of theſe Points, yet, on the whole, the Society would certainly come off very well in Reſpect of the Diſſenters, if they would neither do it Good nor Harm.

But further, probably much more Money hath been given to the Society by the Members of the Church of *England*, on Account of the Proviſion which it hath made for the Epiſcopalians in *Maſſachuſetts* and *Connecticut*, than they would have given if it had made none. Many of thoſe amongſt us, who are zealous for the Support of Chriſtianity abroad, are zealous alſo, though in a lower Degree, for the Support of our own Church there; eſpecially in Places, where, without their Help, it cannot ſupport itſelf. And all ſuch will naturally be more liberal to both Deſigns, when thus joined, if indeed they can be called two, than they

would

would to one of them, if divided? Perſons are not obliged to confine the whole of their Charity to that one Purpoſe, which they think the beſt, but may allowably diſtribute it amongſt all which they think are good. Nor is uniting theſe two Purpoſes what the Doctor would repreſent it [*], preferring or equalling the Peculiarities of the Church of *England* to the Intereſts of the Goſpel, any more than the yearly Contribution of the Diſſenters to the keeping up of their ſmaller Congregations here, is preferring or equalling their Peculiarities to the Intereſts of the Goſpel. They think both may be kept up by one and the ſame Act, ſo do we. They contribute to maintain public Worſhip amongſt their poorer Brethren, without deſigning to *preſbyterianize* England; we contribute to maintain it amongſt ours, without deſigning to *epiſcopize* New England. It would be abſurd in us to charge them with the former; it is equally abſurd in them to charge us with the latter. If indeed the Caſe of the Epiſcopalians in the *Maſſachuſetts* and *Connecticut* doth not, by the Charter of the Society, come under its Care, Bounties to them are at preſent conveyed through wrong Hands. But I apprehend it doth, and think that hath been proved. At

[*] Pag. 90.

leaſt

leaft, the Givers in general have all along had the Opportunity of knowing that Part of their Gifts was applied to this Cafe by the Society, yet they have never fignified their Difapprobation, and therefore it hath underftood itfelf to have been anfwering their Intentions. Nothing hath been clandeftinely kept back, or diverted another Way from what was profeffed. In thefe Circumftances, the Guilt of *Ananias* and *Sapphira* is very unjuftly thrown out *in terrorem* by the Doctor[r], according to the old Cuftom of his Party, which I hoped had been quite laid afide, of difcharging mifapplied Texts of Scripture in the Faces of fuch as happened to offend them. But to return; It is very poffible, that the Defire of fupplying the *New England* Epifcopalians with Minifters, may have produced Donations of as much Money to the Society, as it hath expended on thofe Minifters; now if fo, other Parts have not fuffered on their Account. And fhould thefe Benefactors be brought to think the Society an improper Channel for fuch their Bounty, or fhould it be forbidden to employ in this Manner any Share of what it receives, the Confequence might be, that they would withdraw a Proportion of their prefent Liberality, as the Society hath fignified in a

[r] Pag. 118.

Letter

Letter to the *New Hampshire* Minifters, it hath good Reafon to think they would [g], and eftablifh a feparate Fund, by which Means the Condition of the Epifcopalians might be little, if at all, worfe than before, and the Doctor farther than ever from being pleafed. For the new Managers would certainly be more zealous for promoting the Interefts of the Church of *England,* than the Society have been, even in his own Imagination.

The Doctor fuppofes the Defenders of the Society's Conduct to argue, that it may allowably fupport Miffions for converting the *New Englanders* to Epifcopacy, becaufe this is needful to facilitate the Converfion of the *Indians* to Chriftianity [h]. Now they have faid, and very truly, as the Charter of *William* and *Mary* doth, that bringing our own People to a *good Life and orderly Converfation,* is requifite to win the neighbouring Nations *to the Chriftian Faith.* They may have faid alfo, and very truly, that the great Numbers and great Variety of wild Sectaries, in our Colonies, are a lamentable Hindrance to the Progrefs of our Religion. But I queftion, whether they have ever applied either

[g] See *Beache's* Vindication or Addrefs, p. 31, 32. [h] Pag. 119, &c.

of

of thefe Obfervations to the *New England Prefbyterians* or Congregationalifts ; and yet more,
whether any one of them hath fo much as
hinted, that they muft be made Epifcopalians,
as a Step towards making the Heathens around
them Chriftians. At leaft, the Bifhop of St.
David's, whom alone the Doctor hath quoted,
intimates no fuch Thing. And till he produces
fome Authority for the Affertion, he muft be
underftood to put this Plea into our Mouths,
only as an Opportunity, partly of introducing
his Wit, about fending to convert the *Scotch,*
the *Genevans,* and the Man in the Moon, of
which I leave him without Envy in full Poffeffion; partly of fuggefting in Scripture Language,
that our Miffionaries, *entering into the* New
England *Sheepfold* under this *indirect* Pretence,
are Thieves, and Robbers. But then he is careful to fubjoin immediately, that *he doth not
mean to call them by thefe opprobrious Names, or
to give them any perfonal Affront* [1]. Good Man,
who can fufpect him of it ?

In all that I have hitherto faid, I am far
from intending to affirm, that the Society hath
not laid out in the *Maffachufetts* and *Connecticut* too large a Proportion of the Money put

[1] Pag. 123.

into

into their Hands, confidering the Neceffities of
other Provinces. They have a difcretionary
Power within the Bounds of their Truft; and
whilft they confine themfelves to thofe Bounds,
the Money which they receive is altogether at
their free Difpofal, and fo far *their* own; however the Doctor is pleafed to cavil at that Expreffion [k], when ufed very harmlefsly by Mr.
Apthorp. But ftill they ought to ufe their Power
judicioufly, and in that they may have failed.
For what Society of Men hath not? Even the
Doctor's too blamelefs Societies [l] might poffibly
exhibit fome Tincture of human Frailty, if they
did not warily keep their Tranfactions unpub-
lifhed, whilft thofe of ours lie open to all the
World. Preffing Solicitors are always likelier to
prevail, efpecially if they will contribute freely
to the Undertaking for which they are Suitors,
than thofe who are lefs earneft though better
able. And fuch the *New England* Epifcopalians have been, compared with the Inhabitants
of other Colonies. When the earlier Applications were made by them, it could not be forefeen whether more would follow. So one Miffion was fettled after another, till they became
infenfibly numerous; and when many Requefts

[k] Pag. 116—118.   [l] p. 101, 134.

                                       had

had been granted, it was the harder to refuse others, for which the same Plea could be made. Some Members of the Society approved this Increase, others thought it was going too far. And in Bodies of Men, whose Opinions differ, there must be mutual Condescensions, and Time allowed for one Side to come over into the Sentiments of the other, else they cannot proceed together. But in the last five or six Years, I believe, no new Mission hath been appointed in the *Massachusetts* or *Connecticut*, which had not been promised before, excepting that of *Cambridge*. And now for some Time past, the Society have excused themselves from complying with any Applications from that Quarter. Surely this alone is no inconsiderable Argument, that proselyting those two Districts to Episcopacy hath not been the Point in View.

What is past, as the Doctor observes, *cannot be recalled*. But if Mistakes have happened, they may be avoided for the future, and the Society *is not above altering its Measures*[m]. Doubtless it would have liked, and might have expected civiler and fairer Treatment, than he hath vouchsafed to give it. But however, *fas est & ab hoste doceri.* It cannot desert and abandon

[m] Pag. 133.

th

the Congregations which it hath taken under its Protection, unlefs they fhould become either too rich to need its Affiftance, or too inconfiderable to deferve it. But more Care may be ufed to know, when either of thefe Things falls out. All Forwardnefs in Miffionaries to moleft Perfons of other Perfuafions, and all Encouragement of Parties and Factions in Order to ferve Ecclefiaftical Schemes, may be ftrictly prohibited, and on reafonable Complaint feverely checked. The Eyes of the Society may be turned more attentively to the dark Corners of the Colonies, to the Methods which promife well for the more effectual Inftruction of the *Negroes,* and to the Openings for doing Good amongft the *Indians,* which his Majefty's new Acquifitions will probably difclofe. A friendly Correfpondence may alfo be carried on between fome of the Members of that Body, and fome of the *Prefbyterian* or Congregational Minifters, whofe Difpofitions are mild and ingenuous; and thus Animofities and Jealoufies may by Degrees be extinguifhed, of which, I am perfuaded, the Society is very defirous.

Therefore I proceed now to the laft Part of what I propofed, taking into Confideration the Scheme of appointing Bifhops to refide in our

　　　　American

American Colonies. The Church of *England* is, in its Conftitution, epifcopal. It is, in fome of the Plantations, confeffedly the eftablifhed Church; in the reft are many Congregations adhering to it; and through the late Extenfion of the *Britifh* Dominions, and the Influence of other Caufes, it is likely that there will be more. All Members of every Church are, according to the Principles of Liberty, intitled to every Part of what they conceive to be the Benefits of it, entire and complete, fo far as confifts with the Welfare of civil Government; yet the Members of our Church in *America* do not thus enjoy its Benefits, having no Proteftant Bifhop within 3000 Miles of them; a Cafe, which never had its Parallel before in the Chriftian World. Therefore it is defired, that two or more Bifhops may be appointed for them, to refide where his Majefty fhall think moft convenient; that they may have no Concern in the leaft with any Perfons who do not profefs themfelves to be of the Church of *England*, but may ordain Minifters for fuch as do; may confirm their Children, when brought to them at a fit Age for that Purpofe, and take fuch Overfight of the epifcopal Clergy, as the Bifhop of *London*'s Commiffaries in thofe Parts have been em-

powered

powered to take, and have taken, without Offence.   But it is not defired in the leaft that
they fhould hold Courts to try Matrimonial or
Teftamentary Caufes, or be vefted with any
Authority, now exercifed either by provincial
Governors or fubordinate Magiftrates, or infringe
or diininifh any Privileges and Liberties enjoyed
by any of the Laity, even of our own Communion.   This is the real and only Scheme that
hath been planned for Bifhops in *America*; and
whoever hath heard of any other, hath been
mifinformed through Miftake or Defign.   The
American Diffenters from our Communion,
would think it infupportably grievous to have
no Minifters but fuch as received Ordination in
England or *Ireland*, or to be withheld from the
Ufe of any religious Rite, which they efteemed
as highly as we do Confirmation; or to have
their Churches deftitute of a Superintendency,
which they conceived to be of apoftolical Inftitution.   I fhould, in fuch a Cafe, be a zealous
Advocate for them, as not yet enjoying the full
Toleration, to which they had a Right.   And
furely they ought to afk their Confciences very-
ferioufly, why they oppofe our Application for
fuch Indulgence as they would claim for themfelves; and whether indeed fuch Oppofition is

Y 3

not

not downright Perfecution, and that in a Matter merely fpiritual, without the Mixture of any temporal Concern.

The Doctor is a great deal too vehement to propofe his Objections diftinctly, therefore I will endeavour to do it for him.   He faith, *the State of Religion is much better amongft thofe of his Communion in* America, *than it is even in* England, *under the immediate Eye and Documents of the venerable Bifhops* [n] ; and that, *fhould any be fent thither, it is to be hoped they will have better Succefs than the Bifhops have hitherto had here* [o].   Now certainly, the State of Religion here is far from being what we have Caufe to wifh it were.   Whether it be worfe than in *New England,* I am unable to pronounce ; but fuppofing it to be fo, the Doctor himfelf faith, that *a Rationale might be given of the Fact, without any Reflection on our Church* [p].   And, the Queftion, relative to the prefent Point, is not, where the State of Religion is beft, but whether it will not be better amongft the *American* Epifcopalians, if they have Bifhops to fuperintend their Clergy, and do the other Offices belonging to that Function, than if they have none.   He calls Church Government by

[n] Pag. 39.   [o] p. 40.   [p] P. 39.

Bifhops,

Bishops, *the Yoke of episcopal Bondage* [q]. And certainly Bondage is a dreadful Evil, and religious the worst of all. But what Yoke of Bondage do either Churchmen or Diffenters fuffer in *England,* where Bishops have been fo long? All Church Authority was formerly too heavy; but furely the Epifcopal now is as moderate as any, and it is propofed to be reduced yet lower in *America,* and Diffenters will be no Way fubject to it. He faith, *the Affair of Bifhops hath lately been, and probably now is, in Agitation in* England; *and the Society fpare neither Endeavours, Applications, nor Expence, in order to effect their grand Defign of epifcopizing all* New England, *as well as the other Colonies* [r]. Now moft of the Colonies were originally epifcopal. And I cannot learn, nor I believe will the Doctor affirm, that the Inhabitants of any of them, be they of what Sect they will, groan under that Burthen, or have Reafon to do fo. The Imagination of a Defign to epifcopize the reft, I have fhewn to be altogether groundlefs. But further, they may be epifcopized without fending Bifhops amongft them; and Bifhops may be fent amongft them, without any Intention of epifcopizing them.

[q] Pag. 146.   [r] p. 89.

                    Dean

Dean *Kennett*, confeſſed to be a worthy Man [a], writing to Dr. *Colman* in 1712, concerning the Society's *Deſire to have Biſhops ſettled in the foreign Parts committed to his Care,* ſaith, as Dr. *Mayhew* himſelf quotes him, *I hope your Churches would not be jealous of it* [b]. Certainly therefore, he did not know any Cauſe why they ſhould be jealous of it. Archbiſhop *Tenniſon*, who, though a very good Churchman, is allowed to have meant no Harm to any Diſſenters any where, left by his Will 1000 *l.* to encourage the Appointment of two Biſhops, one in the Continent, and another in the Iſlands of *America*. Biſhop *Butler*, whom the Doctor praiſes ſo highly and ſo juſtly, was a hearty Friend to this Scheme, and left 500 *l.* to the Society. Biſhop ,*Benſon*, whoſe Chriſtian and Catholic Temper is well known to almoſt as many as ever heard his Name, bequeathed to it ſuch a Legacy as he was able, *to be added to the Fund for ſettling Biſhops in our Planta-tions in* America, *hoping* [theſe are his own Words] *that a Deſign, ſo neceſſary and unexcep-tionable, cannot but at laſt be put in Execution.*

The Doctor profeſſes himſelf an Enemy to it, becauſe *of the narrow, cenſorious, and bitter*

[a] Pag. 53.　　　[b] p. 88.

Spirit

Spirit that prevails in too many of the Episcopa-
lians in America ". But may not he think too
ill of their Spirit ? I verily believe he doth.
Or if he doth not, is there not an equal Share
of the same Spirit in too many of the *Presbyte-*
rians and Congregationalists there ? And are
Invectives and Acts of Unkindness the Way to
mend it on either Side ? Or may not the Appointment of proper Bishops, conduce greatly
to mend it on the Side of the Episcopalians ?
But he fears, that *if this growing Party should*
get a major Vote in the Houses of Assembly, Tests
might be obtained to exclude all but Conformists
from Posts of Honour and Emolument, and all
Men be taxed for the Support of Bishops and
their Underlings; and therefore he cannot think
of the Church of England's *gaining Ground*
there to any great Degree, and especially of see-
ing Bishops fixed upon them, without great Re-
luctance ". Now this very Passage implies it
not to have gained Ground, as yet, to any great
Degree : in another, already quoted, he scarcely
seems to think it grows at all; and in a third,
though he falsely supposes the Promotion of it
to be a *favourite Point,* pursued *at a vast Ex-*
pence, he still *hopes in God it will never be car-*

" Pag. 129.   " Ib.

ried.

ried[x]. The Likelihood therefore of its obtaining a Majority, is by no Means confiderable.
Now if it were, would excluding Bifhops be
any mighty Guard againft it? So that either
the Admiffion of them will be very fafe, or the
Doctor muft think of more vigorous Meafures
than have hitherto been ufed, to prevent the
Increafe of this malignant Faction. But fuppofing the Epifcopalians were the Majority
there, why fhould a Teft Law follow? Is there
any fuch Law in the Epifcopalian Colonies?
Or even, though there were, can it be imagined
that if a prevailing Party in *New England* were
wild enough to propofe, his Majefty would ever
be advifed to pafs one for that Country? The
Terror of being taxed for Bifhops and their
Underlings, as he civilly calls the Body of the
Clergy, is yet more chimerical than the former; as an Act for that Purpofe would affect a
much greater Number of Perfons, and in a ftill
tenderer Point. Tithes are paid in *England* to
the Clergy by Virtue of Grants, which laid that
Burthen upon Eftates many Ages before the
prefent Poffeffors enjoyed them. But could an
Act of Parliament be obtained now to impofe
a Tax never known before, of this or the like

-----

[x] Pag. 90.

Nature,

Nature, on this whole Nation, Diffenters not excepted, for the Maintenance of an ecclefiafti-cal Hierarchy ? No-body will pretend it could. And with what Modefty then can the Doctor fuggeft, that fuch a Thing might be feared in *New England?* Befides, would it have been a good Reafon at the Revolution, for debarring the Diffenters from the full Exercife of their Church Government and Worfhip, that, if they obtained it, they might perhaps increafe till they got a *major Vote* in both Houfes, and then might enact no Mortal knows what ?

But indeed the poor Man's Fears, if you will believe him, run to vaftly further Lengths yet. He imagines already himfelf and his Brethren driven to the laft Extremities by thefe favage Epifcopalians, and vents his Lamentations in fuch moving Strains, that I muft tranfcribe them; for they are the fineft Flight of Oratory in his whole Book, though it is adorned with many. " Will they never let us reft in Peace, " except *where all the Weary are at Reft?* Is " it not enough that they perfecuted us out of " the old World ? Will they purfue us into the " new, to convert us here ?—What other new " World remains as a Sanctuary for us from " their Oppreffions, in Cafe of Need ? Where

" is

" is the *Columbus* to explore one for, and pilot
" us to it, before we are confumed by the
" Flames, or deluged in a Flood of Epifco-
" pacy? For my own Part, I can hardly ever
" think of our being purfued thus from World
" to World, without calling to Mind, though
" without applying [to be fure] that Paffage in
" the *Revelation* of St. *John: And to the*
" *Woman were given two Wings of a great*
" *Eagle, that fhe might flee into the Wildernefs,*
" *into her Place, where fhe is nourifhed—from*
" *the Face of the Serpent. And the Serpent*
" *caft out of his Mouth Water, as a Flood, af-*
" *ter the Woman, that he might caufe her to be*
" *carried away of the Flood*[y]." Happily, foon
after, the Doctor recovers from his Panic into
fome Degree of Compofednefs, and faith, *it is*
not his Defign however to difhonour the more
moderate and Chriftian Spirit of the Englifh *Bi-*
fhops fince the Revolution, and particularly of this
Day, by comparing it to the perfecuting Anti-
chriftian Spirit of many Prelates, antecedent to
that glorious Æra of Britifh *Liberty.* But why
then fuch difmal Apprehenfions? why fuch
Outcries? where are the Perfecutors? where is
the Dragon? All the World muft fee, the

<hr>

[y] Pag. 129, 130.

Doctor

Doctor himfelf muft fee, that his Declamation
is quite foreign from the Purpofe; and on his
firft Recollection he fhould have been afhamed
of it, and have ftruck it out.   But paternal
Tendernefs would not let him deftroy fo pathetic a Rant on fo darling a Subject.

Not only the prefent Bifhops, but the prefent
Age is grown milder in religious Matters. Proteftants in general, of all Denominations, in all
Countries, but efpecially in the *Britifh* Dominions, bear with each other far better than they
did a Century ago; and the fmalleft Attempts
towards an oppreffive Enlargement of fpiritual
Power, would immediately be crufhed with
Indignation by our Legiflature. The Diffenters
here know it well; thofe abroad can hardly
fail to know it; and fo far as human Forefight
can reach, both the Moderation of the Clergy,
and the Watchfulnefs of the Laity over them,
are much more likely to increafe than diminifh.
But above all, a Bifhop in *New England* would
find abundant Reafon to be cautious of exerting himfelf too far, and very thankful, if with
all his Caution he could live in any tolerable
Degree of Peace.   Therefore the Doctor would
not need to be at all anxious for the Liberty of
his dear Country, though one were to be placed
there.

there. But to make him perfectly eafy, he may
be affured, that this neither is, nor ever was, intended or defired ; which muft certainly be admitted as another Proof ftill, that epifcopizing
that Province hath not been *the favourite
Scheme,* nor indeed any Scheme, of the Society.
During the Courfe of more than fifty Years,
that 'fending Bifhops to *America* hath been in
Agitation, I believe no fingle Perfon, there or
here, hath once named or thought of *New
England* as a proper Place for the Refidence of
one ; but Epifcopal Colonies have always been
propofed. And this the Doctor might fo eafily
know, that one cannot help thinking he muft
know it. But then alas, if he had owned it,
what would have become, not only of his pompous Harangue already mentioned, but of his
ingenious Suppofitions, that Mr. *Apthorp* was
right-reverendly inclined[z], and that a certain *fu-
perb Edifice,* near *Harvard* College, *was even
from the Foundation defigned for the Palace of
one of the humble Succeffors of the Apoftles*[a] ?
So much Wit and Archnefs, how greatly foever
the Doctor abounds in it, would have been too
great a Sacrifice to make to dull Truth and Fact.

[z] Pag. 149.   [a] p. 89.

We

I

We confess indeed, that we cannot perceive why the *Presbyterians* and Congregationalists in *New England* might not as safely breathe the same Air with a Bishop, as their Brethren in *Old England* do. However, we are unwilling to disquiet any of them, by importing and settling amongst them a Creature, which it seems they some of them account to be so noxious. Only we hope, that his occasionally travelling through the Country cannot infect it very dangerously. *Moravian* Bishops are authorized by Law to live, and act as such, where they will in our Plantations. Popish Bishops reside here, and go about to exercise every Part of their Function, without Offence and without Observation. Dissenting Ministers reside here, and hold their Meetings for Ordinations, and whatever Purposes they think fit; and these Assemblies give us no Umbrage. What we desire with respect to *New England*, is much less: that a Bishop may, not reside there, but resort thither from time to time, to officiate amongst those of our own Communion. His constant Abode will be in whatever Province is willing to receive him, with his Majesty's Approbation: who will certainly, for Reasons of every Kind, send such Persons in this Character, as

are

are leaft likely to caufe Uneafinefs. Surely the Doctor and his Friends cannot thwart a Scheme of this Nature, and call themfelves Patrons of religious Liberty.

It is poffible, though it is ftrange, that when he wrote his *Obfervations*, he might mifunderftand the Society's Intention, both in fending Miffionaries to *New England* and defiring *American* Bifhops. I hope it is now fufficiently cleared up; and if he is ftill diffatisfied, I intreat him to confider, for all Men ought, *what Manner of Spirit he is of*[b]. He hath very good Abilities, and a Zeal that would be highly commendable, if it were duly tempered with Charity. But he feems to have naturally a moft vehement Spirit, and to have imbibed, perhaps in his early Days, equally vehement Prepoffeffions againft the very Name of Bifhops, and every Thing connected with them. I am fenfible that thefe Things plead in his Excufe: for they have often hurried Men, who on the whole meant well, not only into great unfairnefs of arguing, but far worfe Faults. And though I have made ufe of fome Freedom in fetting forth his Miftakes and Partialities, yet if fuch Treatment, as he hath given Mr. *Apthorp*, was de-

[b] Luke ix. 55.

figned

ſigned for *the benevolent End of ſhewing him to himſelf*[t], ſurely my Treatment of Him will not be imputed to any unkinder Motive. If he amends upon Admonition, he will deſerve much Reſpect; if not, much Pity.

But however he may take what I have written, I hope others, particularly the Diſſenters, both *Engliſh* and *American*, as many as happen to ſee it, will conſider it calmly: and neither indulge Fears without Foundation, nor affect Fears which they have not, in order to hinder their epiſcopal Brethren from enjoying what they have a Right to. Our Inclination is to live in Friendſhip with all the Proteſtant Churches. We aſſiſt and protect thoſe on the Continent of *Europe* as well as we are able. We ſhew our Regard to that of *Scotland* as often as we have an Opportunity, and believe the Members of it are ſenſible that we do. To thoſe who differ from us in this Part of the Kingdom, we neither attempt nor wiſh any Injury. And we ſhall gladly give Proofs to every Denomination of Chriſtians in our Colonies, that we are Friends to a Toleration even of the moſt Intolerant, as far as it is ſafe; and willing that all Mankind ſhould poſſeſs all the Advantages, re-

[t] Pag. 145.

ligious

ligious and civil, when they can demand either in Law or Reason. But with thofe, who approach nearer to us in Purity of Faith, and Brotherly Love, we are defirous to cultivate a freer Communication, paffing over all former Difgufts, as we beg that they would. If we give them any feeming Caufe of Complaint, we hope they will fignify it in the moft amicable Manner. If they publifh it, we hope they will preferve Fairnefs and Temper. If they fail in either, we muft bear it with Patience, but be excufed from replying. If any Writers on our Side have been lefs cool, or lefs civil, than they onght and defigned to have been, we are forry for it, and exhort them to change their Stile, if they write again. For it is the Duty of all Men, how much foever they differ in Opinion, to agree in mutual good Will and kind Behaviour.

A LET-

A

LETTER

To the Right Honourable

HORATIO WALPOLE, Esq;

Written Jan. 9, 1750-1,

CONCERNING

BISHOPS IN AMERICA.

ADVERTISEMENT.

THE following Letter was found among the Papers of the late Archbishop *Secker*. It was written in Consequence of a Letter, dated *May* 9, 1750, from the late Lord *Walpole*, to the late Dr. *Sherlock*, Bishop of *London*; which was communicated by the latter to Bishop *Secker*, *Jan.* 2, 1750-1.

It is now printed in Obedience to an Order left with it under his Grace's own Hand (dated *May* 25, 1759) in these Words :

Let the Letter, written by me to Mr. Walpole, concerning Bishops in America, *be printed after my Death.*

THO. CANT.

A

LETTER

TO THE RIGHT HONOURABLE

HORATIO WALPOLE, Esq.

St. James's, Westminster, Jan. 9, 1750-1.

SIR,

I Return You my humble Thanks for the Honour you have done me, in communicating to me your Letter to the Bishop of *London.* I have read it with all that Attention and Regard, which is so justly due to your superior Abilities, and long Experience, and meritorious Zeal for our present happy Establishment, and the public Welfare. But still I cannot see the Scheme, to which it relates, in the same Light that you do. And though, if ever he hath conversed with you on the Subject since, he hath doubtless said every Thing material by Way of Reply, which I can suggest, and much more : yet as he doth not seem to have laid any Thing further before you in Writing, I beg Leave

Z 3

to

to trouble you with what hath occurred to me: which, as the Seffion is not yet begun, you may poffibly have fome Leifure to look upon.

The Thing propofed is, that two or three Perfons fhould be ordained Bifhops, and fent into our *American* Colonies, to adminifter Confirmation, and give Deacons and Priefts Orders to proper Candidates, and exercife fuch Jurifdiction over the Clergy of the Church of *England* in thofe Parts, as the late Bifhop of *London*'s Commiffaries did, or fuch as it might be thought proper that any future Commiffaries fhould, if this Defign were not to take Place. The Queftions that arife on this Propofal, are: Is it a reafonable one in itfelf? And if it be, Are there any fuch Dangers of its being extended to introduce exorbitant Church Powers, or of its raifing Uneafineffes Abroad or at Home, as may notwithftanding, at leaft for the prefent, be juft Objections againft it?

The Reafonablenefs of the Propofal, abftractedly confidered, you feem, Sir, to admit. And indeed it belongs to the very Nature of Epifcopal Churches, to have Bifhops at proper Diftances, prefiding over them. Nor was there ever before, I believe, in the Chriftian World, an Inftance of fuch a Number of fuch Churches,

or

or a tenth Part of that Number, with no Bishop amongst them, or within some thousands of Miles from them. But the Consideration of the Episcopal Acts which are requisite, will prove the Need of Episcopal Residence more fully. Confirmation is an Office of our Church, derived from the primitive Ages; and when administered with due Care, a very useful one. All our People in *America* see the Appointment of it in their Prayer-books, immediately after their Catechism. And if they are denied it, unless they will come over to *England* for it, they are in Effect prohibited the Exercise of one Part of their Religion. Again, if they are to have no Ordinations there, they must either send Persons hither to be ordained, or take such as come to them from hence. Sending their Sons to so distant a Country, and so different a Climate, must be very inconvenient and disagreeable : and taking the Small-pox here is said to be peculiarly fatal to them. The Expence also must be grievous to Persons of small Fortunes ; such as most are, who breed up their Children for Orders : yet not sufficient to bring any Accession of Wealth to this Nation, that would be worth naming, were more of that Rank to come. But in Fact, very few of them

do.

do. Therefore they muſt be ſupplied chiefly from hence. And not many in Proportion will go from hence, but Perſons of deſperate Fortunes, low Qualifications, and bad or doubtful Characters: who cannot anſwer, as they ought, the End for which they are deſigned. And it deſerves Obſervation, that a great Part of them are *Scotch*. I need not ſay what Chance there is that Epiſcopal Clergymen of that Country may be diſaffected to the Government. Now if inſtead of ſuch, Natives of the Plantations were bred in their Colleges, with a View to Orders; notwithſtanding which, their young Men of Faſhion wonld ſtill come to *England* for polite Accompliſhments; this would afford convenient Opportunities to Parents of providing for ſome of their Children handſomely, and Encouragement to the Inhabitants to build and endow Churches, to furniſh Parſonage-houſes, and ſtock Glebes, which now run to Ruin for Want of it. And Clergymen whoſe Families were known, would be more reſpected, and have a better Influence than Vagabond Strangers. As to the Matter of Diſcipline and Juriſdiction over the Clergy, it would ſtand juſt as it hath done hitherto, only with this Difference, that the Exhortations and Directions

of

of a Perfon invefted with the Epifcopal Character, would be more readily and carefully obferved by the Parifh Minifters, than thofe are
which proceed from their Equals: and Mifbehaviours might thus be more effectually prevented, than they can afterwards be punifhed
and rectified.   Nor is this a Point of Confequence only to themfelves and their Hearers,
but to the Public; as the Behaviour of the
Clergy in general is.   And if by reforming
them, and introducing better Order into the
Churches of our Communion, more of the Inhabitants fhould come over to it, as they naturally will, this would be a further public Benefit. For Members of the Church of *England*
will think themfelves more connected with *England*, than others.   And fuppofing them not to
be *Jacobites*, their Acknowledgment of the
King's Supremacy will incline them to be duti-
fuller Subjects than the Diffenters, who do not
acknowledge it.

But allowing the Eftablifhment of Bifhops in
America to be reafonable in itfelf, the fecond
Queftion is, Whether the Danger of increafing
Church Power by Means of fuch an Eftablifh-
ment, be not a fufficient Objection againft it?
Now againft Things evidently right and ufeful,

no Dangers ought to be pleaded, but such as are both very probable and great; and from confirming and ordaining, no Danger of this Kind, I presume, is apprehended. Yet these are the only new Powers that will be exercised. No other Jurisdiction is desired for the proposed Bishops than the preceding Commiffaries have enjoyed; and even that, on this Occasion, may be ascertained and limited more accurately, if it be requisite. But here it is asked, How any Persons can undertake to promise; that no additional Powers shall hereafter be proposed and pressed on the Colonies, when Bishops have once been settled? And strictly speaking, indeed, nothing of this Nature can ever be promised in any Case. But if the Dissenters had been asked, on their applying for a Toleration, how they could undertake to promise, that when that Point was once settled, nothing further, nothing hurtful to the established Church, should ever be proposed and pressed on the Government by them, surely this would not have been sufficient to defeat their Application. And yet what could they have answered? Not more; if so much, as can be answered in the present Case: that no such Thing is at all intended; and that though it were, there would be no

Danger,

Danger, either of the Intention taking Effect, or causing any Disturbance.

But on the former of these Assertions our Sincerity may be questioned. For it is argued, that Bishops doubtless think the Powers, which they have in this Nation, to be strictly just and reasonable; and consequently must be desirous of their taking Place in the Colonies. Now for my own Part, and I believe my Brethren in general are of the same Mind, I have no Imagination, that Bishops are intitled to, or that it would be right to give them, every where, the same Powers, and Privileges, that we happen, by the particular Constitution of this Country, to possess here. Several Parts of that Constitution might perhaps full as well have been formed otherwise. Whether our Share of it might or not, I have never set myself to consider; I hope, and am persuaded, it is on the whole as harmless and useful a Branch, as many others; and I endeavour, so far as I am concerned, to make it so. But were I to live where Bishops were only on the same Footing, on which it is now proposed they should be in our Plantations, I should no more attempt to raise them higher, than I should to overturn the established Form of Government in any other Respect. It may

indeed

indeed be prudent to fufpect Clergymen, Miniſters of State, all Men, to ſome Degree. But it cannot be prudent to refuſe doing Things that are highly proper, on Account of little more than a Poſſibility, that an improper Uſe of them may be hereafter attempted. Some Biſhops may be thought peculiarly fond of Church Power, and it concerns them when they are called upon, to defend themſelves if they can. But at leaſt I hope we are not all ſo fond of it, as to be aiming at that Point now, though we ſolemnly profeſs we are not. Yet I believe there ſcarce is, or ever was a Biſhop of the Church of *England*, from the Revolution to this Day, that hath not deſired the Eſtabliſhment of Biſhops in our Colonies. Archbiſhop *Tenniſon*, who was ſurely no High-Churchman, left by his Will 1000*l.* towards it. And many more of the greateſt Eminence, both dead and living, might be named, who were and are zealous for it: and yet have always been applauded by one Party, and cenſured by the other, for their Moderation. Or if Biſhops, as ſuch, muſt of Courſe be deemed partial, the Society for propagating the Goſpel conſiſts partly alſo of inferior Clergymen, partly too of Laymen. Now the laſt cannot ſo 'well

be

be fufpected of defigning to advance Ecclefiaftical Authority.   Yet this whole Body of Men,
almoft ever fince it was in Being, hath been
making repeated Application for Bifhops in
America; nor have the Lay Part of it ever refufed to concur in them.

'But though fome, or many of the Advocates
for this Propofal, were inclined to ferve wrong
Purpofes by it, is there any Likelihood of its
effecting thofe Purpofes? Some have apprehended juft the contrary, that it will tend to
the Depreffion of the Hierarchy; as it will afford
the Laity here an Example of *Englifh* Bifhops
Abroad, with no other than fpiritual Powers:
which may tempt them to think of reducing us
at Home to the fame Condition.   But I fhould
be very willing, for the Benefit of thofe of our
Communion in the Colonies, to run a greater
Rifque, than I conceive this to be.   For the
Fact is fo notorious, that all our temporal
Powers and Privileges are merely Conceffions
from the State; and the Act of Parliament for
the Suffragan Bifhops, under which feveral
were made in the laft Century, and others may
now, exemplifies fo fully the Poffibility of
Bifhops without Peerages, and Confiftory Courts;
that we need have no Fear of any new Difco-
very

very to our Prejudice, from appointing a few fuch Bifhops in *America*. But then the oppofite Fear, of their growing up to what we are, would it be ever fo great an Evil if it were to happen, feems as unlikely to happen, as moft Things. I do not wonder indeed, that Perfons who were in public Stations at the latter End of Queen *Anne*'s, and the Beginning of the late King's Reign, fhould have ftrong Impreffions remaining in their Minds of the Terrors of Ecclefiaftical Influence, which was then fo grofsly abufed to fuch wicked Purpofes. But whoever attends to the prefent State of Things in this Refpect, muft fee that there hath been a prodigious Change within the laft thirty Years. Though too many both of the Clergy and the Laity are difaffected to the Government on one Account or another; yet of the former, even the lower Part are not near fo generally poffeffed of the wild High-Church Notions, as they were. Nor was a Time ever known, when the upper Part were fo univerfally free from them. And yet it is the upper Part only, that can do the leaft towards fupporting any exorbitant Pretenfions of Bifhops in the Colonies. Then as to the Laity, I hope and believe the Adminiftration and their Friends will always fhew Coun-

tenance

tenance to the Clergy, as far as it is neceffary; but there is vifibly no Danger of their giving them any Encouragement, that may be hurtful. Amongft the Oppofers of the Adminiftration, few, if any, are at all more prejudiced in their Favour. And that Regard, which the Bulk of the People had for Religion and the Teachers of it, is greatly diminifhed, and diminifhing daily, to a Degree, which I wonder wife Men are not alarmed at. For it is as important, even in a political View, that they fhould be able to do Good, as that they fhould not be able to do Harm. Nor do I find, that Bigotry to the Church prevails amongft the Members of it in our Colonies; or that there is any Chance of their making afterwards imprudent Additions to the Authority with which their Bifhops will come to them at firft. On the contrary, one Plea againft the prefent Scheme is, that Bifhops, even with the loweft Powers, will give them Jealoufy and Offence. Now thefe two oppofite Dangers cannot both be confiderable; and I ap-prehend neither of them is: but furely the for-mer is the lefs of the two. The Bifhop of *London*'s Commiffaries, I believe, have gained no Acceffions to what was granted them origi-nally. And Bifhops will be ftill more narrowly

watched

watched by the Governors, by other Sects, by the Laity, and even the Clergy, of their own Communion.   Nor will they have a greater Dread of any Thing, if either so good or so discreet Men are chosen, as I promise myself will, than of losing all, by grasping at what doth not belong to them.   Nor will their Patrons here attempt to defend them, in what they cannot but know will ruin them.   As they will be appointed by the Crown, which, unless I mistake, the Commissaries are not; they will be such Persons, as the Crown can best confide in.   And if it be thought necessary, a Right of recalling them may be reserved to the King. Whereas I believe, he hath not a Right of ordering the Bishop of *London* to recall his Commissaries.   Upon the whole, if the present Disposition of his Majesty's Ministers and Subjects in Relation to Ecclesiastical Authority continues the same, as in all Likelihood it will, there can be no Danger from Bishops in *America*.   And if that Disposition should alter back to what it formerly hath been, which God forbid, they will be established with greater Powers than are now desired for them.

It ought to be considered farther, that an Act of the last Session of Parliament, which

passed

paffed without any oppofition from any Body, hath exprefly eftablifhed *Moravian* Bifhops in *America*; who have much higher and ftricter Notions of Church Government and Difcipline, than we have. Why then fhould there be fuch Fear of eftablifhing Bifhops of the Church of *England?* If for Want of thefe, the *Moravian* Bifhops fhould ordain fuch Minifters for our People as they thought proper; or fhould they, by adminiftering Confirmation, or by the Reverence of their Epifcopal Character, be continually gaining Converts from us; it would be a very undefirable Thing on feveral Accounts; particularly on this, that moft of them refufe taking Oaths, and bearing Arms. Befides, there have been Nonjuring *Jacobite* Bifhops in our Colonies, not very long fince, if there are none now. And Popifh ones alfo, I apprehend, have Recourfe to them from Time to Time. At leaft the Bifhop of *Quebec* hath no fmall Influence in a very important new Settlement of ours. May not then the Neglect of having Bifhops of our own, expofe us to far greater Dangers than the Appointment of them can:

But ftill the Third Queftion remains, and is a very material one, Whether fuch an Appoint-

ment,

ment, however harmless and useful it might be otherwise, would not ftir up dangerous Uneafineffes, Abroad or at Home? And here it is afked, if the Members of our Church in *America* would like to have Bifhops among them, why have they never petitioned for them? Now furely their omitting it may well be afcribed, in Part to the Thoughtleffnefs of Mankind about their religious Concerns; which hath been fo peculiarly great in thofe Countries, that fome of them did not petition for Help, when they had no one Office of Chriftianity adminiftered to them; and partly alfo to this, that probably too many of their Clergy think, they may both live more negligently, and have a better Chance for Preferment now, than if a Bifhop were to infpect them, and ordain Natives to be their Rivals. But the chief Reafon, I doubt not, is, that the Inhabitants of the Colonies, living at fuch a Diftance, and not knowing when an Application to the Government might be feafonable, and being affured, that the Bifhops here, efpecially the Bifhop of *London,* and the Society for propagating the Gofpel, would always be attentive to this Point, have left it to Them. And They, to whom it is thus left, have received abundant Proofs, that very great

Nnmbers

Numbers of the Laity of the Church of *England* in thofe Countries, of higher as well as lower Rank, earneftly defire to have Bifhops fettled there, and think it would be a moft valuable public Benefit. Nor have they found Caufe to imagine that any Oppofition would be made to it from that Quarter. Indeed of Courfe it fhould be prefumed, and none but the very ftrongeft Evidence admitted to the contrary, that all Perfons defire to have within their Reach, the Means of exercifing their Religion compleatly: which thofe of our Communion in *America*, and they alone of all his Majefty's Subjects, have not. It is true, fome of them have provided againft enlarging the Jurifdiction of the Commiffaries: but none of them have expreffed any public Reluctance to the Appointment of Bifhops. I have learned from fome Papers of Bifhop *Gibfon*, that there was a Defign in *Charles* the Second's Time, to place one in *Virginia*; that Letters Patent for that Purpofe are ftill extant; and that no other Reafon appears, why the Defign failed, but that the whole Endowment was to have been out of the Cuftoms: whereas now it is not intended either to burthen the Crown, or tax the Subject. Nor can either be done hereafter but by Confent of

A a 2

both.

both. Nor is it apprehended, that either will be needful. Some confiderable Gifts have been already contributed: and probably more will, when the Scheme appears like to take effect. There are likewife other Methods that might be propofed. And if they who are againft it, think it will mifcarry for want of a Mainte-nance for the Bifhops, they need not take the Trouble of oppofing it. But to go on. For above forty Years paft, the Inhabitants there muft have had frequent Notices, by various Ways, that fuch a Defign was in Agitation: yet I have not heard, that any of them who are Members of our Church, have ever fignified the leaft Diflike of it. Of late indeed, the *Prefbyterians* or *Independants* of *New England* have. But they cannot be intitled to object againft placing Bifhops in any other Province, but their own, in which there never was any Thought of placing them. Whether they would object againft Bifhops coming to officiate occafionally amongft thofe of the Epifcopal Perfuafion in that Province, I know not. If they fhould, and perfift in it, that may be omitted. But it feems hardly poffible that they fhould, unlefs the grofs Mifreprefentations, that have been fo officioufly fent them from hence,

have

have made them deaf to all Reason. It is true, they fled into *America* from the Oppreffions of Ecclefiaftical Power, exercifed by Bifhops. But they cannot fail to know how much that Power hath been long fince leffened; and the Inclinations and the Principles of thofe, who are intrufted with it, altered for the better. If they were here at prefent, they would not think of flying from it. Why then fhould they be afraid of Bifhops reforting to their Country now and then, without any Pretence of Authority over Them, but merely to perform fome religious Acts in a few Congregations of Epifcopal People, that are intermixed with them? This is no more than Diffenting Minifters do here by Law, and even Popifh Priefts and Bifhops by Connivance.

But at leaft, before any Argument againft the Scheme can be drawn from the Opinion of any of the Colonies, it ought to be fairly ftated to them. This was the fole Intention of the Society for propagating the Gofpel, in their late Order for fending Letters into *America*. They apprehended they might take the Liberty of tranfmitting a true Account of the Defign, when others had taken that of tranfmitting a falfe one: and that endeavouring to procure

Evi-

Evidence in Relation to so material a Point in their Cause, against the Time it would come to be tried, was not blameable. However, if they judged ill in attempting it, His Majesty's Equity, and that of his Council, may doubtless be depended on, that they will not reject this Proposal, as disagreeable to the Colonies, till a fair Inquiry shews, whether it be so or not.

But a farther Objection against it, is, That however it may be received there, it will immediately raise Animosities here; produce Declamations in Pulpits, Controversies in Pamphlets, Debates in Parliament; revive the Distinction of High and Low among Churchmen, and terrify or provoke the Dissenters. Now amongst the Clergy, I conceive it can make no Dispute: for every Man of Character amongst them, doth and must wish it Success. If indeed it were to be brought upon the Carpet, and the Administration were to oppose it, some Clergymen might be tempted to say indecent Things of them. But the present Question is not, whether this Affair ought to be attempted, if, after being fully weighed, it be disapproved by the Ministry: that undoubtedly would be very wrong: but whether there be Reason for them to disapprove it. And certainly there is

no

no Reafon to fear inflaming and exafperating the Clergy, by declaring for it : on the contrary, fcarce any thing would pleafe them more univerfally. Nor I prefume, is the Danger from Pamphlets to be thought very great : for moſt virulent ones are publiſhed daily both againſt Church and State, which yet give the Government no Terror at all. Contefts in Parliament indeed would be a Matter of more ferious Concern. But there feems no Neceffity that this Affair ſhould ever come into Parliament. For as the Law now ſtands, Suffragan Biſhops may be ordained with the King's Approbation : and the Biſhop of *London* may fend thofe, inftead of Preſbyters, for his Commiffaries : and they may confirm and ordain, as well as exercife the Jurifdiction which hath been ufual there. But even if the Scheme ſhould be brought into Parliament, it can be oppofed only on thefe two Principles : that Epifcopal Power is a great Grievance in this Nation, and that it muſt rife to an equal Height, wherever Biſhops are : of which two Propofitions, plain Experience proves the former to be falfe ; and I hope I have proved the latter to be fo. Still fome Members may be blinded by Ill-will to the Ecclefiaftical Part of our Conſtitution. But

 furely

furely thefe are not very many. Befides, the
Adminiftration will eafily quiet fuch of them
as are their Friends.　Then the Tories muft be
for Bifhops, if it be only to preferve their own
Credit.　And the Remainder will probably find
themfelves too inconfiderable to ftir.

Therefore the only Danger left, is that of
alarming and provoking the Body of the Diffenters.　Now a few bufy warm Men, are not
the Body of the Diffenters.　And though they
may affect to fpeak in the Name of the Whole,
yet the Whole will neither think it right nor
prudent to do all that thefe Gentlemen are
pleafed to intimate : fome of whom alfo, after
arguing properly with them, have owned, that
they had little or nothing to object againft appointing Bifhops in Plantations of the Epifcopal
Communion.　Dr. *Avery*, if I am rightly informed, hath acknowledged this to the Archbifhop, as Mr. *Chandler* hath to me.　And indeed there is no Modefty in faying, we who are
not of the eftablifhed Church, demand, as a
Matter of ftrict Juftice, the full Exercife of our
Religion here : but at the fame Time infift,
that the King's Epifcopal Subjects in *America*,
with whom we have nothing at all to do, fhall
not, even in thofe Provinces, where they are
the

the eftablifhed Church, have the full Exercife of theirs. Suppofe the *Prefbyterians,* or *Independants* in *America* thought as well of Confirmation as we do, and had not amongft them, a proper Officer to adminifter it : would not they think it infufferable to be denied fuch a one, and put under a Neceffity of fending their Children hither for it, if they would have it ? Suppofing they were obliged only to fend their Candidates for the Miniftry, hither to be ordained ? would they have been patient under it as long as we have been ? Would they not have cried out loudly and inceffantly for Relief ? For my Part, I fhould have thought them fo well entitled to it, as to have been a moft hearty and zealous Advocate for them. It is not merely from my Attachment to the Church of *England,* that I am a Favourer of the Scheme in queftion : but from my Love of Religious Liberty ; which in this Point, the Members of the Church of *England* in our Colonies do not enjoy. And I cannot imagine, how the Diffenters can pretend to be Lovers of it, and wifh it to be with-held from their Fellow-Subjects. God forbid, that we fhould ever be moved, by this or any other Provocation, to wifh it withheld in any Inftance whatever from the Diffenters.

senters. And I believe there never was a Time, when the Clergy of this Land were in so mild a Disposition towards them. Whatever they may plead therefore, it is not Fear that induces them to oppose us on this Occasion; for they well know that we have neither Power nor Wish to oppress them, or their Brethren, in any Way. But it is a Wantonness of Spirit, which we have not deserved from them. It is an ostentatious Fondness of using their Influence with great Persons, to grieve Us, without serving themselves. And instead of being stirred up by their Friends Abroad to what they do, their Friends Abroad have been stirred up by Them. Now this is a Sort of Behaviour which an Administration had much better check by due Admonitions, than encourage its Growth: for how far it may grow, they cannot foresee. The Dissenters are sincere Well-wishers to the Civil Part of our present happy Establishment; and they are to be esteemed and loved for it: but not to be gratified at the Expence of those, who sincerely wish well to both Parts. I am heartily sorry, that all the Members of our Church are not loyal and dutiful Subjects to the King: but much the greater Part of them are; the Bi-shops and upper Clergy in particular: and surely

their

their Defires merit as kind a Regard in this Cafe, as thofe of the Diffenters and their Leaders.   We indeed do not threaten if we are difregarded.   But they have no more Right to threaten than we : nor need they be feared, if they do.   Their Threatnings have been very fafely flighted in a Point which they have much at Heart, I mean the Teft : and fo they may in this.

Permit me to add, that were thofe of our Communion, who are unhappily and unjuftly prejudiced either againft the King, or his Miniftry, worfe, in either of thefe Refpects, than they are, ftill the Endeavour fhould be to make them better in both : for till that is done, our domeftic Affairs will never be on a firm and eafy Footing.   Not that any Thing wrong or hazardous fhould be done to reconcile them : but every Thing that is right and harmlefs.   Indeed fuch Inftances of Kindnefs, when fhewn them, I am grieved to fay it, have not produced, and probably will not produce fo great, and much lefs fo fpeedy Returns as they ought: but fome good Effect they muft produce ; and Perfeverance in a due Regimen will at length compleat the Cure.   On the other Hand, I apprehend, the Rejection of this Propofal will do

the

the Government by far more Hurt amongft the Churchmen, than it can poffibly do them Good amongft the Diffenters. When the Bifhops are afked about it, as they frequently are, by their Clergy and others, what muft they anfwer? We cannot with Truth exprefs Difapprobation of it, or Indifference to it. And if we did, we fhould be thought unworthy of our Stations. Muft we then be forced to fay, that we are all fatisfied of the abfolute Fitnefs, the great Advantages, the perfect Safety of the Thing, and have repeatedly preffed for it; but cannot prevail? Would not this both fadly diminifh our Ability of ferving the Government, by fhewing how little Credit we have with it; make very undefirable Impreffions on many Minds concerning the King, and thofe that are in Authority under Him; as incapable of being won by the Arguments or Intreaties of thofe, who have fo ftrong a Zeal for them, to do an innocent Favour to the Church? Still, if we cannot fucceed by refpectful Applications, I know it is our Duty to make the beft of the Matter; and not difturb the public Welfare, becaufe in this Particular we are unable to promote it. I would fpeak as gently of the Affair as ever I could, where there was Danger

of

of doing Harm :: though I fpeak fo earneftly, where I would fain hope to do Good.' But no Mildnefs or Prudence, will wholly or nearly prevent the above-mentioned Confequences.

I am fenfible it may be argued after all, that the Failure of fo many Attempts on Behalf of this Scheme, is Prefumption more than enough of their being fome infuperable Objection againft it.   But there cannot well be any other Objection, than fuch as are known, and have been produced on the prefent Occafion.   And if thofe have been fufficiently anfwered, we are not to yield up our own Underftandings implicitly to the Judgments of other Perfons in Times paft : efpecially as thofe Judgments differ.   For fome great Men have continued as fteadily to approve of Bifhops in *America,* as others, to difapprove of them.   And poffibly the Reafons of the latter may in Part at leaft, have been only temporary, or they may have had too little ferious Attention to religious Matters ; or more Fear, than they needed, of bringing Difficulties on themfelves by engaging in them.   But whether any of thefe Things be fo or not, in general it is certain, that many Defigns have been long fruftrated, or poftponed, on one Account or other,

which

which at length have been executed, and found beneficial.

I beg your Pardon, Sir, for being thus prolix: But I have gone through each Head as briefly as I could: and fhould you think me ever fo much miftaken, you will do me but ftrict Juftice in believing me to mean well; and to be, with the greateft Refpect, and the moft grateful Senfe o your obliging Treatment of me,

S I R,

Your moft obedient

Humble Servant,

THO. OXFORD.

FINIS.